The Keystone Corner

Also by J.B. Manheim:

FICTION

The Deadball Files

Book 1
This Never Happened:
The Mystery Behind the Death of Christy Mathewson

Book 2
TheGameKeepers:
Whitewash, Blackmail, and Baseball's Darkest Secrets

Book 3
Doubleday Doubletake:
One Ball, Three Strikes, One Man Out

Book 4
The Federal Case

SELECTED NONFICTION

Strategy in Information and Influence Campaigns:
How Policy Advocates, Social Movements, Insurgent Groups,
Corporations, Governments and Others Get What They Want

Strategic Public Diplomacy and American Foreign Policy

All of the People, All the Time:
Strategic Communication and American Politics

The Keystone Corner

THOMAS EDISON TURNS TWO

BOOK FIVE of The Deadball Files

a novel by
J. B. Manheim

MILFORD
HOUSE
an imprint of Sunbury Press, Inc.
Mechanicsburg, PA USA

MILFORD
HOUSE

an imprint of Sunbury Press, Inc.
Mechanicsburg, PA USA

FIRST MILFORD HOUSE PRESS EDITION: January 2024

Set in Adobe Garamond Pro | Interior design by Crystal Devine | Cover by Lawrence Knorr | Edited by Sarah Peachey.

Publisher's Cataloging-in-Publication Data
Names: Manheim, J.B., author.
Title: The keystone corner : Thomas Edison turns two / J.B. Manheim.
Description: First trade paperback edition. | Mechanicsburg, PA : Milford House Press, 2024.
Summary: Thomas Edison didn't invent baseball any more than Abner Doubleday did. But he was a big fan of the game. Fresh from his victory in *The Federal Case*, young attorney Andy Dennum and his cartographer girlfriend Keiley Barefoot use Edison's love of baseball to uncover the secrets hidden in the estate of the inventor's last surviving offspring, "Uncle Frank" Culbertson. You won't believe what they find.
Identifiers: ISBN : 978-1-934597-96-5 (paperback).
Subjects: FICTION / Thrillers / Legal | FICTION / Sports | BIOGRAPHY & AUTOBIOGRAPHY / Historical.

Product of the United States of America
0 1 1 2 3 5 8 13 21 34 55

For the Love of Books!

From one who weaves the story
To those who pull the threads

The Lineup Card

The Box Score

keystone 1. *adj.* Describing second base. 1. Terms include "keystone bag," "keystone corner," "keystone cushion," "keystone hassock," "keystone sack," and "keystone station." . . . It is often claimed that the term is a play on the fact that many important, or "key," defensive plays involve second base.

Author's Note

Baseball fans speak with nostalgia of what they term the Deadball Era, roughly the years between 1900 and 1920, when pitchers threw hundreds of innings, home runs were rare, and the game was played spikes up. Those years were marked by the consolidation of Major League Baseball, the first legal moves toward its antitrust exemption, the development of the Doubleday creation myth, and the arrival of The Bambino—all things that would change the game forever.

But baseball has always been a reflection of the times in which it is played, and the Deadball Era was much more than a frame for the game. It was a time of seismic technological, social, and political change in the United States and elsewhere—an era of firsts. The first powered flight. The first large-scale assembly line. The development of mass-audience media. The first World War, and not coincidentally, the first U.S. government ministry of propaganda. The opening of the Panama Canal and the birth of the American Empire. The Federal Reserve System, and the first income tax. The first pandemic of the modern era. Women's suffrage. Prohibition and the rise of organized crime. The Boxer Rebellion. The Russian Revolution.

And just as baseball had its larger-than-life personalities during these years—Christy Mathewson, Ty Cobb, Walter Johnson, Honus Wagner, and of course, Babe Ruth, to name just the first five inductees into the Hall of Fame—so, too, did the larger world. Teddy Roosevelt. Henry Ford. The Wright Brothers. Susan B. Anthony. Albert Einstein. Marie Curie. Vladimir Lenin.

But there was one man of an earlier day who nonetheless stood out well into this new era, perhaps because he literally invented much of early twentieth-century life. That man was Thomas Edison.

Thomas Alva Edison was widely viewed as the greatest inventor America and the world had ever known. By many accounts, he was also a poor organizer and manager, boorish, standoffish, and not especially pleasant to be around. In the popular imagination, a successful inventor is a tinkerer of sorts until, one day, a light bulb of an idea flashes in his or her head. There are surely many such innovators, but Edison was not among their number. Rather, his method was to identify a commercial need that might be addressed by developing or improving some form of technology, then to lay siege to it, exploring a sometimes-overwhelming number of potential solutions until the walls of innovation were simply knocked over by the weight of the assault. In the case of that now mythic incandescent light bulb, for instance, Edison once claimed to have tried more than three thousand different approaches to perfect the device, while other sources place the number at double that. Years later, he orchestrated tests of some ten thousand combinations of materials in an effort to perfect a rechargeable battery for automobiles.

Edison's commitment to practicality over theory may best be evidenced in a third-hand story published in the *New York Globe* in 1919. According to the story, which may be apocryphal but has the ring of truth, Edison had in his employ a young college valedictorian who was schooled in mathematics and wanted to become an electrician. Edison removed a light bulb from its socket and handed it to the fellow, telling him, "Find the cubic contents of this." The shape of the bulb made this a difficult problem, but after several days and several false starts, the young mathematician presented Edison with his result. Edison claimed the answer was off by at least ten percent. To prove his point, Edison picked up a small hammer and knocked the tip off the blown end of the bulb. He then filled the bulb with water, weighed it, and, based on the known weight of water, calculated the true volume of the bulb. As he had indicated, the mathematical calculations were at least ten percent off.

Another aspect of Edison's character may be seen in the text of a letter he dispatched to George Flint & Company, a furniture manufacturing firm, on April 9, 1901. The company, it seems, had asked Edison for his recommendation regarding one Charles N. Jenks, a corundum miner and one-time prospective customer of Edison's separator technology for iron ore, though the purpose of the request is not clear. Edison wrote:

> I beg to state that I only know good of him, if you want to know the bad part, see Mr. R.N. Dyer, 31 Nassau Street, New York, also Mr. Luther Steringer, Electrician of the Pan American Exposition of Buffalo, New York.

It does not take a particularly sophisticated read to see that, his disclaimer to the contrary notwithstanding, Edison did in fact know other than good things about Mr. Jenks but did not want his fingerprints apparent on any such assessments.

But it is another item of correspondence, with a different Flint, that set the current tale into motion. Before we turn to that, however, it is worth mentioning a bit about this second Mr. Flint, whose name, unlike that of Edison, is not common currency.

Charles Ranlett Flint was born in Thomaston, Maine, in 1850, the son of a successful merchant. His family moved to New York City, where Charles graduated from Brooklyn Polytechnic Institute (now part of New York University), and in 1871 he entered the shipping business in a firm that was later merged into W.R. Grace. But his real claim to fame was as a business consolidator, forming U.S. Rubber in 1892 to control the trade in that vital commodity, then combining Adams Chewing Gum, Chiclets, Dentyne, and Beemans in 1899 to form market-dominating American Chicle. For good reason, Flint was often referred to as the "Father of Trusts."

Perhaps his most lasting amalgamation came in 1911, when he drew together the Tabulating Machine Company, International Time Recording Company, Computing Scale Company of America, and Bundy Manufacturing to form the Computing-Tabulating-Recording Company, or CTRC. In 1924, CTRC was renamed International Business Machines, more commonly known as IBM.

Not long before that last binge of mergers, at the very end of 1907, Flint received a brief letter from Edison. It read: "If your commercial working days are not over, & your ambition is still of continuing passion get into your automobile & come over to see something that I am not going to take commercial advantage of but which you could."

It is at this point that imagination must take over from historical fact. What was it that Edison shared with his friend Flint? What was it that made the drive from the financier's New York office to the inventor's New Jersey laboratory worth the forty-five minutes each way? We could speculate, but for our present purpose we need not do so. All we need do is take Edison at his word: He had stumbled across something Flint would find interesting, and something he himself had no interest in exploiting.

While such disinterest might seem out of character for the Edison we know from schoolbooks, in his real life, by 1907 the inventor had largely moved on from his electrical and electro-mechanical focus. More than that, earlier in the year, Edison had announced that he was giving up his work on commercial development of his inventions altogether to concentrate on his role as a laboratory scientist. He had closed his laboratory at Menlo Park after the passing of his first wife in 1884, and, after remarrying two years later and moving to a new and expansive home in West Orange, New Jersey, had opened a much more extensive facility nearby. By the time in question, he was more focused on such projects as building superior mining and milling equipment, improving the quality of cement and, of course, making motion pictures, eventually with the addition of sound. In 1898 Edison had even produced the very first motion picture showing a game of baseball in progress.

It is entirely possible, then, that the man who had invented the stock ticker, the electrical vote tabulator, a version of the electric typewriter, and so many other devices of the kind might find yet another such advancement to be somewhat boring or a mere distraction.

But for a man such as Flint, who might even then have been considering ways to consolidate companies engaged in electrical measurement, tabulation, and the like, some critical innovation in this field could be the very key to success, perhaps the focal point or conceptual core of yet another trust. And to receive such a "gift" from Thomas Edison himself, well, that might indeed be worth the drive.

Consider, then: If Edison's favor turned out to be the linchpin of Flint's next success, how might the Father of Trusts reward his friend once that success was imminent? Perhaps your imagination will point in the same direction as mine, and from that common ground we can begin.

Our tale here is pure fiction. Unless otherwise documented, the words, deeds, and motives ascribed to Edison and his contemporaries are an invention of the author, and all the other characters and their words, thoughts, and actions are altogether fictitious, perhaps even the result of an Edison-like exercise of sorting through the many to isolate the few that work.

In particular, because several of the legal and historical documents referenced here refer specifically to the Committee of Managers that governs the Llewellyn Park community, it was not feasible to rename that entity for purposes of this tale. But to be clear, unless otherwise documented, any actions or motives attributed to the Committee of

Managers, its members, or any other formal body operating within or on behalf of that community are fictitious, and nothing here should be taken to suggest that these entities or individuals acted either inconsistently with their respective charters or in any way contrary to the interests of their constituencies. Any resemblance to actual persons in any such roles is strictly coincidental.

That said, the correspondence and apparent friendship between Edison and Charles Flint were real. Who really knows where that might have led?

And as for baseball? As we shall see, Edison himself was a fan of the game, and there are many subtle ways in which one game might influence another.

Game Notes

Today's contest between the players representing Reality and those on the side of Fiction is being played at storied Llewellyn Park, about a dozen miles west of New York City. Llewellyn Park was the nation's first planned, gated community, and the long-time home field of Thomas A. Edison.

Superstar inventor and self-proclaimed baseball crank (fan) Edison, an American icon who set many records during his career, leads Team Reality into this game, with a supporting crew that includes:

- Charles Ranlett Flint, financier and industrial amalgamator, who has already been introduced;
- Mary Edison, first wife of Thomas and mother to his three oldest children, Marion, Thomas, Jr., and William, who makes only a pro forma appearance in today's matchup;
- Mina Edison, second wife of Thomas and mother to his three youngest children, Madeleine, Charles, and Theodore;
- Samuel Edison, father of Thomas, appearing here as the closer;
- Miller Reese Hutchison, AKA Hutch, a one-time Edison friend, the inventor's one-time chief engineer, a man of surpassing ambition, and something of a hustler;
- Georgine Shillard-Smith, AKA Georgine Northrup Wetherill Smith, a painter and patron of the arts who, like Edison, lived seasonally in New Jersey and Florida, and who shared with Edison membership in the Theosophy Society, a

religious-philosophical organization that was popular with leaders of the arts, business, and politics before and during the Deadball years;

- James McNeill Whistler—yes, that Whistler—who makes a brief appearance as Shillard-Smith's mentor and a fellow theosophist;
- John Eyre Sloane, American industrialist, whose marriage to Madeleine Edison was the only match among Edison's offspring to produce grandchildren for the inventor, none of whom, then, bore his last name;
- Otto Schott, German chemist and industrialist, who invented borosilicate glass, an improved composition that revolutionized the optical and scientific uses of the material;
- Frederick Miller Harry, Edison's private secretary from 1908 until 1910, who succeeded the inventor's personal aid for the prior three decades, John F. Randolph, following his predecessor's suicide;
- William Henry Meadowcroft, who entered the game as a replacement for Harry in 1910 and stayed in the lineup until Edison's death in 1931;
- Mel Fisher, famed twentieth-century treasure hunter, who was long dead by the time he appeared in our game;
- Henry Pedder (and wife, Louise), who commissioned and built Glenmont, the Edisons' Llewellyn Park estate, but were forced to surrender it shortly afterward when Pedder was caught absconding with funds from the company owned by his employer, Arnold Constable;
- Frank Sprague, one-time Edison employee who went on to invent the electric traction motors that revolutionized urban railroading;
- Louis Comfort Tiffany, prominent jeweler, designer, inventor of new techniques for making and using stained glass, and close friend of Thomas Edison;
- Andrew Mellon, Secretary of the Treasury under President Calvin Coolidge;

- guest appearances by the 1909 Brooklyn Edisons, the Edison Club team of Orange, New Jersey, the 1929 Edisons, the 1927 Philadelphia Athletics, the 1931 Brooklyn Robins (also known as the Dodgers), and baseball greats Joe Judge, Kid Gleason, Al Simmons, Ty Cobb, and Connie Mack;
- and a variety of other lesser players who storm the field at assorted critical moments; plus
- shout outs to some other playing grounds: Olympic Park, Sprague Field, Elysian Fields, Edison Field (1 and 2), Washington Park, Visitation Oval (by its varied names), West End Oval (Bath Beach Baseball Field), and even old Yankee Stadium.

Team Fiction is led today by Andy Dennum, a young night-school-trained lawyer with a record of 1–0, coming off a stunning victory over Major League Baseball in his debut appearance in *The Federal Case*. Andy is joined by:

- Keiley Barefoot, professional cartographer, semi-pro genealogist, and Andy's battery mate;
- Betty, last name unknown, whom Andy inherited from his now-deceased law partner, Lou D'Antonio, and who serves the practice as secretary, receptionist, treasurer, paralegal, IT consultant, friend, confidant, and occasional gossip lover, which is to say, she keeps the place running;
- Max Tomhoff, auction master at Marbury House Auctioneers, who makes his customary cameo appearance throwing out the first pitch;
- A. Francis Culbertson, AKA Uncle Frank, who enters the game early only to die in his first paragraph, leaving behind an estate that proves more mysterious than expected;
- Sam Patrick, Frank's nephew and sole heir, and Andy's client du jour;
- John Culbertson, AKA Sam's Grampa John, long-time Edison Company employee and star batsman on the company's semi-pro baseball team;

- Jennifer O'Connor Culbertson, AKA Sam's Grandma Jennie, short-time Edison Company employee, John's wife and Frank's mother;
- Hiram (Hi) Burlmeister, professor and chair of the chemistry department at Rutgers University;
- Art Escalon, director of the Edison Papers Project at Rutgers University;
- Audrey Templeton, professor of archeology at Rutgers University;
- Rudy Gallegos, specialist in the use of ground-penetrating radar (GPR);
- Stanley Golden, Gallegos's business partner;
- Ray Cordova, GPR technician;
- James Cashman, chair of the Llewellyn Park Committee of Managers;
- Ephraim Cook, superintendent of the Thomas Edison National Historical Park;
- Peggy Morse, park ranger;
- Ed McVay, representing the U.S. Environmental Protection Agency;
- Maggie Harmon, representing the New Jersey Historical Preservation Office;
- Jackson Drummond, representing the West Orange Historic Preservation Commission;
- Doris Mayo, representing Preservation New Jersey, a nonprofit group advocating for historic preservation;
- Anne Driscoll Smith, representing the U.S. Secretary of the Interior;
- Tina Winston, property specialist with the National Park Service;
- Barley Acres, representing the New Jersey Attorney General's Office;
- Ross Rubin, representing the U.S. General Services Administration; and
- Jim Grey, Andy's stockbroker and friend.

Play Ball!

"Baseball is the greatest of American games. . . . [I]t is my firm belief and it shall always be that baseball has no superior. . . . I don't believe you can find a more ardent follower of baseball than myself, as a day seldom passes when I do not read the sporting pages of the newspapers. In this way I keep close tab on the two major leagues and there was one time when I could name the players of every club in both leagues."

—Thomas Edison, 1927

Framing the Pitch

Max Tomhoff looked nervously over the room. *Schoolboy jitters*, he thought. *I've got the first-day-of-school jitters.* It was a strange sensation for a man who had spent literally decades standing at this very podium in this very room. But for Max, the auction master at New York's prestigious Marbury House Auctioneers, it was, in fact, another first day. Almost two years earlier, he and Frederick, the acquisitions director, had been called to testify before a congressional investigating committee looking into irregularities in the market for baseball memorabilia. Max had never done anything remotely like that before, and though he and Frederick were merely called as witnesses and there was never any indication of wrongdoing on their part or that of Marbury House, the experience had been nerve-wracking. He had not appreciated just how anxious he'd become until the ride back to the City on the Acela later that same day. Just as the train had pulled out of Wilmington, Max had felt an odd sensation of floating followed by a sharp pain in his chest. He'd passed out. Lost consciousness.

Next thing Max knew, he was in a hospital bed in Philadelphia. Frederick, who'd had the good grace to stay with him, was seated across the room, dozing in a chair. Philly-Hugh, or Phil Houston as he was more formally known, the Marbury House attorney who'd accompanied the pair to Washington, was nowhere to be seen. Max vaguely recalled that the lawyer had made for the bar car as soon as the train had rolled out of Union Station. Perhaps he didn't even know his colleagues had left the train.

1

The truth was, Philly-Hugh had missed all the excitement, not even realizing a paramedic team had met the train in Philadelphia and dispatched Max to the nearest hospital in an ambulance. But he surely knew it by then, because that was not the first day of Max's stay, but the third. He'd been out for quite a while.

What Max had suffered, of course, was a heart attack brought on, the doctor supposed after Frederick described their most recent experience, not only by the tension that had been building inside him for weeks in anticipation of his command performance on Capitol Hill, but by the sudden and unexpected release of that tension when the Chair of the committee had suddenly terminated the session without explanation. *What was the point?* he wondered. *Why did that son of a bitch put us through all that? For nothing?*

Max had never had occasion to give much thought to his health, and yet there he was, tubed up, wired in, and flat on his back. When the news that he was awake had brought the doctor back to his bedside, Max had learned something else, something that had stayed with him. He was in danger of a relapse unless he took several months off from work to rest, and then found ways to reduce the stress of his job. Max had resisted, but his bosses at Marbury House had insisted. They did not want to risk losing their most valued employee.

So here he was, nearly two years later, sitting to the side of the raised platform that served as a stage of sorts for the auctions, reading the room. As Max rose from his seat and took his customary place behind the podium, a familiar male voice from deep in the crowd broke protocol. "Welcome back, Max!" he shouted, and the other regulars in the room provided a smattering of applause. Max stood silently for a moment, finding himself deeply touched by this surprising show of affection. He held back a tear, then found his voice.

"Thank you so much. It is wonderful to be back at this podium. And now let us open today's auction.

"The first lot before us today is number 25-126D17, a very special pair of early Tiffany lamps. As you will have read in the catalog, Louis Comfort Tiffany was by 1889 one of the world's most prominent designers and manufacturers of stained-glass windows. His work was displayed at the 1889 Paris Exposition, where the American industrial exhibit space was dominated by the electrical lighting and other inventions of Thomas Edison. Edison and Tiffany knew one another from their work on a common project five years earlier, and had already become fast friends. It is believed that, after seeing the Edison display in Paris, Tiffany became interested in merging their commercial interests by creating decorative electric lamps. An innovator in his own right, he produced his first lampshade employing colored handblown glass, which he termed Favrile glass, in 1893, and, with his designers Clara Wolcott Driscoll and Alice Carmen Gouvy, produced the first applications of his foil and stained glass mosaic technique to a shade for an electric lamp in 1898. The matching shades on the two lamps in this lot are believed to trace to this early period of development, though the design itself was never commercialized.

"Of greater interest are the electrical sockets in the two lamps, both of which fitted the Edison bulbs then in use, but which are not a matched pair. In fact, the sockets are unique among Tiffany lamps; neither design was put into general use. After consulting with Tiffany's historical corporate records, our in-house experts have concluded that, once their designs were rejected, these two prototype lamps were dispatched by Mr. Tiffany to Mr. Edison as gifts. Based on that confirmatory research and on the markings on the lamps themselves, this pair of 1898 prototype Tiffany lamps will convey with full Marbury House certification. The bidding will open at five hundred thousand dollars."

A. Francis Culbertson—Uncle Frank—lay on the table, stone-cold dead. The cause of his demise was obvious: a brutal assault on the poor fellow by ninety-six years of life. The fluid that now filled his veins could preserve for a time, but it could not protect. The last fruit in Thomas Edison's orchard had fallen from the tree.

The first of these facts was known and obvious to all. The last was known to none, or at least to no living soul, including to Frank himself, if the formaldehyde could somehow have reinvigorated him, brought him back to life. There had been only two people in this world who had ever shared this isolated bit of biological truth. The first, who, perhaps unsurprisingly, had briefly resisted the fact before accepting it, was his father, the esteemed inventor. That half of the secret died with Edison on October 18, 1931. The second was Grandma Jennie, Frank's mother, who had herself preceded her oldest son in death by a quarter century and taken the other half of the secret with her.

Frank's younger siblings from Jennie's marriage to John Culbertson, Robbie and Rosalind, were never, ever the wiser, nor was their long-deceased father, who had accepted young Frank as his own even though the child's true father was unknown to him. Robbie had passed away of a bad ticker five or six years earlier, and, like Frank, he had never married. Roz, long ago divorced from Mason Patrick but still carrying his name, had followed Robbie over the finish line about two years later.

That left Sam Patrick, Roz's only child and Jennie's only grandchild, alone in the world, or at least on that bough of the family tree. For his part, Sam had been more successful in marriage and more prolific than any of his immediate forbears, with a loving wife, Sara, and three younger Patricks, now mostly grown up themselves. Sam had been close with his Uncle Frank, at least in recent years, and had visited him often, even helping him with the sale of his old rambler of a house and the move into senior care. But even then, he could not say he knew the old man well.

According to the letter Frank had given him in an envelope to be opened only upon his death, Sam Patrick was Uncle Frank's executor and sole heir. Of what, he could not imagine. Uncle Frank had lived a frugal existence, wearing clothes that were decades old, cooking in pots that were blackened and thinned from age, and driving a car—while he still could—that was scratched, dented, rusted and rattling, its maker uncertain and perhaps anonymous by choice. Sam always chuckled when he thought about that clattering bucket of bolts, which reminded him of an old Johnny Cash song about an auto worker who, over time, had built himself a car out of parts from different makes and model years that he had smuggled out of the factory where he worked. Add a couple of decades of bad roads, bad weather, and serious neglect, and it could have been Frank's ride.

The house had brought only a modest return, since consumed by Frank's expenses, and there had been precious little of any apparent value that had made the transition to the old folks' home. Some sturdy old furniture that looked like it had come out of a workshop somewhere, a couple of well-worn oriental-style rugs, a painting of some pasture or field with a farmhouse framed on either side by a row of trees in the distance, and a pair of dusty old stained-glass table lamps, both with what looked like their original century-old wiring intact. In life, Frank never seemed to pay them much mind and, at least in Sam's presence, had never so much as switched them on—perhaps with good reason. Now, it was too late.

In his letter, Frank let Sam know he had left instructions for his burial and had even prepaid the funeral home and cemetery for his coffin, his memorial service, his plot, and a modest headstone. That was back in the '90s, and Sam had to chuckle as he thought of the losses against current value that some poor funeral director would have to explain to his now-corporate bosses. "But sir, the man was already in his seventies when we signed that contract!" Served the vultures right. But there was more to the letter, though just what it meant Sam could not immediately discern.

———

Grandma Jennie had always been a bit of a mystery to her family, or at least to Sam, who, if he had ever met her, had no recollection of the event. He knew her mainly through the occasional stories Uncle Frank would tell. Roz, his own mother, had never spoken of her. Mothers and daughters, he supposed.

He had seen a few old photographs in family albums and surmised that she had been thin and fair in her youth, with a pretty face that was still discernible into her later life. Like so many, she had come to this country sometime in the 1920s to escape the famine in her native Ireland. She almost surely had booked steerage on one of the great liners and been deposited upon Ellis Island, but any effort to learn more than that of her origins or arrival would become instantly entangled with the details of the hundred and forty-seven others named Jennie or Jennifer (or in its traditional form, Seannafair) O'Connor who had reached these shores in that same time, place, and manner.

According to Uncle Frank, Grandma Jennie had found her way to New Jersey and had worked as a maid or a servant of some sort. By the time he was telling these stories, Frank's memory was no longer as firm as it had once been, or perhaps he was mixing and matching the memories he retained. So Sam was not sure whether this work had been in one of the great houses of the era or in some sort of commercial or industrial setting. Whatever the case, she had somehow met and married John Culbertson, Sam's grandfather, who had, in the cliché of that era, taken her away from all that.

Of Culbertson, still less was known. But it was intriguing, nonetheless. Grampa John. Sam had never thought of him that way and, in truth, had seldom thought of him in any way other than as an old man he had never known except through a small number of ancient family photos. Grampa John had been a skilled workman, probably a carpenter, and he'd had the good fortune to work for one of the true titans of his era, the inventor Thomas Edison. Edison, Sam knew, had built an invention factory—literally, a factory for inventing things—over in West Orange, where he employed an army of tinkerers and testers. But Culbertson had been neither. Instead, he was on the maintenance staff, tasked with building what needed to be built, repairing what needed repair, replacing what someone or other had broken beyond redemption. It was gainful and stable employment for its day, and he was lucky to have it when times turned hard.

Edison had long since surrendered control of his electrical patents and manufactures to JP Morgan and other financiers, who had combined and shaped them into what became General Electric, and had stepped back from his other commercial interests—in motion pictures, storage batteries, Portland cement, and the rest. Perhaps for that reason, he was little impacted by the onset of the Great Depression. But it was a short test, as he succumbed to the effects of diabetes in 1931, leaving behind his widow, Mina, his Glenmont estate in West Orange, and a legacy of technical insights and accomplishments that endured. This much Sam knew, as would any product of the public education system in the state of New Jersey, let alone anyone who lived within a few miles of what is now the Thomas Edison National Historical Park. It was the school field trip magnet to end all magnets.

Alas, the Depression was not at all kind to John Culbertson. The Edison laboratories had always been guided as much or more by economics and sensed opportunities as by scientific or technological advance, as the cart must be guided by the horse, but under hard times, new pressures, and more remote leadership, decisions were made that Edison, were he alive, might have eschewed. Maintenance was deferred to save money, and one vital mechanism for such a deferral was the reduction of staff. Culbertson was not the first to find himself jobless, but neither was he the last, and at some point, he was cast off from the great venture with few prospects but, by then, a wife and three children to feed, clothe, and house. He began to drink.

Uncle Frank had fond early memories of his father, and whenever one of his stories brought him to this point in the family history, he faltered, often with a tear in his eye. But from what Sam had pieced together in these conversations, Grampa John had simply disappeared for a very long time, only to return to the family when he was, as they say, at death's doorstep. He came home to die, and in short order fulfilled his destiny.

Through all of this, Grandma Jennie somehow managed to keep the family together. Frank, a boy of perhaps ten when his father died, never understood how she did that, but he remembered that he, Mom, Aunt Roz, and Uncle Robbie never thought of themselves as destitute. They never went hungry, they never wore rags to school, and their small house was somehow warm through the coldest winter days. The woman was a miracle worker.

It was a sleepy Monday morning at the smallish office just off Main Street in Mendham, a bedroom community on the edge of New Jersey's little-known horse country. The usual smells—fresh coffee and stale paper files—filled the air. Around ten, the silence was broken by a persistent electronic ringing sound that served to bring everyone up to the present moment.

As usual, it was Betty who answered the phone.

"D'Antonio and Dennum. This is Betty. How can I help you?"

"Uh, Betty . . . my name is Sam Patrick. I'd like to speak with Mr. D'Antonio, please."

"I'm very sorry, Mr. Patrick. Mr. D'Antonio passed away not long ago. But I'd be happy to connect you with Andrew Dennum. Mr. Dennum was Lou's partner. May I ask what this is about?"

There was silence on the line for a beat or two as Sam internalized this unexpected information. Then he picked up the thread. "Okay, sure. My Uncle Frank, that's Frank Culbertson, died a couple of weeks ago. He left me a letter with some instructions, one of which was to contact Mr. D'Antonio. I guess he has—or had—the official copy of Frank's will. Uh, is that going to be a problem?"

"No," replied Betty. "No problem at all. We have all of Mr. D'Antonio's files, so if Mr. Culbertson's will is in there, Mr. Dennum will be able to put his hands on it. Shall I put you through?"

Andy had explained that he would be out of the office the next day, Tuesday, getting advice on another matter from a friend who worked at the state capital in Trenton, but said he would be happy to meet with Mr. Patrick at his convenience on Wednesday. If they could do that after about ten in the morning, he would have a chance to review the file on Mr. Culbertson before they spoke.

At the subsequently agreed hour of eleven o'clock, the front door opened, and a tallish man with a receding hairline came into the room. Betty judged him to be in his mid-forties. As he turned to her, he flashed a pleasant smile.

"You must be Sam Patrick," she said, returning his with one of her own.

"Is this a detective agency? I was looking for the law office," he offered in response.

They shared a laugh.

"Please have a seat, Mr. Patrick. I'll let Andy . . . uh, Mr. Dennum, know you're here. Can I get you something? Coffee? Water?"

"Shot of your best tequila?" he replied. "No thanks. I'm fine."

"Añejo?" Betty shot back. "Guzano?" She enjoyed this sort of banter, and she wasn't going to settle for second place. But then she picked up

8

the telephone receiver and pushed a button. There was a ringing sound behind one of the two doors off to Sam's right, then a man's voice.

"Andy, your eleven o'clock, Mr. Patrick, is here."

A moment later the door opened, and Andy Dennum stepped out into the reception area with his hand outstretched. Dennum was in his early thirties and only a couple of years out of law school—the gritty kind of law school, the kind that held classes only at night. On another day, he'd have been dressed in khakis and shirtsleeves, but knowing that he'd meet and need to impress a new client, he'd dipped into his newly acquired professional wardrobe, chosen with the aid of his shopping consultant (and girlfriend) Keiley Barefoot—which is to say, chosen by her—and donned a gray suit, chalk-white shirt, and complementary tie. At her urging, he'd even shined his shoes. "Mr. Patrick, it's a pleasure to meet you. Please come into my office. Did Betty offer you some coffee?"

Sam and Betty shared a glance.

Andy directed his new client to one of the chairs facing his desk, closed the door, and took his own seat. "How can I be of service today? This has something to do with the passing of your uncle . . . ah . . . Frank Culbertson?"

<hr />

As he grew older, Edison found that he spent less and less time in Building 5 of the lab complex, which housed the library, music room (for recording), machine shops, and the inventor's private office, though he still enjoyed the occasional moments when his hands and his brain were singing in harmony. These, he had long ago determined, seemed to come more frequently at night, when no one else was around, than during the day with its many competitors for his attention. Perhaps it was the absence of distraction that solitary work allowed, or perhaps—and he hated to admit this—he just valued his time away from Mina. He still loved his wife, as he affirmed whenever the question occurred to him, but he did consider at times that the marriage had been strong for so many years precisely because he had been so often on his own and doing the *things* he loved.

By midnight or one on such nights, he could focus. The only source of annoyance came from the cleaning crew, three or four workers who showed up in the early hours of the morning to make ready for the following day's voyages of discovery. It was all part of the system he had put in place years before, the one that had produced light, sound, motion, and so much more—the system that had created the modern world. Or so he liked to think. The captain was seldom on the bridge these days, but the ship sailed onward.

The engineers, machinists, craftsmen, clerks, and their aides who filled the space during the day were diligent, perhaps even intimidated, and for such a large and complex enterprise, their chatter was limited. But in a building filled with machines, large and small, powered by a system of overhead belts, things were never quiet. For Edison, though, in his ever-increasing deafness, it was all simply the white noise of invention. He scarcely noticed it. The cleaners, on the other hand, whose tasks were equally essential yet menial to Edison's way of thinking, and who arrived when the background rattle and clatter and grinding of the machines had been silenced for the day, loved to jabber away as they passed the time, and they were always sliding furniture around. He remained blissfully unaware of the chatter, but the screech of sliding chair legs did break through from time to time.

Over the years, and especially as he had moved toward working later at night, he had trained himself to tune out even this limited noise. But that ability to focus his attention depended on a certain continuity. So long as the scraping of chairs as they were moved aside then restored, the squeaking of the trash carts, and the like were the same from one night to the next, his brain could easily isolate and ignore them.

But in the course of his work on the phonograph, Edison had discovered that, though his deafness was even then nearing totality, there were certain frequencies of sound that somehow penetrated his consciousness. Even late into his life, for example, Edison could hear his wife's words clearly because of some singular quality of her voice. And on one particular night, the essential continuity of silence in which he lived was broken. A new voice carried across the workshop, a feminine voice with a bit of an Irish lilt that somehow resonated at just the right pitch. *New maid*, he judged. Such a transition happened with a good bit of regularity on the cleaning crew, but it was one he seldom noticed. This time, however, the voice came closer, and he looked up for a moment to see an attractive young girl of perhaps eighteen or twenty with dark hair surrounding a well-formed face. She was singing as she worked. Though it was out of character, he smiled and nodded in acknowledgment as their eyes met, though as soon as she realized he was there, she muttered an apology, turned in embarrassment, and scurried away.

The same thing happened the next night, and the night after that, until it became something of a routine. On the fourth such night, as the maid turned to leave, Edison spoke to her for the first time.

"Stop, girl! Don't be afraid. What's your name? Please speak up loudly." He turned his head slightly to the left as he faced her.

"Jennie, sir. I'm very sorry to have bothered you. It's just that I'm supposed to clean up this area here, and—"

"Nonsense. Of course you are. Please don't let me interfere with your work. Do you know who I am?"

"Yes, sir, Mr. Edison, sir. Everybody knows who you are, sir!"

"Yes. Well, then you know that I place a great value on hard work, and I can see that you are a good worker. So you feel free to come clean over here every night, and don't you be frightened of me."

"Yes, sir. Thank you, sir," was all the response she could muster. She proceeded to make a big show of mopping the floor in Edison's personal space, and he made an equal show of lifting his feet for the mop.

"Now, you be careful, sir. That wet floor will be slippery for yet a while."

"Thank you, ah . . . Jennie. You keep up the good work, and I'll see you again tomorrow night."

Such encounters in the workplace are far from rare, and over time, they can lead to other sorts of encounters between the parties to them. That is apparently what happened in this instance once Edison had passed the word that he found Jennie's work superior, and that only Jennie was henceforth to be responsible for tending to his personal spaces, including the so-called hideaway office in a corner of the second floor of the building that he had maintained under lock and key for many years. It was a small space, as these things go, but it could take a remarkably long time to clean. Edison was an old man, to be sure, but he was a truly great one, perhaps the greatest of his time, and the appeal of such power and fame can be its own source of attraction. Or perhaps the power in question was a narrower and darker one, the power to control someone's prospects and well-being, or perhaps even simple intimidation. The record is silent on that, and we will never know. What is clear, though, is that Edison very much looked forward to Jennie's efforts in his office.

But there came a time some months later when a nervous Jennie approached her employer.

"Mr. Edison," she said. Whether he preferred it, or she was naturally timid, or it was simply the way things were, she had never, ever called him by his given name. He was always "Mr. Edison."

"Yes, my dear. You look troubled. What is it?"

"Mr. Edison, sir . . ." she mumbled, "I am with child."

"Speak up, girl," he replied. "I can't hear you."

"I am in the family way, sir."

"And you are telling me this because . . . Come now, Jennie. I am an old man, as you can plainly see. Surely you don't think—"

"Begging your pardon, sir," she whimpered, clearly on the precipice of losing her composure, "but I just . . ." At this point, she broke into tears, which Edison, to his credit, took to be genuine. "I'm all alone here. I have no one. And I just don't know what to do."

"Come here, my dear. Come here," he said less harshly, and he held her to him.

Edison was in earlier than had become his custom, and as he sat at his bench, he surveyed the workshop. Finally, he settled on his quarry. He was a heavyset man whom Edison judged to be in his thirties, with dark hair and dark eyes in what the inventor thought of as the "Irish way," but with a light gait, an agile grace for one his size, and a pleasant smile.

"Mr. Culbertson," he said loudly and, when the man looked up from his work repairing a broken cabinet drawer, continued, "Come here, would you please?"

Culbertson was surprised to be summoned in this way by the great man himself, but if anything, more surprised that Edison knew him by name.

"Yes sir, Mr. E," he said as he approached the inventor. Culbertson was more than a little concerned at being singled out but could not think of how he might have transgressed. At least he remembered that he must speak loudly and close to Edison's right ear. All he said was, "How can I be of service?"

"Culbertson, we've not spoken much, you and I, but you have been working here for several years now, have you not?"

"Yes, sir. Ever since I mustered out of the Army, sir. So that would be ten years or so, I reckon."

"I want you to know that I have been very pleased with your work. Very pleased indeed. You will know that, of course, because you were retained even as we were forced to reduce the staff by many thousands over the last few years. And needless to say, I remember your exceptional play with the Edisons baseball team. You were quite the batsman back in the day. Some said the very best in the league."

"Thank you very much, sir. That means a lot to me."

"I remember one game . . . must have been around 1920. My old friends at the General had just built Sprague Field there in Bloomfield, and we went over there for a game. I remember you hit a ball so hard that it almost knocked a hole in the outfield fence." He smiled at the memory.

"Do I recall that you even made the bat the fellows used?"

Though years had passed, Culbertson began to suspect the reason he had been called out. Edison was, after all, known to have a long memory.

"Mr. Edison, sir, if this is about my using company supplies and the woodshop to—" He never had the chance to finish the sentence.

Edison threw his head back and gave a hearty laugh. He held up both hands as if in surrender to the joke. "John!" he exclaimed. "It has been years. Have you been carrying that with you all this time? For goodness sakes. It was the company team!"

"Well, sir," Culbertson began, but again Edison interrupted him.

"How old are you, John?"

"I'm thirty-six years old, sir, nearly thirty-seven."

"Married? Children?"

"No, not married, sir. I guess I just never met the right woman and never had the time to look."

"Yes," replied Edison, "we all go our different directions, I suppose. I've married twice, you know." He paused, either lost in thought or for effect. "Culbertson, I need you to do something for me. It is something that I believe very important, and if you do it, I will be forever in your debt."

"Sir?"

"There is a young woman on the evening cleaning crew. Very good worker, very pleasant person. Quite pretty in her way, I suppose. I've had a few occasions to chat with her briefly, and I suppose I have taken a liking to her. Rather like a daughter, perhaps. The other evening, she approached me in tears. I don't know why she felt she could do that. Many people seem to feel I am, ah, remote or unapproachable. But approach me she did, and I am not ashamed to admit that it has touched me deeply. It seems she has a problem. You can rather guess what that might be.

"John, I would like to help this young woman, but I do not wish to be seen to be doing so. I suppose I have become accustomed to a certain, ah, reputation for crustiness, shall we say, and at this point in my life, I do not wish to be seen as a soft touch. And that is where I need your assistance. I'm afraid I am about to ask you to do something very, very . . . unusual."

Culbertson tensed as he listened.

"I would like you to meet this young woman, and if you find her in the least agreeable, I would like you to court her and make her your wife. Were you to do so, you would make this woman's life much easier than it would otherwise be, and you would spare an innocent child the ignominy of its current fate. You will also, I hope, find companionship in your own life. Companionship is very important, especially as we get older."

Culbertson was suddenly lost in confused contemplation. Was Thomas Edison—*the* Thomas Edison—trying to play matchmaker?

"John, I know this is a very great deal to ask. But should you see your way to granting me this favor, and should things work out accordingly, as they may or may not, I assure you that I will be eternally grateful. As a token of that, I can promise you that you will have employment here as long as I am alive. In addition, I will arrange the purchase of a house for you and your bride and will establish a modest fund to ease any financial burdens you might encounter.

"I can guess what you might be feeling just now. And I confess that I have never made such a request or such an offer before. But for some reason the plight of this young woman has reached my soul. And old as I am and wealthy as I am, I suppose I see it as an opportunity to help someone I know and think deserving rather than merely continuing to subsidize my worthless children or simply giving funds to anonymous charities. So . . . what say you?"

"So, I have this letter that Uncle Frank gave me a year or so back," Sam began after settling himself across the desk from Andy. "And basically, it says that I'm his only heir, and I'm his executor, and Mr. D'Antonio is holding his will, which I guess now means you are, and there's some other stuff with it, which seems kind of mysterious. And that's why I'm here."

"Okay. Just to set your mind at ease, we did find your uncle's file. It's right here," Andy replied, tapping a legal file on his desk. "But before we get to that, why don't you tell me about Frank Culbertson?"

"I can tell you what I know," said Sam, "but I'm afraid that's not very much. I saw him a few times over the years, like at family events. But it's just in the last few years that I really spent any meaningful time with him. He was getting on in years—the guy lived to be ninety-six!—and I was the only one around to help him out. Plus, in his way, he was interesting to talk to. Beyond that . . ." Sam proceeded to share with Andy what little family history he knew, with an emphasis on Frank's earlier life. Then he cautioned, "Now I have to tell you that, by the end, Frank's mind had a tendency to wander, and I'm not sure how much of what he said he really remembered and, of that, what he remembered accurately."

"Fair enough," inserted Andy. "And that's a good place to start.

"I've had a chance to review the will, and I can tell you that it pretty much confirms what Frank told you in his letter. It's a fairly straightforward document, as these things go, and you are his sole heir and his personal representative, which is the term we use these days for an executor. But before we can move forward or determine the nature or extent of any inheritance, there are some legal steps we need to take. For one, we'll need to order some copies of the death certificate, maybe a half-dozen or so. You'll need those to establish his death with any banks or insurance companies, and certainly the IRS and the state tax people. Chances are the funeral home will do that automatically if they haven't already, but I can have Betty check to make sure. Also, we'll have to advertise his death in the local newspaper. We do that just in case some other unknown claimant steps forward, which is unlikely in this case, but also to give any merchants a chance to make claims against the estate for outstanding debts. Do you know anything about Frank's finances?"

"Actually, I do. I've been managing his finances for the last couple of years. Helped him sell his house, move into Solitude House. That's an old folks' home over in Middlesex County. I can tell you there's not much. He pretty much used up the proceeds from selling the house. That and Social Security was about what he had."

"Personal belongings? Any jewelry, art, collectibles, that sort of thing? Or personal papers?"

"Well, there were a few odds and ends. Some furniture, a painting, some old cufflinks, and a watch. But that's about it. I don't think any of it had any value."

"Okay, that's something we will need to look into, especially if there is art or jewelry. Sometimes people are surprised by the current values of such things, and we'll need to lock them down when we file the estate with the courts. But if you're right, that will be pretty straightforward. With your permission, I'll bring in an appraiser who can have a look and write up a report. From what you say, that shouldn't cost too much. We usually use the Jersey City office of Marbury House, the auction firm across the river. If you don't object, we can get them started and see what they have to say. They do a lot of high-end auction sales, but they're usually pretty reasonable in a case like this."

"Speaking of cost, how much is all of this going to run? I mean, it seems silly to spend a lot of money to inherit nothing of worth. Sorry, I know that sounds crass, but. . . ."

"No, not at all, and that's an entirely fair question. There are a few things we are legally required to do when someone passes, but we can keep a tight lid on those expenses. And as for my own fee, well, that is established by law and controlled by the court. It's a fixed percentage of the estate, and in cases like this, where there are very few assets and none of great value, it's quite minimal."

"Okay. Well, I guess there really is no choice, so let's get this done."

"Now, there is one more thing we need to discuss," said Andy. "In addition to the will, Frank left a couple of other documents with my late partner. One is a receipt from Martini and Cage, a funeral home over in Montclair, showing all the details for his burial, which he seems to have prepaid many years ago."

"Yes," Sam said. "He'd told me about that. That's who I've been talking with about the arrangements. So that's one less thing to worry about, I guess."

"Good. Well, that's helpful," said Andy. "And there is also a letter addressed to you and to Lou, my old partner. I need to hold on to the original for a while until everything gets filed, but I can make you a copy. There is some family talk, but the main point seems to relate to a painting. Presumably that's the one you mentioned a moment ago. The letter says that Frank was told by his mother, a woman named Jennie Culbertson, that the painting had been a wedding gift from a dear friend who said that she must never let it pass out of the family because someday it might be valuable and might be their means of rescue in times of need. See, this is why we need to do an appraisal of everything. Sometimes there are surprises. Let me ask you, is the artist anyone you've ever heard of? Is the painting especially beautiful?"

"There is a signature of some sort," Sam replied, "but it's mostly covered by the frame and there's no way to read it. As for beauty, I suppose that's in the eye of the beholder. But to my eye, it's just a very plain painting of an old farm. A big green field and a house and trees in the distance. Oh, and there's a dab of yellow paint on the house—maybe like a light in the window? But it's all very small and indistinct. Certainly nothing I would pay for at a gallery."

"Interesting. You know, art can be tricky. But we'll get that sorted out. The last thing in the file was this ring."

Andy held out a small men's ring to show Sam. It was a squarish gold ring with some sort of weird symbol on it, maybe something Masonic.

"Does that symbol mean anything to you?"

After a brief inspection, Sam indicated he had never seen the ring on Frank's finger, or at least never noticed it, and that the symbol meant nothing to him. So far as he knew, Frank had not been a Mason.

"The only other feature," Andy added, "was this little bit of engraving on the inside of the ring. I had to use a magnifying glass to read it. It's just one word: TEA. Maybe somebody's initials. With the symbol and all, and with your grandmother having come over from Ireland, as you said, maybe this is some old Celtic piece that has come down in the family. That's something we can try to figure out.

"Whatever it is, it'll be yours before too long."

⸻ ⬥ ⬥ ⸻

It was the worst day of Edison's life. The worst. Yes, the death of his first wife, Mary, had been hard. Hardest at the time, of course, but that was more than twenty years ago. He scarcely thought of her now. The battles for his patents, perhaps. Poor Randolph's suicide. The fellow had been with him in one role or another for, what, three decades? The fire at the battery plant two years ago. The explosion, the inferno. And three months later, the same again when the gun cotton being manufactured for the Navy exploded and took thirteen buildings with it. That was bad. Edison did not believe in God—not in the traditional sense—but he believed in karma and in the force of nature that could turn against one in an instant.

And here it was again, but this time, men had died. Men had been scarred by the flames. It wasn't at the laboratory, thank goodness. But in its way, it was worse. The Navy's newest E-2 submarine, under construction at the Brooklyn Navy Yard, had exploded and burned, and the Navy was blaming the incident on hydrogen escaping from his Edison Batteries.

How had he gotten into this mess? Ah, yes. It was Hutch who had done this. His dear friend, Miller Reese Hutchison. When was it . . . 1910. Yes. July? Hutch showed up with some Navy officers—submarine captains as he remembered it. Said they had been using open-topped lead-acid batteries in their boats, but they couldn't dive at any sort of steep angle because the acid would spill, and everything would go to hell.

Somehow Hutch had convinced them Edison could redesign his auto batteries on a massively larger scale and solve their problem. And Edison had let them talk him into doing that.

Hutch wouldn't have known, but years earlier—1898, if he remembered correctly—he'd let his curiosity get the better of him. He'd allowed Captain Frank Cable, who was connected with the Electric Boat Company and Holland Submarine, which together designed and built the boats, and John Philip Holland himself, to talk him into boarding a submarine with them and taking a trip from Fiftieth Street in Brooklyn down the bay and back, all the while submerged. He laughed momentarily, recalling how he had pledged both men to hide the trip from his family lest they worry about his safety. But then his mind snapped back to the present day, and his sense of mirth dissipated instantly.

Damn the batteries! They'd been having this problem for years— almost since he'd formed the battery company back at the turn of the century. In 1904, he'd even shut down all production for a time because of leaks and loss of capacity. And ever since then, he'd been looking for new components. He'd spent ten years testing various configurations of nickel flakes to serve as positive electrodes. He'd investigated cobalt. He'd played with new ways to process iron. He'd tried casing after casing until he thought he had it. Had it! So, in 1910—July, he seemed to recall— he'd told the Navy he could build batteries for their submarines. Hell, he'd run off the competition. And now this.

Whether it was guilt or simply fear for his reputation, he could not say. Perhaps both. What he *could* say was that he felt like crap. He was getting too old for this!

How ironic that it was the letter from that German, Otto Schott, that had brought him to this place.

Andy, now back to wearing his customary khakis, ushered Sam Patrick into his office and offered one of the chairs on the client side of his desk, then he took his own seat and settled into his best lawyer's pose.

"Thanks for coming in today. As I mentioned on the phone, we now have the report of the appraisers we asked to value the non-cash assets of your uncle's estate, which is to say, just about everything that was left. I wanted to share those results with you in person, because there were a couple of surprises.

"The furniture was pretty much what it looked like—a couple of old upholstered pieces that don't really have any residual value but might easily go to a homeless shelter or someplace like that, where they still might get some use, and the three tables and two wooden-frame chairs that were obviously do-it-yourself projects sometime in the past, either made by Frank or by an earlier relative. Quite possibly your grandfather John. They were, according to the appraisers, well constructed and still functional, but again, unless they have some sentimental value to you, not of any economic significance.

"Now the rugs are quite interesting. They were both pretty worn and faded, but the appraisers were able to identify them as what's called Pinde Bokharas. They come from Turkmenistan—which I'll tell you I had to look up on a map—and they are apparently regarded as quite rare and valuable, though the condition of your rugs is not very good. They placed an auction value of seven thousand to ten thousand dollars on the smaller of the two, and twenty to twenty-five thousand on the larger one."

"No kidding?" Sam interjected. "I'd have never guessed that in a million years."

Andy picked up his narrative, knowing he had yet another surprise in store for his client. "That takes us to the matched pair of stained-glass lamps. Several things to know about those. First, the markings indicate that these lamps were made not only by Tiffany and Company but by Louis Comfort Tiffany himself."

"No shit?" exclaimed Sam, who had watched enough episodes of *Antiques Roadshow* to recognize the significance of this statement, and whose full attention was now focused on Andy and the report in his hands.

"No shit. But it gets better. From the shape and design of the shades, the appraisers could determine that these were not production models. Both are similar to models the company later retailed, but Tiffany never sold lamps with this particular shape and pattern. And that got them looking at the bases. The patina on both is what they described as 'right,' meaning it had just the sort of brownish film that's indicative of aging in the bronze Tiffany used in their bases, and the metal is pure bronze. There's also a heavy lead ring in the base, which, they tell me, was also typical. Apparently, solid bronze was too expensive even for Tiffany back then, but the lamps tended to be top-heavy. So they added a lead ring for stability. But it turns out that the lamps are not quite identical. The shape and patina on the two bases were identical, but the sockets—the parts where you would attach the bulb—were not the same, and neither one ended up being used on production models. One has a flip-type switch and the other has a very subtle pull chain. But Tiffany's early production models almost all had a turn-paddle knob for switching the lamp on or off. When you add all this up, the report says, it puts the manufacturing date sometime in the late 1890s.

"That, of course, leads to an obvious question: What was your uncle doing with a pair of non-production Tiffany lamps? And odd as it seems, there may be an obvious answer. I remember you told me that your grandfather, John Culbertson, at one time worked for Thomas Edison, or more correctly, for Edison's West Orange laboratory. The thing about these lamp sockets is that, although they were never production models, both were designed to fit only light bulbs manufactured by Edison, or later General Electric. So it would not be a stretch to think that just maybe Edison gave these two lamps to Culbertson at some point. Edison lived with a clutter of old gifts and awards he'd received, and probably a lot of prototypes of various devices sent to win his favor. Maybe he had a garage sale or a big giveaway of some sort or simply gave things away to favored employees when the mood struck him. Or for all we know, maybe your grandfather stole them. It's a possibility we can't dismiss out of hand, though based on the rest of what I have to tell you, that's not likely.

"As for value, you might want to grab the arms on that chair. Based on recent sales, the appraisers estimate the value of each lamp, sold individually, at $350,000 to $400,000. But you have an almost-matched pair. If you sold them together, they think you could get an additional hundred thousand dollars or so. But there's more. If we were somehow able to prove that these lamps had once belonged to Thomas Edison, and perhaps even been prototypes sent to him for testing or some other purpose by Louis Comfort Tiffany, well, the sky is apparently the limit. At the very least, it might be worth our looking into this and seeing if there is any connection we can establish. It might be as simple as Tiffany and Edison having known each other, perhaps even been friends. We can do a little research on that and see what we can learn.

"But speaking of Edison, that gets us to the ring. Two things about that. First, there's that really strange design on the ring, the one we thought might be Masonic. It's not, though there might have been some connection. The appraisers said that design is the logo of the Theosophical Society, which was some sort of religious-philosophical-scientific movement that was prominent back around the turn of the twentieth century. All those things on the ring have some sort of symbolic meaning. According to their report, that algebraic-looking business at the top is a Hindu symbol for creation, and the backward swastika was an old Scandinavian symbol for positives and negatives, maybe good fighting bad or some such. The snake swallowing its tail around the outside stands for the cycles of time, and the Jewish star-looking triangles have something to do with spiritual renewal. And that legless stick figure thing in the middle is actually an old Egyptian cross that was a symbol of resurrection. So it was all deep stuff. Apparently rings with this logo are not very common, so again, we have the question of what your Uncle Frank was doing with it. But again, there might be an answer of sorts.

"You remember that, inside the ring, someone had inscribed the word 'TEA.' Well, it turns out that's not what that was. The print was very small, but the appraisers were able to magnify it, and what they found was that the E in the middle was slightly larger than the T or the A. So, it was almost surely a monogram, with the last initial in the middle, just like you find on lots of sterling silver dinner services. So it seems that the original owner of this ring had the initials TAE. I don't know if Edison was tied in with that society or not, though the ring would seem to suggest so. All I can say at this point is that, once again, we are left to wonder about a possible connection between Edison and John Culbertson."

Sam had sat quietly through Andy's summary of the appraisers' report, but at this point he was unable to control himself. "Are you saying—" But he never had the chance to finish.

"Hold on," said Andy, holding up his right hand. "Because I've been saving the best, or at least the strangest, for last. Remember that painting?"

Sam nodded.

"You had said that the frame covered so much of the artist's signature that you couldn't make it out, and the appraisers had the same problem. But it goes without saying that in order to arrive at a valuation, they had to see who the painter had been. So they removed the backing and then carefully separated the painting from the frame. They found that the piece was signed by Georgine Shillard. They tell us that her full name was Georgine Shillard-Smith, and she was a pupil of James McNeill Whistler and something of a well-known Philadelphia and New Jersey artist in her own right. Unfortunately, her paintings today do not have much of a market, and one like yours would sell for a couple of hundred dollars, give or take.

"However," and here Andy paused for effect, "there was a notation on the back of the painting in something called 'dried black,' which, they tell us, looks like it is made with a brush used for black paint that has not fully dried onto it. Apparently, that's a technique painters sometimes use to name a picture or state a price or send some other message. We'll be able to see what that is when we have a look ourselves. Anyway, on the back of the painting is a date—January 1, 1915—and a title or description of the work, which reads, 'He brought Light into the world.' Maybe that's a reference to that speck of yellow you said stood out from the farmhouse in the picture. But we are not quite done yet. Because, when the appraisers removed the craft-paper backing from the painting to get at the frame, attached to the back side of the painting itself, they found this."

Andy slipped a single sheet of paper across his desk to Sam, who studied it intently for a few moments.

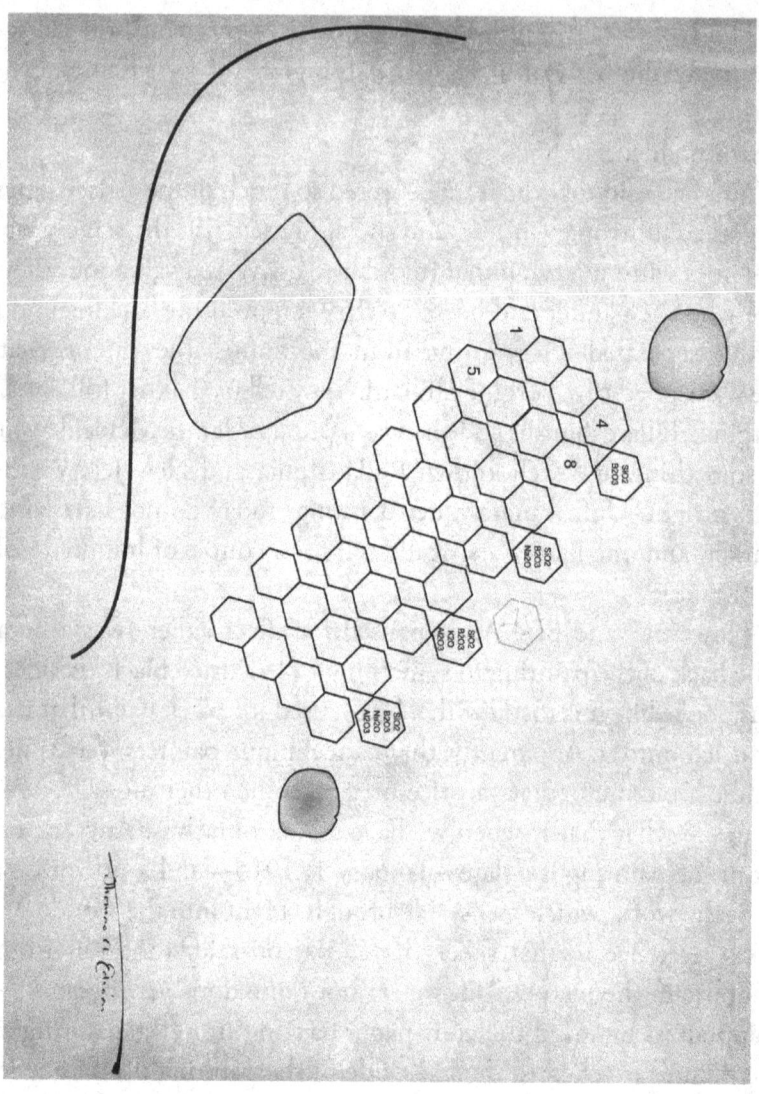

"Is that what I think it is, down in the corner?" Sam asked.

"Sort of intriguing, isn't it?" Andy asked in response.

"I think we need to take another look at that painting," was about all that Sam could offer.

"I couldn't agree more."

"Thomas," she had said—the she, in this instance, being Mina, his second wife. "The grandchildren are getting older, and we simply must have more room for their visits. The time has come for you to clear out all those boxes of yours in the upstairs back bedroom."

The upstairs back bedroom in question was one of twenty-three rooms in Glenmont, as the Edisons called their home in the exclusive New Jersey community of Llewellyn Park, located close at hand to the inventor's laboratories in West Orange. Edison had purchased the home in 1884 from Arnold Constable, owner of a major New York department store.

Edison had six children: three—Marion, Thomas, Jr., and William—by his first marriage, and three—Madeleine, Charles, and Theodore—by his second. But the grandchildren, four boys, all belonged to Madeleine, the only one of the six to have children of her own. Madeleine had married John Eyre Sloane, an American industrialist who had established one of the country's first airplane manufacturing companies, in 1914. Edison's own sons were thus the last of his line to carry the family name, although all four of his grandsons bore Edison as their middle name. Since, he was forced to admit, he left the management of their visits to Mina, as he had the better part of his children's upbringing, he recognized the justice of the rebuke implicit in her "reminder" and vowed that he would address the matter. Indeed, no time like the present.

So America's greatest inventor, the creator of modern life, as he thought of himself with but a touch of humility anchoring no small measure of justification, climbed the stairs, took the turn, and headed for the offending chamber. Opening the door, he was stunned by the magnitude of the task that awaited. "Put that upstairs," he had said to a generation of aides, maids, movers, contractors, and others. And put it upstairs they had. It would take days, he realized, to turn Mina's glower into any more neutral expression, days he hated to waste away in the detritus of the past when the future continued to beckon. Alas, he had little choice.

It was in the second week of clearing the room—most of which simply meant instructing one minion or another to move a set of boxes from Glenmont to a storage room in the laboratory complex—that he came across a box that brought him up short. The label simply read "CYLINDERS."

The box was heavy, far too heavy for a man of eighty years to lift. So he pushed it across the floor to his chair and sliced open the paper tape that had sealed it for . . . goodness, was it nearly a decade and a half? Where did the years go? Folding back the flaps, he saw, as expected, the ends of a dozen glass cylinders, each one nearly a half-inch in thickness, six inches across, and, he recalled without removing one, some sixteen inches long. A tide of bad memories came flooding in, and for a moment all Edison could do was close his eyes and relive a part of the past he had managed to isolate and pretend away.

It was the damned batteries again. And suddenly, it might have been yesterday.

Edison had always prided himself on his skills as a chemist. Though hardly a theoretician, he enjoyed the mixing and matching, the cooking, as he thought of it. In short, his approach to chemistry was much like his approach to any of his other interests: test enough possibilities and you just might find an optimum solution to a given problem. And with the rapid development of automobiles, the commercial potential for a market-dominating rechargeable storage battery to power the infernal things, the embodiment of industrial chemistry, seemed unlimited. Plus, there were so many other potential uses as well. It was just the sort of opportunistic play that had always appealed to him. *No time like the present*, he'd thought to himself. So even as he was building his new Portland cement works in Stewartsville and moving his motion picture work from New Jersey to Twenty-First Street in New York, in May 1901, he had committed himself once again to the chemist's bench, organized the Edison Storage Battery Company, and only a couple of months later worked a stock deal to get some fresh capital and at the same time cement his own control. Edison had been working on battery design since the 1890s, and as always, he had ideas—alkaline batteries, nickel-graphite conductors, other new materials, and glass jars or cylinders to hold them. The time had come to make definitive progress. In 1901, he went so far as to consolidate the research from all his companies into a new engineering department at the West Orange laboratory complex. He eventually put his friend Hutch in charge as chief engineer.

But others had ideas, too. And patent claims. So the better part of 1902 was lost to a struggle to determine whose patents would hold, a struggle that Edison won in no small measure through effective lobbying. He was, after all, Thomas Edison, and that counted for something. Still, it was a hollow victory. By the time he had control of what he thought to be a workable product, the auto industry had passed him by on its way to relying on the internal combustion engine. And if that was not enough, the product itself failed. By 1904, it was clear that Edison's alkaline batteries were prone to leaking and loss of capacity. He shut down the whole works for five years and began a decade of experimentation with reagents and new designs for electrodes.

His first thought was that it must be the seals. He understood the basics of rubber chemistry, and he knew that Charles Goodyear had figured out how to harden the stuff using heat, but that was nearly a hundred years earlier. Much could have changed in the interim. Perhaps he needed to look more closely at any new developments that might affect the vulcanized rubber material he was using for the seals on his batteries and might point toward improvements. *Flint,* he thought. *Flint's the guy who put together the U.S. Rubber Trust. He's no chemist, but he probably knows somebody I can ask about this. And he does owe me a favor.*

As fortune would have it, that was about the same time he received a letter, or rather, when it was brought to his attention by Frederick Miller Harry, who was in his last days as Edison's private secretary. His own departure was one of the few plans in Edison's professional life to which Harry himself was not privy. The letter sent his mind in an entirely different direction, and he all but forgot about the seals and contacting Flint.

"Mr. Edison," Harry had said. "We've just had this memorandum from the Cement company. It seems they have received an inquiry from a German industrialist, asking if our milling equipment is available for licensing. Fellow named Schott. Otto Schott."

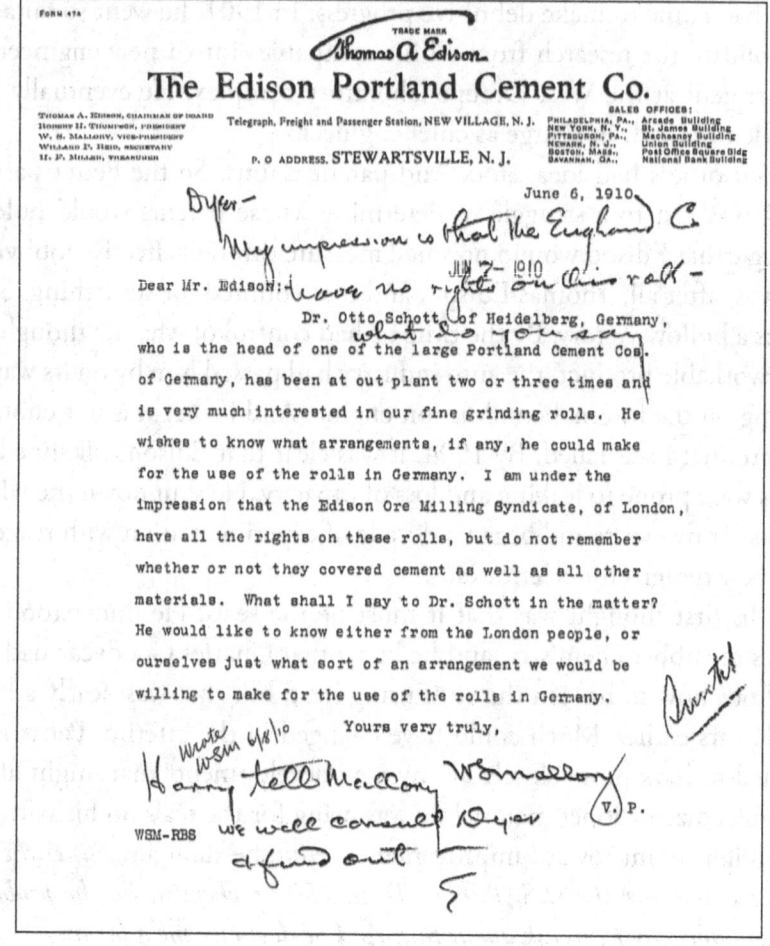

"Schott, you say?" Edison responded. "Is that Schott in Heidelberg, by any chance?"

Harry consulted the paper in his hand. "Yes, sir, he is. Do you know him?"

Edison grabbed the missive out of his secretary's hand. "Leave this with me," he instructed.

Father Brendan Culhannon declared Jennifer O'Connor and John Culbertson man and wife in the eyes of God at St. Joseph's Church in

East Orange, which had recently celebrated its twentieth anniversary, a hopeful omen. An anonymous donor had provided a beautiful spray of white and yellow flowers for the occasion. Jennifer was resplendent in a white dress she had sewn for the service, loose-fitting in the manner of late 1920s fashion, while John wore a borrowed suit in which he felt distinctly out of place. A few friends of the bride and groom attended the ceremony, and afterward the wedding party retired to a nearby establishment that was not committed to enforcing the prohibition laws then in effect. A celebration ensued.

Edison did not attend.

But when the happy couple returned to their new home—small but more than adequate for a family soon to number three—they found waiting on the front stoop three boxes, two of medium size and one a good bit larger. Attached to the largest box was a typed, unsigned note that read:

> All good wishes as you begin your new life together. To light your way, you will find here a pair of lamps that were manufacturer prototypes testing the latest socket designs. And to brighten your walls, you will find a painting which I hope you will treasure. Sometimes works of art become repositories of great value. As this may be one such, I most strongly urge that you never allow it to leave your family.

Though the note was unsigned, both Jennie and John felt sure they knew the author—each for their own reasons, unknown to the other.

"What lovely gifts," Jennie offered after she and John had opened all three boxes. They revealed a pair of table lamps with some sort of fluted metal bases and matching floral-patterned stained-glass shades, and a landscape of no particular distinction, about sixteen inches by twenty—an oil-on-canvas rendering of a distant farmhouse in a simple frame with a brown craft paper backing. A pinpoint of yellow light in the farmhouse window was the only element that truly drew the eye. The artist had signed the work in the lower right-hand corner, but the greater part of the signature was obscured by the frame. "I wonder who might have sent them."

———

Otto Schott's name, while a mystery to his private secretary—one of many, it was coming to seem—was well known to Edison. And this inquiry about grinder rolls for milling cement might offer just the opening that could solve the inventor's real problem—the damned batteries.

Herr Schott might now be . . . what did the memorandum say . . . head of one of the largest Portland cement companies in Germany, but his real claim to fame was in a different area altogether. Glass. Otto Schott was the world's leading innovator in the improvement of glass for scientific and optical purposes. The Thomas Edison of glass, as it were.

Edison himself had a great deal of experience in the commercial manufacture of glass. After all, every Edison light bulb was encased in the stuff. In 1878 he'd added a dedicated building, dubbed The Glass House, to the old Menlo Park complex, and the next year, he'd hired glassblower Ludwig Boehm to work on ways to improve vacuum pumps for his bulbs and other applications. For most of the day-to-day glassblowing for the bulbs, the inventor relied on a large number of female glass technicians, whom he thought took particularly well to the delicate work. But producing glass for light bulbs and glass for scientific and industrial use were very different things. It didn't matter much in 1878, but twenty and thirty years later, when Edison was trying to corner the market in storage batteries and was coming to the conclusion that suitable glass containers could well be the key to his success, it mattered a great deal. And that is where Herr Schott came in. The guy had even written a doctoral thesis on the stuff.

Edison had once read an article about Schott, and remembered something of his life's story. Schott, as he recalled it, was born into a family of glassblowers but aspired to be a chemist. As a result, he was perhaps the one person in the world other than Edison himself who kept up with trends in both fields. His interest in the chemical properties of glass had been spurred onward by two events—the development of the periodic table of elements by Russian chemist Dmitri Mendeleev in 1869, and the publication of a paper by physicist and astronomer Ernst Abbe seven years later that argued that new compositions of glass were needed to improve its optical qualities for scientific applications. In 1882 Schott had partnered with Abbe and microscope maker Carl Zeiss to experiment with various chemical modifications of glass. Two years later he started a company, Schott & Associates Glass Technology Laboratory, to make and sell specialized glass. By some accounts, that may have been the origin of the term "shot glass" to describe a small glass of whiskey, an Americanized version of the German "Schott Glas." Be that as it may, it was Schott who first thought to add boron to his mix. That insight created an altogether new type of product, known as borosilicate glass, with important properties that could be purpose-designed by varying the amount and particular compound of boron that was added.

For their part, American glassmakers—and Edison included himself in that group—knew of borosilicate glass, but without Schott's knowledge and techniques, they found themselves unable to produce it to the same standards. So in his battery design experiments, and most especially in his recently begun work on storage batteries for the Navy's new submarines, Edison had been unable to use the very type of glass widely judged as the world's best. Now, he saw in an instant that just such an opportunity might have landed on his desk in the form of Schott's unrelated inquiry. Perhaps a trade might be in the offing.

Edison sat staring at the box of Schott's glass cylinders. These, he recalled, were the last of the five dozen that he had commissioned during and after Schott's 1912 visit. A dozen each of five different formulations. Edison had been so confident in the first cylinders that he had used them in the construction of the batteries he had sent to the Navy for its submarine program. It was those very batteries that had been blamed for the Brooklyn Navy Yard disaster in 1916. He tried to remember: Had he mentioned the submarine project to Schott during his stay? He thought not. But if he had slipped, and if Schott, a German industrialist after all, had any inkling that his country might be moving toward war . . .

could that have been an act of sabotage? Edison rejected the idea immediately. He had regrets enough without giving credence to so dark an interpretation.

That accounted for only a dozen or so of the cylinders. The others—what had become of the others? Suddenly Edison realized that they were still out there, out where he had buried them nearly fifteen years earlier to test them against one another and against the elements. That was just before the West Orange fires, which were followed only two years later by the Brooklyn explosion. In all that chaos and dismay, had he simply forgotten about them? Was that possible?

After Sam had left his office, Andy sat staring at the browned-out paper that had accompanied the rather pedestrian painting through the better part of its existence. A squiggle, some gray blobs, a bunch of hexagons, some with strange notations on them. The only thing on the paper he could make sense of was the signature, Thomas A. Edison, and that made sense only in the context of Uncle Frank's backstory, the ring, and the pair of Tiffany lamps. Then there was the admonition from Sam's Grandma Jennie that the family should always hold on to what now appeared to be a worthless piece of art. There had to be more to this than met the eye, or at least Andy's eye.

It was at that moment that Keiley knocked lightly and pushed open the office door. "How'd your meeting go?" she asked. There were few secrets in an office administered by Betty, and Keiley was more than Andy's nearest and dearest. She was part of the team, at least for certain cases. Keiley was a professional cartographer—a mapmaker—with her own company and studio. When she wasn't working on maps, she enjoyed doing genealogical research and mapping the results for a growing group of clients. Space. Time. Either could be captured in one of Keiley Barefoot's charts.

"Pretty routine," Andy replied. "The report of the appraisers for the Culbertson estate came in yesterday, and we were going over it. It turns out there is more to the estate than we thought, like the fact that it might actually be one. One name keeps coming up again and again.

Thomas Edison. Frank's father, John Culbertson, worked for the man for some number of years, so it makes sense there might be a reference of some sort. But we have several pieces of property—a ring, a painting, a couple of valuable lamps—that have Edison all over them. And then there's this," he added, pushing the cryptic paper across the desk. "I have no idea what this is. But it was attached to the back of the painting."

Keiley picked up the well-aged paper for a closer look. A smile spread slowly across her face. "I know what this is."

Andy waited five seconds, then five more. She was toying with him, and he knew it.

"Are you going to share?" he finally asked in exasperation. One point for Keiley.

"It's a map of some sort. The squiggle and the gray blobs are landmarks. The squiggle could be a road, or a river, or a pathway, or the outline of a garden . . . almost anything. The gray blobs are markers—rocks or bodies of water, for example. In any event, it's a representation of some specific place.

"The truly interesting part, maybe, is the hexagons. We don't know how big they are, but they're all the same size. If Edison really drew this, that's probably not accidental. If I remember right from school, he was a very detail-oriented guy, very precise. So, if we ever figure out the dimensions of one of them, we'll have a basis for measuring this . . . I guess you could say this 'field' of hexagons. Or if we were somehow able to locate the landmarks—if they're even still there—we could use their common dimensions to locate each hexagon.

"You know, I've seen something similar to this before. Give me a minute to think."

The minute turned out to be nearly five, but the investment in time proved worthwhile.

"I thought at first it was in one of those Ed Tufte books I have at home. You remember those. But it was somewhere else, and I finally remembered where. Google melfisher.com," she instructed. Andy complied and found himself on the home page for Mel Fisher's Treasures, which billed itself as the "World Leader in Historic Shipwreck Discovery."

"Sorry. I'm confused. You think Edison was diving on a shipwreck?"

"No. Here. Let me come around and play with your mouse for a moment."

"That sounds like fun," Andy said playfully.

"Shut up and move over, you idiot!" she replied, laughing as she dragged her chair around the desk to a point where she could reach the mouse and see the screen. "Let me think."

Keiley clicked on the header for "Latest News" and began scrolling down the page. "There! See that?" she exclaimed when the first of several maps came into view. As she continued paging down, more similar maps appeared on the screen.

"Who the heck is Mel Fisher, and what am I looking at?" Andy asked.

"Mel Fisher was a treasure hunter down in Florida back in the last century. I think he died about thirty years ago. He's mostly famous for finding one particular shipwreck down in the Florida Keys, an old Spanish galleon called *Nuestra Señora de Atocha*, which most people just call the *Atocha*. That was like fifty years ago. The ship was carrying tons of treasure from the New World back to Spain—silver from Bolivia and Peru and Mexico, gold and emeralds from Colombia, pearls from Venezuela—maybe half a billion dollars in all."

"Half a *billion*?" Andy interjected.

"That's what they say. Anyway, the ship somehow got separated from the rest of the Spanish fleet, and then it got caught in a hurricane and sank. Most of the fleet suffered the same fate. That was in 1622. When the news got back to Spain, the Spaniards sent out a salvage mission using indigenous slaves to do the diving, and they recovered about half of the lost treasure from the fleet, but they never were able to locate the *Atocha*. So there it sat for the next three and a half centuries."

"Hold on," Andy said. "This sounds familiar. Wasn't there a movie about this? Owen Wilson, maybe? They found some old treasure map that was left by the captain?"

Keiley laughed. "Oh, you're thinking of that Matthew McConaughey film . . . *Fool's Gold*, right? And yes, it's the same ship as in the movie."

"And you think Edison found it?"

"No, silly. But look at these maps. Especially this one from 2011. See all the circles? Those mark out the areas that were searched by this company that still bears Fisher's name, and the types of items that were found. Together they show the track of the shipwreck as the vessel broke up back in 1622 and as the ocean has impacted it over the years since. It's the circles we're interested in. They're generated by GPS, and they mark out a grid of sorts and the locations of the prizes. They look for patterns that might suggest where to search next. When I saw your map there, my mind just flashed to these treasure charts. I'm not saying that Edison was burying treasure, and he obviously wasn't using GPS. It was one thing he *hadn't* invented. But I think he was burying *something*, and this was how he kept track of it."

"Wow," Andy said. "I never would have figured that out."

"Well, Lawyer Man," Keiley continued, using one of her pet names for Andy, one that he seemed to find amusing, "there's more where that came from. See those notations in the four hexagons that are sort of top-right on the chart? Those are chemical labels, though I couldn't tell you what they mean. It's probably worth having someone figure that out. The numbers down the left, the way he's done them but then not repeated them . . . If I had to guess, I'd say they might be sets of eight similar or identical things, whatever those are. But unless we find whatever this is, that's something we may never know.

"But the other thing I noticed is that there's one hexagon that's separated from the rest. The one with the tiny lines on it. I'd say that one was added at another time. It's pretty hard to read, much harder than the others. The ink is different—it's set apart—and it's the only one where you see a diagram like that. There might be some kind of special significance to that one."

"So," Andy asked once he was sure Keiley had finished her soliloquy, "that leaves only one question. Where do we find this chemistry experiment if it's still there?"

"No clue," was all she could offer. In that, the pair was equally enlightened.

Painting the Black

When Andy had taken over the law practice from Lou D'Antonio the year before, he could only hope for a steady enough flow of work to provide a reasonable living. After all, Lou had been in declining health for quite a while before he passed away soon after the two formed their partnership, and his caseload and clientele had been trending in the same direction. Andy knew he would need to energize things by seeking out new clients and new challenges. Then he'd unexpectedly ended up representing himself in a major case against Major League Baseball that had earned him massive publicity, not to mention several million dollars. And suddenly, there was more business than he could easily handle. The long, slow professional climb he had anticipated suddenly became long hours, followed by more long hours as expected, but serving a different purpose—not generating demand but struggling to meet it. If he did not have Keiley working part-time in the office next to his, keeping him centered, he might have felt the crush of work even more.

They had met on his very first foray into what is euphemistically called "business development," a fancy term for hustling for clients, at a seniors' community just outside Mendham, where she was doing the same while building her genealogy clientele. A mapmaker by trade, Keiley was turning her attention more and more to mapping family ties, and her research had been crucial to winning his big case. Now, the two were inseparable . . . except by work.

As far as Sam and his uncle's estate were concerned, things had pretty well reached a natural stopping point. The appraisal was done, and other things being equal, Andy could go ahead and file for probate. Soon Sam would have his inheritance and, he expected, some nice money from auctioning off those lamps. But he kept going back to that diagram, that map. What the heck was that? There was certainly enough work on his desk to keep him busy, and the chances of any billable hours, the lifeblood that pumped through every legal practice, coming from pursuing that question were pretty low. Yet he was deeply curious about that, and he thought that somehow there must be more to it than met the eye. Maybe a payday, maybe not. But if the money he'd made from his last case had any meaning, it was in the freedom it gave him to follow a hunch now and then. And this was just such a hunch.

Andy knew he would need some time out of the office just to clear his head, but he couldn't afford to take real downtime. Then he hit upon a compromise. He needed to find someone who could interpret the chemical symbols on Sam Culbertson's map, if that was, in fact, what it was. And he knew just the place to find such a person. Best of all, it was only about a half hour away. He asked Betty to call the chemistry department at Rutgers University and arrange an appointment with the department chair for the next day.

With his meeting set for two in the afternoon, Andy set out an hour beforehand for Piscataway, where the university's science programs had a campus more or less to themselves. Midday traffic was light, and he even found parking not far from his destination—all good omens. He found Doolittle Hall in short order and walked into the chemistry office five minutes early, only to be informed that the Chair had been called to a last-minute meeting with the dean but should be back shortly. It was about half an hour later when a bearded gentleman who looked to be about sixty walked up and introduced himself.

"Mr. Dennum, is it? I'm Hiram Burlmeister, the Chair here. I understand you had something you wanted to discuss with me?"

"Yes, yes, I do. I'm Andy Dennum," he responded, handing the professor one of his business cards. "Very nice to meet you."

Burlmeister took a quick look at the card, noting at once that his visitor was an attorney. "We're not in any legal trouble, are we?" he asked hopefully.

"No, nothing like that. I'm just looking for a little help with a chemistry question that's come up."

"Well, in that case," the Chair responded, showing some relief, "do come back to my office."

The pair retreated to a large office lined with overflowing bookcases and a table with what Andy took to be plastic models of elements or molecules or some other chemical thing. He had not done well in the two science courses he'd been required to take in school.

"Please have a seat," said Burlmeister, pointing to a settee and coffee table arrangement near the one window, "and tell me how I can be of service."

Andy set the browned-out document on the table. "I have a client," he began, "who inherited this rather strange document, and we are trying to figure out what it might be and why it might be important. We think it's some kind of a map, perhaps one showing the location of a large number of containers represented by the rows of hexagons. We don't know where this location is or how big the containers are, let alone what might be in them. But if you look closely, five of the hexagons have symbols written on them. Unfortunately, our high school chemistry got us only far enough to make a guess that these are chemical formulas of some kind. I was hoping you could tell us what they are."

Professor Burlmeister picked up the paper by opposing corners for a closer look.

"This," he said, "is very interesting. These are indeed chemical formulas. They represent various compounds—all but one of them include SiO_2, which is silicon dioxide, and B_2O_3, which is called boron trioxide. Then there are some other things mixed in: Na_2O, or sodium oxide, which is an alkaline metal; K_2O is potassium oxide, a base; Al_2O_3, or aluminum oxide. Did you want to know more about those compounds?"

"What I really want to know," Andy responded, "is what these are, or what they have in common. Why are they all together here?"

"Well," said the professor, "I don't know if I can answer all of that. But I can tell you that whatever these are, they all have the silicon and boron compounds in common, and that suggests very strongly that each of these various groupings uses a slightly different type of glass. It's been about a hundred and fifty years or so now, but after years of trial and error, scientists finally figured out that they could improve the strength and the optical qualities of glass, for example, to use in magnifiers or laboratory experiments, by mixing boron compounds into the molten glass. Fellow named Otto Schott discovered that and made himself a fortune, as you can imagine. The result is called borosilicate glass, and there's no single formula for it. So, what you might have here is someone playing around with different formulations to find the best one for some particular purpose. Of course, that's just a guess. Let me take a closer look. . . ."

Burlmeister sat forward and turned the paper in his hands. It was then that he noticed one of the corners that had initially been covered by his right thumb.

"Is that Thomas Edison's signature?" he asked somewhat incredulously.

"Yes," said Andy. "We aren't sure yet, but we have reason to think it is."

"My goodness!" Burlmeister responded. "This is remarkable. Where did you say you got this?"

"It was attached to the back side of a painting that my client's uncle left to him in his will. We found it when the backing was removed from the painting so that it could be appraised for the estate."

"Remarkable," said the professor. "And it makes me think of three things you might find of interest. First, you should get in touch with someone at the university library on the New Brunswick campus. Rutgers is the repository for Edison's papers, and they may either know what this is, or even have a copy of it in their collection already, or they may covet it, which could be helpful for your client, depending on his circumstances. I'll see if I can get you a name before you leave.

"Second, if what you have is, in fact, some kind of a map or guide, then the several ranks of objects make good sense. People tend to think of Edison as someone who continually tripped over good ideas. Nothing could be further from the truth. Edison was a different kind of inventor—a very . . . commercially oriented one. He would identify a potential or emerging market opportunity and then try to invent practical things to exploit it. And he would try hundreds or even thousands of possible solutions until he found one he liked. He used to refer to the process as 'mucking' and to the researchers he employed as 'muckers.' So what we are looking at here might be a master drawing of one of his experiments. He might have been testing four different compositions of glass—probably glass cylinders of some sort, which would have been a common application for the boron compounds—perhaps under different environmental conditions, or perhaps with different contents. That numbering scheme that is suggested off to the left? That could mean there were eight different conditions being tested for each of the four compositions of glass. Maybe those labeled hexagons would have been a ninth condition or, more likely, those cylinders would have been empty to serve as controls. I can't say for sure, but if this truly was Edison's work, something along those lines would be a good bet."

He paused. "Give me just a moment." Then he continued, "Do you know off hand the date associated with this document, which is to say, when it was created?"

"No," said Andy. "We don't have even a guess at that just yet. The only thing we believe is that the hexagon up there at, I'll call it the top, the one with the lines on it, was likely added at a later date. The ink looks different, and it's the only one with that kind of symbol. Plus, it's set aside. But we have no idea of its significance."

"Well, if you could somehow date this document to sometime between about 1907 and 1915, I might be able to guess what these are. From early on, Edison ran an operation that manufactured glass. He had his own factory and a staff of women who handled much of the work, and I think he even had a master glassmaker. After all, all of those light bulbs and tubes required a lot of the stuff, and he was not one to farm out a big job like that if he could make money from it himself.

"Now, one of Edison's big ideas was to control the market for batteries to power the newfangled automobiles that were becoming ubiquitous on the roads at the time. Most of them at the beginning were electric. So he got into designing and manufacturing batteries in a big way, almost exclusively alkaline storage batteries because they could be recharged and they would last longer. He was convinced it would be a huge and highly lucrative market. But by the time he figured out how to solve some major design problems, like leakage and loss of charge, the industry had moved on. Almost all the autos by then were being powered by internal combustion engines.

"But there was another mode of transportation gaining in importance in those days in a big way—the submarine. Navies around the world were beginning to build them in significant numbers, and they all depended on electric power to operate. They needed batteries—big, powerful, reliable batteries. It was just the sort of opportunity Edison was always watching for, and he became a supplier to the U.S. Navy. But his early designs still had serious flaws, and he was looking for new and more reliable ways to build them.

"Again, I can't be sure. But if the dates work, I suspect what you might have here is a chart showing Edison experimenting with different glass containers that he hoped to optimize as containers for his batteries or some of their components. We know, for example, that his early nickel-iron batteries used thick glass housings for the potassium hydroxide electrolyte—the chemical that made the battery function. Knowing Edison, he was probably experimenting with all sorts of glass if he thought he could make an improvement. If that's the case, and if what you have here is a one-off document, I think it is something of real historical importance. Some collector would surely want it, or some museum if your client is so inclined, and that's all the more reason you should talk to someone at the library."

"Okay. I'll be sure to follow up on that. But before I go, you said this glass and battery explanation applied to four of the five sets of symbols. But what about the fifth? What about this B with the lines and the O's? What's that about?"

"Now, that one is a little strange. It's the molecular structure of a borate ion, or more specifically, orthoborate, and the thing is, you don't find it that way in nature."

"Beg your pardon?" said Andy.

"Well, it's what's called an oxyanion of boron, a negatively charged ion that includes boron and oxygen, but it only becomes a stable compound when you combine it with some other element, like, say, hydrogen. But in the form that's shown here, about all I can say about it is that it's a very strong base. You know about acids and bases?"

"I've heard of them," was Andy's droll response. "I never took a chemistry course myself," he admitted. "But I have a general sense of what acids can do."

"Okay, well, bases behave in a similar way. A strong base can cause chemical burns just like a strong acid. And this borate ion is one of the strongest bases there is. Hold on and let me just pull up a table . . . yes. I'm looking at a table of the most common acids and bases that would have been known in Edison's time, and it's right here. Borate ion was the second strongest of all the commonly known bases.

"Now, if you want to get technical," Burlmeister was about to continue.

"We weren't getting technical yet?" Andy offered in dismay.

The professor began by ignoring him, but then paused. "Fair enough. I'll just say that if we are looking back at what Edison might have been up to, it's worth noting that combining a base with a hydrogen source like water creates what's called an alkaline solution, and remember that Edison was trying to perfect alkaline storage batteries. So there might have been a reason for him to be experimenting with the BO_3^{3-}, sorry, the orthoborate."

"Okay," said Andy, "so this outlier cylinder with the chemical diagram on it was probably filled with this borate stuff?"

"Actually, no," corrected the professor. "Because on its own, this BO_3^{3-} is unstable. So the cylinder could well be empty. And whatever this label meant, it could not have referred to the simple contents of a glass cylinder.

"I hope that's helpful," Burlmeister concluded rather doubtfully.

"I think," said Andy, "I'm glad I never took chemistry!"

* * *

As it turned out, the Edison archivists at Rutgers were not housed in the university's library on the main New Brunswick campus, but rather in a nondescript office building on the Livingston campus that overlooked a massive parking lot covered by solar panels. *Clever idea*, thought Andy as he made his second sojourn to Piscataway, this time adding a mile or two to reach his destination. In fact, the collection was not part of the library at all, but a project of the arts and sciences school. And the building itself, he discovered from a plaque just inside the door, was a much-remodeled version of a World War II edifice that had once served as the officers' club at Camp Kilmer.

This time Andy was a few minutes early for his appointment but found the bespectacled director of the project waiting for him. "Art Escalon," he said, reaching out to shake Andy's hand.

"Andy Dennum," came the reply. "Thank you for agreeing to meet with me on such short notice."

"To the contrary, I'm very interested to see what you have. Please, take a seat." He pointed to a chair across from the business side of his desk.

Andy sat down, opened his briefcase, and pulled out a thin file.

"As I mentioned on the phone," he said, "I'm an attorney over in Mendham. I have a client who has just inherited an estate that includes an old oil painting, and in the process of determining a value of that for probate, we found this document fastened to the back of the canvas."

He opened the file, took out the map, and handed it across the desk.

Escalon's eyes were immediately drawn to the signature in the corner of the document, and they opened wide. Then he studied the drawing itself.

"And you think this is . . . what?" he queried.

"I have a cartographer colleague who tells me it is most likely a map, and that it resembles in form the maps that treasure hunters use to identify and characterize locations that interest them. I have no reason to think there is a treasure being represented here, but I do think it identifies a specific location where there are, or were and might still be, some kind of objects buried. Your colleague in the chemistry department, Professor Burlmeister, studied the notations on the four . . . what would you call them . . . master locations, which he said represented different formulations of borosilicate glass. He indicated that, depending on whether we could date the document to sometime in the decade before about 1920, these might be testing vessels for containing corrosive components of alkaline batteries. I guess that Edison was working during that time to solve problems he was having with his battery designs."

"Now that," said Escalon, "is really quite interesting. You know, Edison was a prodigious notetaker. In our archive we have many examples of his research notebooks, including at least a couple on his battery work. Coincidentally, I have a page from one of those notebooks right over . . . here." Escalon found a photocopy on a corner of his desk and passed it to Andy.

"You can see that he was a highly structured thinker. But I have never seen a document quite like this one. What I am wondering, though, is whether we might have in our archive a key to this map, as you describe it—some rough diagram or list that we have never understood or perhaps even noticed. If you don't mind, I'd like to take a few days to look into that. Perhaps set a graduate student on the trail. They're quite good, you know, in tracking down this very type of esoterica."

"That would be great. I can't leave the document with you, but I can let you make a copy if you promise to return it."

"That would be fine. I understand. But I must tell you: If this document turns out to be genuine and links to something in Edison's notebooks or leads to the discovery of some lost Edison experiment, which seems to be what you're suggesting, we would be very interested in acquiring it for our collection. Perhaps that's something you could discuss with your client when the time comes?"

"I certainly will," Andy replied.

Experiments with Iron in the new
Concave smooth Crimping die with
drying & subseqt pressure with Concave
Corrugating Die July 16 1942 —

Reg 8+2 mix does not crimp strongly
on account of the lack of flowing
properties possessed by Nickel —

Now try following expmts to increase
the flowing properties so can get a
good light crimp

$\mathcal{N}^o$ 1

(2 of Each)
N° 1 Iron 4 6 grm cake, made at 500
press — Calipers 81 This now is 7 of
Iron and 3 of graphite, no 47 jum —
This is pretty thin + will not work I think
The crimping is no good can take side and
move it — Cake entirely too thin —
Crimped callipers in middle 56 — Edge
106·5 — We now make a cake 6 grams
without wetting it with the extra water to see
how cake Callipers are compared with the above
of 81/1000 = It callipers 91·5
This show that the 81 Calliper cake has less Iron

[1]

"In looking at this," Escalon continued, "I'm struck by one more thing, and perhaps it will be helpful. I'm looking at the larger shape at the bottom here, just above that curving line. If this is a map, then it might be that the shapes that seem to establish boundaries on the hexagonal spaces are rocks. They must be some sort of landmarks, and that seems most likely. And if you look at the larger of the three, it almost resembles the shape of home plate on a baseball diamond.

"You may not know this, but Edison was quite the baseball fan. He attended games, he sponsored teams . . . why, he even made the very first motion picture showing a baseball game. I believe it's in the Library of Congress.

"Now, the fact is that we don't have any significant holdings that relate to baseball. We do have some family correspondence and the like, but most of our emphasis here is on Edison as inventor and industrialist. So there is not much I can do to help you advance that particular line of inquiry using the archive. But you might want to contact someone at the Edison Innovation Foundation. They are, how shall I say it . . . less formal than we are, both in their structure and in their interests. They just might have some kind of information you can use. As you can imagine, we work with them from time to time. Let me get you the name of a contact over there."

And with that, Andy thanked his host, headed out to the parking lot, and drove back to Mendham. *Baseball again*, he was thinking. *Why do all my cases keep coming back to baseball?* But he knew a good lead when he heard it, and Escalon was right. That rock—if it was a rock—did look a lot like home plate. But where?

"Okay," Keiley was saying to Andy a couple of days later as they walked into the office following a breakfast of pancakes and coffee at the diner. "You asked me to see if I could find anything about Edison and baseball. So I started by looking at Edmund Morris's biography of the guy. You know Morris, right? Did those books about Teddy Roosevelt?"

"Afraid not," Andy replied. "I never find the time to read anything I don't have to."

"Well," she retorted. "You missed some good reads. Get a life! But as I was saying, I started with his Edison book. What a brick! Weighs about five pounds. It was published a few years ago, just shortly after Morris himself died. A lot of people consider it the best of the Edison bios, of which there are quite a lot. Given what's going on here, you probably need to read it right away.

"The book is encyclopedic about almost all things Edison, but I don't remember seeing a single word in it about baseball. That could mean that the guy had no interest in the sport, or it could mean that Morris simply never looked in that direction.

"But boy, that book sure tells you a lot about Edison the man. I started with the index in case there was some reference that would save time. It was very thorough, which isn't always the case, but it may be the strangest index I ever saw. One of the oddest categories was a listing of all the guy's personality traits, complete with page references. I wrote some of them down: absent-minded, aloof, attention-loving, blunt-speaking, calm in a crisis, charming and charismatic, cheerfully agnostic, cold handshake, contrary and obstinate, domineering, unaffectionate, generous, gregarious, distant, honest, humorous, incapable of self-doubt, patronizing, perfectionist, poor judge of character, risk-taker, impatient, stingy, ruthless, willful."

"Sounds like a hell of a guy," noted Andy. "I don't think they taught us all of that in school."

"Wonder why," Keiley replied. "Now, I have to say, I came across another biography, a contemporaneous one by a guy named Kennelly. That one was published by the National Academy of Sciences in 1932, the year after Edison died. And Kennelly described him very differently—energetic, frank, courageous, kindly, simple, modest, direct, and above all, tenacious. But again, nothing about baseball. I guess we all have our strengths and weaknesses. But whatever his were, they didn't have anything to do with baseball. At least according to Morris and Kennelly. But like I said, I was just getting started.

"The next thing I did is I went online and searched that archive of Edison's papers at Rutgers. I know your contact there said they didn't have anything of that sort, and he was almost right. I found two documents. The first," she said while placing a document on his desk, "was this long letter from the president of some Canadian telegraph company, and most of it had to do with trying to work out some sort of royalty arrangement for one of Edison's inventions. But then the telegram goes on to propose that the two collaborate to develop incandescent lighting for baseball fields so games could be played at night. That was in 1885, when Edison was still focused on his lighting products. I didn't find any follow-up or response, so we don't know whether Edison ever even considered the proposal. And that doesn't really get us anywhere.

ERASTUS WIMAN, President.   E. F. DWIGHT, General Manager.

THE GREAT NORTH WESTERN TELEGRAPH CO.
OF CANADA,

OPERATING THE LINES OF THE MONTREAL, DOMINION, AND MANITOBA TELEGRAPH COMPANIES.

President's Office:
854 Broadway, New York.
P. O. Box 727.

NEW YORK, AUGUST 7TH 1883,

THOMAS A. EDISON ESQ.,

65 FIFTH AVENUE, NEW YORK,

MY DEAR MR EDISON:

YOURS OF AUGUST 6TH IS RECEIVED, IN WHICH YOU SAY THAT IF I CAN PUT THE WESTERN UNION WAY WIRE AFFAIR THROUGH THIS QUARTER YOU WILL ASSIGN TO ME ONE QUARTER OF THE ROYALTIES. THIS IS INDEED A VERY LIBERAL OFFER ON YOUR PART, AND I ACCEPT IT GRATEFULLY, AND I PROMISE TO USE MY BEST AND MOST ACTIVE INFLUENCE IN THIS DIRECTION. I HAVE BEEN QUIETLY WORKING AT IT FOR SOME TIME, AND WILL DO THE BEST I CAN. NOTHING WOULD BE SO INFLUENTIAL IN ACCOMPLISHING THE PURPOSE WE BOTH HAVE IN VIEW, AS A PRACTICAL DEMONSTRATION OF THE EFFICIENCY OF YOUR INVENTION. THERE IS NO PLACE IN THE WORLD WHERE IT COULD BE DONE BETTER THAN IN CANADA. MR DWIGHT, THE GENERAL MANAGER, IS, AS YOU KNOW, IN THOROUGH SYMPATHY WITH YOU, HAS THE BEST POSSIBLE FACILITIES, AND WOULD GIVE A PRACTICAL AND ANXIOUS OVERSIGHT TO ANY PRACTICAL DEMONSTRATION OF YOUR VIEWS. WOULD IT NOT BE POSSIBLE, FOR INSTANCE, TO PUT YOUR DEVICE ON THE WIRES BETWEEN TORONTO AND HAMILTON, A DISTANCE OF 40 MILES, AND ILLUSTRATE BY PRACTICAL DAILY WORK THE ADVANTAGES WHICH YOUR INVENTION PROMISES? IT IS TRUE IT MIGHT BE UNWISE TO APPLY FOR A PATENT IN CANADA PRIOR TO YOUR APPLICATION HERE, AS THAT MIGHT INJURE IT OWING TO THE RULE IN REGARD TO FOREIGN PATENTS. WE HAVE, HOWEVER, LINES IN THE UNITED STATES BELONGING TO THE GREAT NORTH WESTERN CO., FOR INSTANCE IN NORTHERN NEW YORK, AND WE COULD USE THE DEVICE BETWEEN WHITERALL AND WATERTOWN. ANYTHING YOU SUGGEST IN THIS REGARD I WILL BE PROMPT TO CARRY OUT, ONLY, LET US GET TO WORK AT IT AND GET IT DEMONSTRATED. WHY SHOULD YOU NOT TAKE A RUN UP TO CANADA AND HAVE A CONFERENCE WITH MR DWIGHT ABOUT IT? I SAW HIM LAST WEEK FOR THREE DAYS AT THE THOUSAND ISLANDS AND HE WAS VERY MUCH IN EARNEST OVER THE WHOLE MATTER. HE ASKED ME MANY QUESTIONS ABOUT IT WHICH I WAS UNABLE TO EXPLAIN. HE HAS SOME FIRST RATE ELECTRICIANS IN HIS EMPLOY.

DID YOU NOT RESIDE LONG ENOUGH IN CANADA TO BE A MEMBER OF THE CANADIAN CLUB? THE ENCLOSED SPEECH MAY HAVE SOME INTEREST FOR YOU.

I HAD GREAT PLEASURE IN ENTERTAINING JOHNSON AND OUR FRIEND COSTER AT MY HOUSE THE OTHER NIGHT . JOHNSON THINKS THERE IS NO DIFFICULTY IN ILLUMINATING BASE BALL GROUNDS AT NIGHT BY THE INCANDESCENT LIGHT, SO THAT THE GAME COULD BE PLAYED. IF THIS COULD BE DONE WE HAVE A BONANZA IN THE GROUNDS AT STATEN ISLAND AND TRANSPORTATION TO AND FROM THEM BEYOND THE DREAMS OF AVARICE. LET THE SUBJECT OF ILLUMINAT-

ERASTUS WIMAN, President.   E. F. DWIGHT, General Manager.

THE GREAT NORTH WESTERN TELEGRAPH CO.
OF CANADA,

OPERATING THE LINES OF THE MONTREAL, DOMINION, AND MANITOBA TELEGRAPH COMPANIES.

President's Office:
854 Broadway, New York.
P. O. Box 727.

ING GROUNDS FOR ATHLETIC SPORTS HAVE SOME THOUGHT FROM YOU NOW AND AGAIN.

I TRUST YOU WILL HAVE A PLEASANT VACATION, WHICH I AM SURE YOU GREATLY NEED.

I AM,

FAITHFULLY YOURS

Erastus Wiman

"The second item I found was much less detailed, but it got me thinking in a different direction. It was a news clip from the *New York American* from 1912, reporting that Edison and his family took a day off to go to something called the Edison Field Day Games. About two hours into the festivities, there was an intramural baseball game between the company fire department and a bunch of white-collar types—clerks and managers. Let me come back to that in a minute.

"At that point, I wasn't sure if that meant baseball was a big deal, or if this was just some employee picnic he happened to attend. So, I looked into that a bit, and I found out that it was a little of both. It seems that, for years, Edison used to sponsor an annual Field Day for his workers, with all sorts of competitions, including baseball. But that's when things started to get interesting.

"Andy, you know better than most people that the professional leagues were in full swing back in 1912, and of course, it wasn't long after that when your great-grandfather made his arrangement with that Ban Johnson fellow, though we still don't really know what that was about. But what I discovered in my reading is that there was this whole other thing happening on the amateur and semi-pro side. Baseball was a big deal and a good way for workers to blow off steam, and a lot of the big companies had their own teams. The newspapers even had regular columns they would devote to semi-pro ball—results, standings, even the players on the teams. Sometimes it was a rivalry among different departments or parts of the company, like the Field Day games only with entire leagues. But a lot of times those leagues were made up of different companies that competed against one another. They called them industrial leagues, and there were quite a lot of them. And the competition could be pretty intense. Then, during World War I, it seems like a lot of big league players went to work for some of the companies in the defense industries to avoid getting drafted, and lots of them spent most of their supposed work time playing for the company teams in these industrial baseball leagues.

"Now, what's interesting is that Edison seems to have sponsored teams at both levels—both interdepartmental and between companies. And it looks like he took the whole thing pretty seriously. Could have been as a matter of interest, or out of some sense of obligation, or it could just have been a matter of pride. That certainly would have fit with his personality. But it got me to broaden my search, and that's when I started to find evidence that baseball really was one of his interests. I discovered that there was an Edison Club baseball team that was founded in Orange in 1911. The team president was a guy named Clarence B. Hayes, who, as it happened, was Edison's Music Room supervisor at the West Orange labs, and one of his top aides. And at least one of the other team officers, A.B. Meserlin, the treasurer, was also an Edison employee. In fact, he was the secretary to Miller Hutchison, Edison's chief engineer between 1912 and 1918. So this team looks like it was directly connected to Edison, or at least to his company, at a pretty high level. But oddly, even though most of his operations were in New Jersey, his company teams seemed to play mostly in Brooklyn. So they must have been tied in with the Edison Electric Illuminating Company. That wasn't one of his manufacturing companies; it was started back in 1887 to provide electricity for homes and businesses there.

"I found this old 1909 photo of one of those teams, and their uniforms identify them as the Brooklyn Edisons." Keiley passed the photo to Andy.

"They must have been pretty good," she continued, "because somewhere in this picture is a player named Joe Judge, who got started with the Edisons, then in 1913, got himself a tryout with the Giants, the real ones in New York, and went on to play for several years with the Red Sox and Washington in the majors. Apparently, from what I read, the Yankees even tried for several years to get him away from the Senators."

She placed an old news clipping on the desk.

BROOKLYN EDISONS NINE WINS INTER-CITY CONTEST

In one of the most exciting games ever played at Edison Field, Henry and Lorraine streets, yesterday, the Brooklyn Edison baseball team, one of the fastest independent clubs in the East, took the nine of the Philadelphia Electric Company into camp by a score of 5 to 3. The contest was witnessed by hundreds of rooters, and they were on edge all during the contest.

Townsend, who at one time drew pay from the Philadelphia and Washington American League clubs, was on the firing line for the visitors, and except in two chapters he was at his best. In the breakaway the Brooklyn ball-tossers gathered three runs on some timely hitting, and in the eighth, after the Quaker lads had tied the count, batted out a victory by sending two runners into the registration office.

Matty Sheridan, who was on the St. Louis American League team two years ago, did the delivery act for the winning combination, and he turned seven back to the bench on strikes.

The batting of Manley and a running catch of Finley were the features of the lively tussle.

A silver loving cup and gold watches were presented to the winning club players.

This afternoon at Edison Field the home team will tackle the famous Havana Red Sox, with Pop Watkins and King Kelley in the batting order. They are the funniest coaches in the world. A big crowd of fans will no doubt be on hand. The score:

BROOKLYN EDISON.

	R.	H.	O.	A.	E.
Sweeney, l. f.	1	2	1	0	0
Ennis, r. f.	0	2	0	0	0
Riley, c.	1	2	8	1	0
Springman, 3d b.	1	0	1	0	0
Kaselman, 1st b.	0	0	0	0	0
Finley, 2d b.	0	1	2	2	0
Manley, c. f.	1	3	2	0	0
Maires, s. s.	0	0	4	3	0
Sheridan, p.	1	1	0	12	0
Totals	5	11	27	14	1

PHILADELPHIA ELECTRIC CO.

	R.	H.	O.	A.	E.
Rapinger, l. f.	0	0	0	0	0
Miller, 1st b.	0	1	10	0	0
Wilson, c.	0	1	4	2	3
Townsend, p.	0	1	2	0	0
Kelley, r. f.	1	0	3	0	0
Brenner, c. f.	0	0	0	1	0
McCauley, 3d b.	1	2	3	2	0
Schwaub, 2d b.	0	0	1	4	0
Eirenbrey, s. s.	0	1	1	4	0
Totals	3	6	24	14	3

Phila. Electric ...0 0 0 0 0 0 3 0 0—3
Brooklyn Edison ...3 0 0 0 0 0 0 2 *—5

Left on bases—Philadelphia, 5; Brooklyn, 8. Two-base hits—Miller, Sweeney. Sacrifice hits—Sheridan, McCauley. Bases on balls—Off Sheridan, 3; off Townsend, 3. Struck out—By Sheridan, 7; by Townsend, 3. Hit by pitcher—Sweeney and Schwank. Umpire—Mr. Hassett. Time of game—2 hours and 5 minutes.

"Now it looks like Judge didn't play in this particular game, but you've got to read this writeup from one of the 1911 Brooklyn Edison games. It's a hoot. Plus, it shows that both teams had players who had played in the major leagues, so Judge wasn't the only one. And look how complete the coverage is!

"And here's another one. This one's from 1929, and it doesn't say Brooklyn, but it's still the Edisons. Maybe the New Jersey group. No way to be sure. But it does show that the company must have been fielding teams for a long time.

"And here's one from 1921, so in between the team photos, that shows Edison throwing out the first pitch for a game. I couldn't find out where this game was, but if you look at the grandstand there, it looks pretty substantial. And you'll see what might have been the same grandstand in another picture in just a second. Since a lot of the Field Days were at a place called Olympic Park in Irvington, New Jersey, I'm guessing that was it.

"There's even this grainy old snapshot from 1912. This had to be that game that got written up in the New York paper, and it's the one with the similar grandstand in the background. Edison was maybe fifty years old here and he's pitching to an actual batter. Somebody even went to the trouble of drawing in the flight of the ball and the path of the bat in this one. The old boy obviously had swing-and-miss stuff." Keiley smiled broadly, and Andy had a good laugh.

"I found an article about this game, too," Keiley continued. "It was in the Newark paper, and it talked about how the game was between the Edison Club and the fire department, and Edison threw out the first pitch. Let me find the quote . . . Here it is."

Stepping on the pitching slab with the air and grace of a Marquard or a Johnson, Edison wound up in true league style and shot the ball across the centre of the plate for a clean strike. The proud catcher stationed behind the plate said that Mr. Edison had speed to burn. He also used a curve ball that nearly worked havoc with the receiver, who was expecting a slow, straight one.

"Somebody was sucking up," Andy said. "But maybe Edison wasn't satisfied being a famous inventor. Maybe he had his own dream of making it in the majors."

"Funny you should mention that," said Keiley, picking up her narrative. "Because it turns out that the Edisons had a winter place down in Fort Myers, Florida, which happened to be where the Philadelphia Athletics held their spring training sessions from 1925 until the mid-thirties. Place called Terry Park. Connie Mack, who owned and managed the team, laid out the specifications, and the local government built the park. Edison was known to watch games there, but it gets better. In 1927, Ty Cobb signed on to play for the Athletics, and there's a photo of Cobb and Mack with Edison at the ballpark. This one." Again, she handed Andy a photo.

"I don't really follow baseball, but even I've heard of Ty Cobb. But I thought he had a pretty bad reputation."

"Yeah," said Andy. "People used to call him the meanest guy in baseball. I think he used to get into all kinds of fights, on the field and off."

"Well, here's a shocker for you, then. I found this old newspaper article from one of the Florida papers back in 1927, so right at this same time. Edison actually wrote the article himself. And he really loved Ty Cobb. I wrote down this quote: *It certainly is wonderful to think of a man like Cobb running around the bases with the speed and dash of a youngster barely in his twenties. If every youth who aspires to become a baseball player*

follows the career of Ty, they won't go wrong. He is an immaculate man, one of the cleanest the game has ever known."

"Offhand," Andy observed, "I'd say that Edison did not subscribe to the conventional wisdom."

"You've got that right. And here's another photo. Cobb's not in this one, but it turns out he was part of the action.

"There's a fun story that goes with this picture. Supposedly, Edison, who was eighty at the time, challenged Cobb to pitch to him, and Mack stepped in as the catcher, which I think must have been his old position when he was a player. Cobb stood about halfway between the mound and home plate and tossed in a few balls. There're two different versions of what happened next. In one version, Edison didn't make much contact. In the other, he hit a line drive that knocked Cobb down, and a bunch of reporters who were on hand had a good laugh. And Edison said to Cobb, 'Think you can hit them like that when you're eighty?' Take your pick. Either way, Edison was obviously a fanboy.

"There's even a third take on this same story. In this one, Edison showed up at the Athletics' training camp the previous year, 1926, and

was challenged by Kid Gleason, one of their best pitchers, to try to hit one of his tosses, again with Mack behind the plate. Edison reportedly popped the pitch over first base for what would have been a hit. Then, in 1927, according to this telling, Edison drove his car right up to the third base line and got out. After a minor negotiation, he borrowed one of Al Simmons' bats—that would be the bat in the picture—Cobb tossed a pitch from in front of the mound, and Edison smashed a line drive off Cobb's shoulder, knocking him down. In this version, the two shared a laugh and a handshake, and some observers started shouting, 'Sign him up!'

"Whatever version you want to believe, a few days later, the entire Athletics team showed up for a lunchtime visit at Edison's place. I found a photo of that, too. You can see Connie Mack right there behind that bush," she said, pointing, "and Ty Cobb is the guy in the V-neck sweater off his right shoulder. Apparently, the Edisons invited the team to come to their Florida home, which they called Seminole Lodge, and gave them a personalized tour. Then supposedly Edison regaled the players with stories about alligators. He also gave each player a cigar, but he noticed that rather than smoke them, each man put the cigar in his pocket. When he asked about that, they explained that they wanted to keep the cigars as souvenirs of the visit, so Edison sent off for more stogies, presumably to be put to their original intended purpose. At that point, the story goes, Mina announced that punch was being served, but Edison teased that she hadn't put anything in it. Guess the guy was not a teetotaler.

"At least the Athletics had the good sense to show up. I found another article that said that a couple of years later—1931, to be exact—the Brooklyn Robins were in Fort Myers during spring training, but for some reason, they couldn't get themselves organized to pay the Edisons a visit. One of their coaches had wanted to do it, and another one was very much in favor. As he put it, 'It might be a good idea at that. It will take an Edison to invent a new way to lose ball games. We know all the ways there are now.' And of course, Edison died not long after that, so there was no rain date the next year.

"And one more thing, though it's kind of indirect. I read an article that talked about Theodore, Thomas's son, and how he had a baseball card collection that he carried around with him in a special wallet. The cards were all from around 1909 or so, when he was about eleven or twelve, and he had what seemed like a lot of them. But the thing that impressed the writer was that they were all from something called the T-206 set, and apparently that's a big deal. You might have read about a baseball card that sold for millions of dollars? I guess it was one of those. But the reason I mention it is that the only way to get those cards was by buying cigarettes from one of the tobacco companies, and chances are that some eleven-year-old kid wasn't into that habit. And his father hated cigarettes—he even banned his employees from smoking them at work. He thought they were toxic—that smokers were less efficient workers, more prone to accidents, and even at risk of brain damage. Of course, he was always smoking cigars himself, and he was big into chewing tobacco. But not cigarettes. So somebody had to give all of those cards to Theodore. It wasn't likely Edison. Could have been his driver or some staff person at the house, I guess. No way to ever know. But he had to have known about it and approved."

As Keiley paused to catch her breath, Andy could only express admiration for her effort. But he did see one problem.

"That's really amazing work, hon. So now we can be pretty sure that Edison was a fan of the game. But I'm not sure it gets us any closer to figuring out where it is that our map references. Where's home plate? You're the cartographer, right? So where is this place?"

"Yeah, I was afraid you'd ask that," Keiley responded resignedly. "I guess there's more research to do."

That was when Betty's phone rang in the outer office, and after a moment she called out, "Andy, it's that fellow from the Rutgers archive for you. Should I put him through?"

Testing. Massive testing. It was always Edison's way, and no different this time. So much would ride on his ability to compare the qualities of these different glass formulations Schott had produced, to find the one solution that would make Edison storage batteries not merely superior but dominant, essential. For that, he needed a place—private, secure, and, above all, safe from some unsuspecting fool exposing himself to noxious chemicals. The lab complex simply would not do. There was too much activity, and there were far too many people around, to allow the requisite isolation. Then the inventor had a thought.

The Edisons' home in West Orange—Glenmont—was a remarkable property in itself: eleven wooded acres, a beautifully crafted house, a garage, a barn, a greenhouse. Designed in the Queen Anne style by architect Henry Hudson Holly, the house was originally built by Henry and Louise Pedder in 1880 to 1882. Edison acquired it as a distressed property—he always loved a bargain!—from Arnold Constable in 1884 after the Pedders had been forced to turn it over in the course of settling their legal troubles. Pedder, it seems, had been Constable's confidential secretary and was found to have been siphoning resources from his company. The statistics of the home told the tale: twenty-three rooms at the time of purchase, including two and a half bathrooms, a conservatory, twenty-three fireplaces feeding seven chimneys, ninety-four exterior windows, 157,000 bricks, and five tons of iron and steel framing. Edison wired the house for electricity in 1887 and added six more bathrooms over the years. It was quite the house.

But more remarkable still was the community in which Glenmont was situated. Llewellyn Park had been established in 1853 by businessman Llewellyn Haskell in the New Jersey countryside about a dozen miles west of New York City. It was a "romantically landscaped," planned, gated community in a park-like setting with hills, streams, and forests—the first of its kind in the United States—and it eventually extended to almost five hundred acres. Large portions of the land were set aside to preserve the ambiance of the community, while the remainder was divided into lots of no less than one acre and no more than approximately ten for residential construction. Almost from the outset, the Park was governed by a committee elected by the owners, with maintenance covered by an annual assessment, initially set at ten dollars per acre.

The community was divided into four areas which are still evident today: the Ramble, a mile-long scenic wooded area following a central streambed set aside for walking paths, seating areas, and visual enhancements; the Glen, an area of mostly open, gently sloped former farmland featuring some of the earliest development and the largest houses in the Park, including the aptly named Glenmont at its highest point; the Forest, steeper and heavily wooded; and the Hill, with the steepest slopes of all. Though augmented with various lighted paths, benches, gazebos, fences and other manmade visual features, the land itself remained fairly open, with no walls or fences marking the boundaries among the individual properties. Forested spaces, particularly surrounding the larger properties, along with the size of the lots, assured a high degree of privacy.

Just what Edison needed.

Sitting on eleven acres and surrounded by dense forest, Glenmont offered open space aplenty for the tests he had in mind. More than that, because a corner of the property sloped down toward the stream, there was land available in an area that would present the greatest challenge to the integrity of Schott's cylinders—the outer confines of an active wetland. If they could retain their viability in water and mud and all manner of weather conditions, without leaks, cracks, or signs of decomposition, well, those cylinders might be the answer he had been seeking for housing the most corrosive components of his storage batteries.

So it was that, on an unusually warm, moonless November night following a day of ground-softening rain, America's greatest inventor had set out with a barrowload of glass cylinders, a suitably sized auger, and a pair of rubber boots. Only days before, the Edisons had engaged in the one ritual that assured their popularity with their neighbors, or at least with their neighbors' children, one that had become a cherished Halloween tradition. As one resident of that era related, one of the children's fathers would drive a small group to the house, where they would be invited into the library. Edison would be seated before a fire, wrapped in a blanket, with a horn-shaped hearing aid in one ear. Mina would draw the visitors closer and ask for an explanation of each costume, then Tom would give each child a ten-dollar gold piece and Mina would give each the chance to choose one of the small toys she had purchased at FAO Schwartz and placed in a basket.

And now, here he was, sneaking down the hill in the dark of night with his collection of test containers in a wheelbarrow. Some of the cylinders were empty, allowing for a pure test of the structural integrity of the glass, while others were filled with various combinations of the metals and acids they would be expected to contain. Each canister was etched with symbols to indicate its contents, and some of the end caps were marked as well. By the time the task was completed after an expected night or two of what Edison thought of as his "fall plantings," each of Schott's various borosilicate compounds was to be represented.

One problem the inventor had not anticipated manifested itself right away. He knew that his property sloped down toward the stream, but as he soon realized, because there were no fences or other boundary markers, it was unclear where Glenmont ended and one or the other of the neighboring properties, owned by what he thought of simply as "The Douglases"—Douglas Cox and Benjamin Douglass, Jr.—not to mention the recreational area of the Ramble owned by the community at large, began. True, there was a much-traveled road just before the land fell sharply away toward Wigwam Brook, but roads were known to wander into places they ought not to be, especially where boundary lines were left somewhat ambiguous by design. Well, he thought, I am here, and I am not pushing this wheelbarrow back up that slope. Besides, once I am done, no one will notice.

Over the course of what turned out to be four suitable nights spread over two weeks, Thomas Edison "planted" some three dozen glass cylinders, each one about six inches in outer diameter, a touch under sixteen inches long, and between a quarter and a half-inch thick. As he worked, he drew a rough sketch of the location of the cylinders, including some rudimentary landmarks, which he would later reproduce more formally, and took copious notes as to their contents. He covered each cylinder with three to four inches of dirt, then used a rake to scatter leaves across the entire test field. Finally, to mark the area, he placed two medium-to-large rocks—the heaviest he could maneuver by himself—into a pair of shallow pits that he hoped and expected would prevent their rolling downhill into the stream over the six months or so he intended his experiment to last.

It was not long afterward that events overtook him, and Edison promptly forgot about the entire episode.

———※———

"Thank you for coming back over to the campus," said Art Escalon as he guided Andy to the same visitor's chair as before and then settled behind his desk.

"Well," Andy replied, "thank you for following up on our visit. I can't wait to hear what you discovered."

"I'm afraid that what I have for you is rather mixed news. We have conducted a very thorough review of our digitized collection of Edison's laboratory notebooks, and we have not turned up anything that looks like a guide or a key to your document. There are many other notebooks around outside of our collection, and there are still quite a few microfilm files we have not yet been able to process fully, and one of those might well include such notations. But alas, so far as we know, we do not have it.

"That's the bad news. The good news is rather more nuanced, but it might still give you encouragement, and it certainly enhances our own interest in acquiring that document. You had mentioned Professor Burlmeister's belief that your document had something to do with Edison testing a variety of formulations of borosilicate glass, quite probably in the context of his efforts to reduce leakage and loss of charge in his alkaline batteries, especially the larger scale ones he wanted to sell to the Navy. Though, as I said, we did not find notes relating specifically to your map, as you describe it, we did locate some battery-related notes that would seem to reinforce Burlmeister's notion. I have brought you the two best examples."

At that, Escalon placed two photocopies on his desk and turned them so Andy could read them.

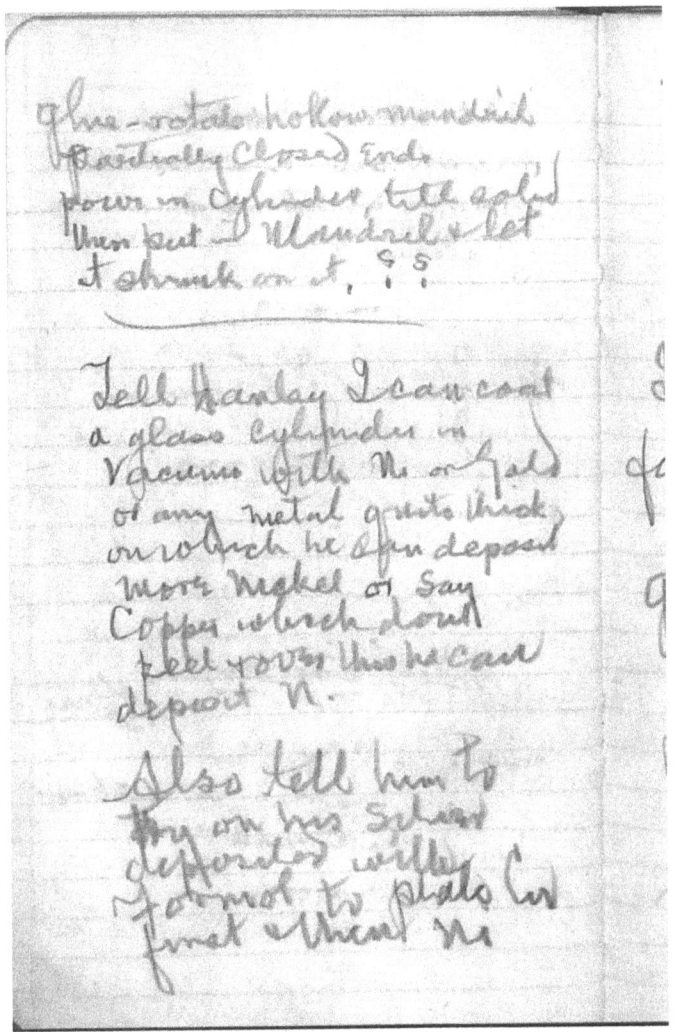

"This first page is from a 1921 entry, and you can see there in the middle that Edison was experimenting with glass cylinders, probably of the same type Burlmeister has in mind. By this point, he was obviously looking at metallic coatings of varying thicknesses, but it's the fact that he was using glass cylinders that seems most germane. And again, this passage is from his lab notes on battery construction.

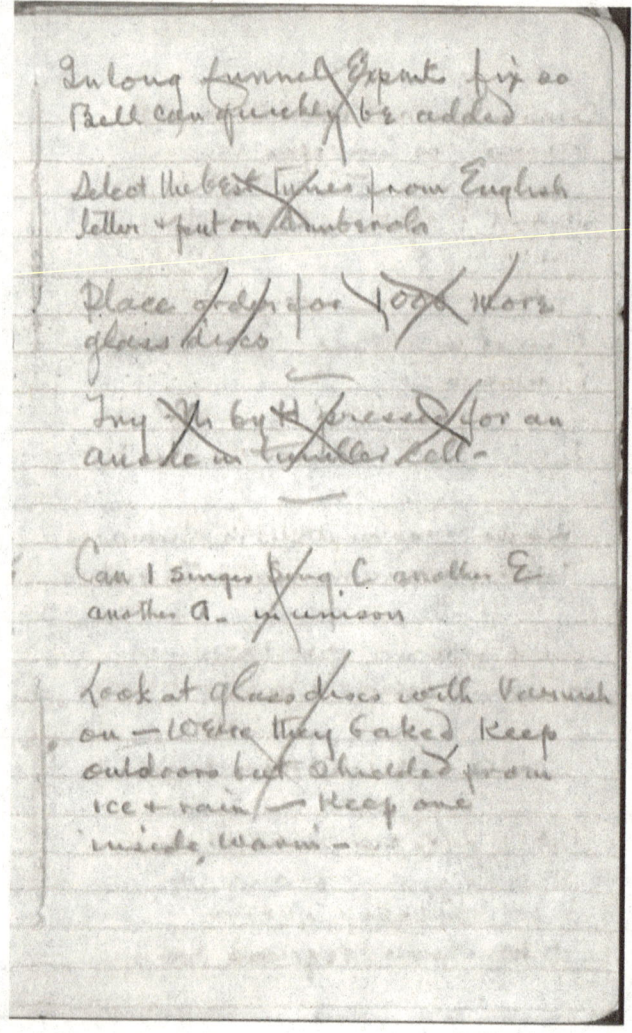

"This second page, also from his battery development work, is perhaps less directly on point, but of interest, nevertheless. This one is earlier, from 1919, and what you'll see here is that he was again testing glass, this time in the form of discs rather than cylinders. More specifically, he was advising one of his staff to test the glass outdoors under varying conditions, such as ice and rain, while retaining comparable samples indoors as controls. If what you have is indeed a map of the placement of varied types of glass cylinders in a structured manner, possibly with controls in the form of empty exemplars, that would seem to be entirely consistent with the method he advances here.

"I didn't bring it along, but we also located a letter that Edison wrote to the shareholders of his battery company in 1908. The company had been having all sorts of quality control issues with their batteries, even to the point where Edison shut down the factory in 1904 until they could make design improvements. By the end of 1908, they were back in production. The reason I thought you might find that of interest is that, in this letter, Edison spells out how they switched over from using charged plates, which they welded in place, to using cylindrical tubes. They were still using metals for those cylinders at that time, which is why I didn't think this particular document spoke to your problem. But the fact that they had switched to cylinders from 1908 onward did seem consistent. It might well have been that the cylinders were still not a perfect solution, and that could be why Edison was testing out various formulations of borosilicate glass. Of course, the 1919 notebook seems to suggest he was back using plates, or discs, instead. But that is how the man worked. Try this, try that, try the other thing.

"The bottom line is this: Based on what we were able to turn up, I believe my colleague in the chemistry department is most likely correct in his supposition. I think you have come across a document that details the placement of some kind of glass objects outdoors in one of Edison's experiments with materials for use in his batteries. Of course, as I am sure you have already grasped, that does not help in the least to identify a location where this experiment might have been conducted, let alone whether, somehow, its components are still in place."

———

Since her last conversation with Andy, Keiley had embarked on something of a voyage of discovery of hundred-year-old ballparks in New Jersey, and she was frustrated. She had learned that a park in Hoboken, Elysian Fields, had a reputation as having been the site of the first organized baseball contests between amateur clubs, though that primacy of place was no longer taken for granted. Still, Hoboken wasn't that far from the many New Jersey-based Edison enterprises, so it seemed entirely possible that one or more of his teams might have played there. The problem was that, even if that were true, it would not likely point to a solution to the current problem. After all, the baseball grounds at Elysian were part and parcel of a public park complex, one that was used by many different groups. Such a location would not seem to offer Edison the security he would require for an important and presumably long-running experiment. Moreover, the last baseball game documented to have been played at that location took place in 1888, at a time well before Edison would have been experimenting with borosilicate glass for use in batteries.

She thought her second discovery, Sprague Field in Bloomfield, New Jersey, might be more promising. Sprague Electric was a subsidiary of General Electric, which was, of course, the latter-day incarnation of Edison's original electrical enterprises. The company was named for its founder, Frank Sprague, a native of Milford, Connecticut, who had gone to work for Edison in 1883. Edison was focused at the time on building a central power station for his lighting system in Sunbury, Pennsylvania, but Sprague was more interested in working on electric motors. So a year after joining Edison, Sprague left to form his own company, where he invented electric traction systems that were in use or in planning by one hundred ten electric railways around the world within a mere five years. But it was Edison who actually manufactured much of Sprague's equipment, and in 1890, Edison bought him out and acquired the company.

As for the ball field, Keiley learned that Sprague Electric bought a plot of land near its factory and built the athletic complex for the off-hours use of its employees, much the model at the time. The company's team played the first game there against the Orange Athletic Association, which put it well within the geographic reach of many of Edison's facilities, not to mention the Orange-based Edison Club team Keiley had discovered earlier. Sprague's team then went on to capture the championship of the North Jersey Industrial League, which suggested that there was a suitable league within range. Unfortunately, all of this happened in 1919, which, if Professor Burlmeister's theory was correct, and if the date inscribed on the rear of the painting that had hosted the map all these years had any significance (admittedly an unknown), meant the field might not have been constructed until after the mystery cylinders had been set in place.

Finally, she knew that Edison had staged that series of Field Days at Olympic Park in Irvington. That one, she discovered, was still there—sort of. The park was permanently closed, but you could still find it on online maps, and in the satellite views, you could still make out a baseball infield and the location of home plate. But when she sought out more information, things became confusing. In Edison's day, Olympic Park had been a massive complex, at one time or another incorporating a rollercoaster and other amusement rides, a harness racing track, an Olympic-size swimming pool, a concert venue and dance floor, and much more. The perfect place for a large company outing. But the baseball field she could see online was surrounded by houses now, and the block it was on, while not small by any means, was nowhere near large enough to accommodate all of those activities. But then she found a 1912 map of the park, and looking more closely, she realized that, although the park had indeed been located at the point on Fortieth Street indicated on contemporary satellite maps, it had been *on the other side of the street*. And that land was now occupied by a maze of large commercial and industrial buildings. The Olympic Park in the photos was no more.

New Jersey was turning out to be a dud, so she turned to the only other location that had been referenced in what she'd read: Brooklyn. If it seemed like a reach, it proved to be anything but. In fact, others had already done Keiley's work for her.

Almost by accident, she stumbled across a website called BrooklynBallParks.com, which was a storehouse of information on the teams, parks, games, and more that captured the early history of the game in that borough. In particular, she found a page that summarized the history of Brooklyn's semi-pro, which is to say, industrial league, fields. And not only did she find that Edison company teams played there from about 1907 onward, either as Ampere A.C., the Edisons, or the Voltas, depending on the year, but that one of the fields was known as Edison Field (among several other names). In fact, there was a *second* Edison Field elsewhere in Brooklyn, at Washington Park. And for one year, in 1914, the company fielded teams at a different location called West End Oval. Best of all—essential, really—the website identified the specific locations of each park by listing the streets that bordered them. *Aha!* Thought Keiley. *Maps!*

Now it all came flooding back. The cylinders. The test. The damned batteries! The consequences. Edison was a man of few regrets, but this . . . this still affected him.

And there was now that other regret, the one he could never acknowledge publicly. Poor sweet Jennie and her newborn baby. Thank God Culbertson had stepped up. Still, there was more he could do.

Edison pulled out one of the remaining glass cylinders from the box on the floor before him. He had an idea.

Over the course of his remarkable lifetime, he had accumulated many honors and gifts. Perhaps he might share some of these with his other, secret family. Perhaps someday they might have value in their own right. And if that value was somehow enhanced by an association with himself, the Great Inventor, well, so be it. Any such association would be vague, ambiguous, and, most important of all, posthumous, his secret secure. He returned down the hallway to his personal study and began to contemplate his selections.

"Road trip!" Keiley said loudly. She had been up half the night with thoughts of baseball diamonds rolling around in her brain. Perhaps not the kind of diamonds most young women her age might see featured in their dreams in the circumstances, but there they were.

"Road trip!" she said again, this time leaning over Andy's sleeping form on the bed.

One eye flicked open, then the other.

"What? It's Sunday, for heaven's sake. What time is it?"

"Early," she replied, dropping her voice to a more conversational level. "It's about six thirty. Wake 'em and shake 'em, Lawyer Man. We're going on a road trip."

"What are you talking about? Where are we going?"

"Brooklyn. And we need to get going because it's going to be a long day."

"And we're going to Brooklyn because . . . ?"

"Ballparks, you slug. Ballparks. You've had me chasing down ballparks to the point where I'm starting to dream about them, and that, sir, is unacceptable. Even after all that wine, I couldn't sleep, so I got up an hour or so ago and started to map out a route. You want to figure out where Edison might have buried these cylinders or whatever they are, and we need to go see where all of these fields are, or were, that he might have used. And it seems they might be in Brooklyn. So get some clothes on, and I'll make some coffee. Move it!"

Half an hour later, they were in his atomic silver Lexus LX 600—the one indulgence he had allowed himself when the millions from his settlement with Major League Baseball had rolled in—and heading down Route 24 toward the interstate. Keiley was in her element—the cartographer as navigator—and she had the whole trip plotted out. They reached I-78 in about a quarter of an hour, and that took them all the way through Jersey City and the Holland Tunnel into lower Manhattan. Things slowed appreciably as they exited onto Laight Street and circled back to the west. Then it was left onto the Greenway until they picked up the ramp to I-278, then I-478 and the Hugh Carey Tunnel. Andy was remembering why he hated driving in Manhattan; Keiley was having a great time. Part of that, of course, was the sense of accomplishment that came with figuring out such a complex trip—a challenge even for the best navigation software—and it was only going to get more so. But part, she had to admit, was having this great opportunity to boss Andy around . . . just a little.

They took the exit for Hamilton Avenue, crossed the expressway, made a left at the light onto Hamilton, then a quick right onto Huntington. They crossed Court Street, then made a left under the IND Culver Line tracks onto Smith. Then it was right onto Third Street.

"Where the hell are we?" Andy wanted to know. "Do you even know?"

"Oh, ye of little faith," was Keiley's only rejoinder. "Drive on!"

They crossed the Gowanus Canal, something Andy thought he would never do in this life, and continued across Fourth Avenue.

"Pull over," Keiley said. "We're there."

There, it turned out, was Washington Park, or what was left of it. The park, known originally as the Fifth Avenue Grounds, had been used for amateur baseball games as far back as the Civil War, but by the 1880s, it had long been used as a skating venue. It had stretched in an easterly direction to Fifth Avenue—hence the original name—and more or less north-south between Third and Fifth Streets. The newly formed Brooklyn Base Ball Club, which eventually evolved into the Dodgers, took over the property in 1883 and built a field with a grandstand that could seat twenty-five hundred "cranks," as fans of the day were known. The park was built around the historic Old Stone House of Brooklyn, which resembled nothing so much as . . . an old stone house. Built in 1699, the house had played an important role during the Revolutionary War. But the baseball club had a different purpose in mind, and used the building as a "ladies' house," presumably for those of the fair sex who were either overcome by the heat of summer days or simply uninterested in the contests just adjacent.

That was then, of course, and while interesting, perhaps not the immediate concern of Andy and Keiley. For them, it was enough to know that the Edisons had played there for a time. Their question: What is left of the old grounds, and is there a place Edison might have buried his experiment? The answers came quickly. Not so much, and no. The Old Stone House was still there, or at least a reconstruction from the 1930s. But much of the park had been either built up or, at the very least, hardscaped. This was, after all, Brooklyn. There was still an open field, though its dimensions struck the pair as rather long and narrow for baseball, at least for today's game. But more to the point, there was no obvious landmark indicating a home base, and the early dates and short time the park was used by the company team also seemed unpromising. Andy was sure they could cross this one off the list.

Next up: Edison Field. They had a good feeling about this one, if only because of the name. Of course, they knew from Keiley's research that the place had had other names as well: Visitation Oval, Visitation Park, St. Mary's Field. But she had also turned up an old 1911 photograph of the ballpark that showed a grandstand and extensive bleachers that even seemed to suggest where home plate might have been, and that gave them hope. This had been a serious ball yard and they had a good lead. Better still, it was not that far away. Off they went.

Keiley directed Andy to Sixth Avenue, then right to Ninth Street, and right again to Court. Left on Court, right on Lorraine, and there they were. The good news was that they found themselves smack in the middle of the extensive Red Hook recreation area, replete with soccer fields and even baseball diamonds. The bad news? The block bounded by Lorraine, Clinton, Bay, and Henry Streets, the block that had housed Edison Field, was now occupied by the Red Hook Recreation Center and a massive outdoor swimming pool, with some bleachers, formal landscaping, and hardscape thrown in for good measure. Another dead end.

That left only the West End Oval, or Bath Beach Baseball Field, where the Edison teams had played their games for just one year—1914. It was the longest of long shots, and also a long drive. But if Edison had been experimenting with battery containment options in the middle of that decade, as seemed to be the case, Andy felt they must take a look.

In the event, it was a waste of time. The blocks from Cropsey Avenue to the Shore Parkway, or Shore Road as it would have been in 1914, were long ones, but the block between Bay Nineteenth and Bay Twentieth Streets, where the field was reportedly located, was not only very narrow but was also thoroughly built up with row houses and commercial buildings. Finding home plate at the West End Oval—if there had ever been one—was simply out of the question.

It all made the hour's drive home that much more depressing. Like Mighty Casey, Andy and Keiley had struck out.

"I hate to mention this," Keiley said as they wound their way back to Mendham. "But you should know that there was one more connection between Edison and a ballpark."

"Oh?" Andy replied warily.

"Yeah," she continued. "One of Edison's most successful inventions was a particular way of making Portland cement, and they used sixty-eight thousand bags of the stuff when they built the original Yankee Stadium. So if Yankee Stadium was called the House That Ruth Built, he built it with Edison's cement."

"Don't even think about it," Andy said. Those were the last words either spoke all the way back to Mendham.

———

Both Andy and Keiley were disappointed that their long, looping drive through a dark corner of Brooklyn's baseball history had gained them precisely nothing. But neither was really surprised. The whole thing had been a stretch. Andy had a desk full of work on other cases, and he had an easy time setting Frank Culbertson and his nephew Sam aside for a while. Keiley returned to her studio and started catching up on some genealogical mapping projects that had been lying in wait. One particular effort fascinated her. Following up on an idea that Andy had given her with a simple passing reference some months before, she had made contact with the official historian of one of the oldest New Jersey corporations, and she was preparing a graphic to illustrate its various mergers, acquisitions, lines of business, and other important developments over the one hundred and seventy year time period since its founding. They were planning to use the illustration as a foldout in their next annual report to shareholders, and that could lead to all sorts of new opportunities for her. But she kept coming back to Edison and his map. Why would such an orderly man leave a map as ambiguous as that one in a place where he must have known it would remain undiscovered for years? And once discovered, lead to . . . what? There had to be more to it. They had to be missing something. She reached for her phone.

"Andy, it's me."

"And all this time," he replied, "I thought my Caller ID had been hacked."

"Okay, smart ass. I deserved that. But I've been thinking. You remember that map?"

"What map?"

"Are you done busting my chops yet, mister?"

"Sorry. I'm just buried in this awful divorce case. You won't believe what some people will do. Apparently, the wife's brother arranged a double date for himself and the husband with a couple of strippers, then used his phone to shoot a video of the husband taking full advantage of the opportunity. He then texted the video to his sister, who immediately paid a visit to Rich Pristello over at OLPS—Olson, Lazareth, Pristello and Smith in Morristown—and had him file divorce papers. It's all those guys do over there to the point where they're known in the trade as Our Lady of Perpetual Separation, LLP. Anyway, I've got the husband. But that's where it gets weird. He says that the whole thing was a setup from the start because he just got a big bonus—make that a really big bonus, like six figures—at work that she had known was coming, and by waiting, she gets to claim half of the money. Plus, he says it was all planned out. So, he wants to counter-sue for something, but we haven't yet figured out what."

"Any kids?" she asked.

"Two from his previous," Andy replied. Then he skipped a beat and added, "Thirty and thirty-three."

"Beg pardon?" Keiley responded. "How old are—"

"He's sixty-four. She's thirty-eight. Kind of puts a different light on it, eh? Marriages might be made in heaven, but this is a hell of a mess. But you wanted to talk about that map."

"Yes. I've been sitting here, trying to figure out why Edison would have attached something like that to an old painting when he would likely have known it might never be discovered. And if it was, somebody would have to work through the very puzzle that we're struggling with now."

"Well," Andy said, "there's one more piece of this, which is that someone, and we are assuming it was Edison, told one or both of Frank's parents that they should never dispose of the painting. They should keep it in the family forever. It was in Frank's letter that he left with Lou. Which is weird, because the painter was never all that famous, and the painting . . . now, I confess I do not know much about art, but that painting is just plain boring. There's simply not that much to it."

"You know," said Keiley, "I've seen the map, obviously, and I've heard you talk about how it was found. But I've never actually seen the painting.

Maybe a fresh set of eyes would see something that's been missed so far. Do you have it at your office?"

"No, Sam took it home with him. But let me give him a call. I'll ask him to drop it by so you can take a look. I should have it by noon tomorrow at the latest."

"Actually, would you ask him if I could pick it up and bring it over to my studio? You know I have all of these art books, and the lighting upstairs is set up for just the sort of close inspection I'd like to do."

Keiley retrieved the painting from Sam and carried it to the world headquarters of her company, Barefoot Mapping, which happened to double as her house. She carefully maneuvered it up the stairs to her second-floor studio, where she set it on an easel in the well-lighted center of the room.

She began by walking around to the rear of the piece and gently leaning it forward on the crossbar. There, as expected, she saw the dried black notation, "He brought Light into the world," and the date, January 1, 1915. She assumed quite naturally that the "He" in question was Edison, though she realized that a reasonable alternative was that it was a religious reference to God. *Let there be light.* She moved the painting back to its resting position and circled back to the front of the canvas.

Andy was right, she thought. *It's pretty nondescript.* Big green field. Distant farmhouse. Trees on either side. Light in the window. There didn't seem to be anything special about the colors—mostly lots of greens. And though it was certainly not painted in the impressionist style, the overall impression was kind of gauzy and imprecise, almost like a watercolor in oil. The first thing to do, she decided, was to look up the artist whose name she had never encountered in any of the art history classes she had sat through in school. *Georgine Shillard, who are you?*

When Keiley typed the name into a Google search box, she got a surprise. The first site that popped up was something called Theosophy Wiki. This rang a bell. Something she had read about Edison . . . not in Morris, but somewhere. She brought up a separate search window to check it out, and sure enough, there it was. Thomas Edison had joined the Theosophical Society on April 4, 1878, a date that was shown beside his signature on a pledge card. Even the pledge was interesting. It read, "In accepting fellowship with the above named society, I hereby promise to maintain ABSOLUTE SECRECY respecting its proceedings, including its investigations and experiments . . . and I hereby PLEDGE MY WORD OF HONOR for the strict observance of this covenant." Keiley wasn't sure what Theosophy was, but she was excited that she might have found a link between Edison and this painter. *Now*, she thought, *back to Shillard*.

Georgine Northrup Wetherill Smith, she discovered, was indeed a member of the Theosophical Society. In fact, she was something of a major donor. She gave the society some land and art works, and apparently commissioned murals for its headquarters building. She was born in 1873, Keiley read, so she would have been about five years old when Edison signed his pledge card, but that would have made her about forty when she dated the painting. When she was twenty, she married Charles Shillard Smith, who was a wool merchant and into banking and finance. That must have been where the money came from, and also the name. From what Keiley was reading, the whole Wetherill family, at least in Shillard-Smith's generation, seems to have been into Theosophy. Georgine and Charles had several homes, including residences in New Jersey and Florida, so between geography and philosophy, and perhaps even Charles's business interests, there's a good chance they would have crossed paths with Edison.

The more she read, the more curious Keiley became. It turned out that Shillard-Smith, as she styled herself, had joined the Theosophical Society on July 2, 1914. That was precisely six months before she apparently presented Edison with her painting. She made a note to herself to figure out what Edison was doing during those months.

One odd thing was the painting itself. Shillard-Smith had studied art with Cecilia Beaux, who was a portraitist, and then with James McNeil Whistler. Whistler is well remembered for a single portrait, that of his mother, but he did develop a style called tonalism that was influential among American landscape painters: earthy colors, soft lines, abstract shapes. To Keiley's eye, the painting before her did not fit with that movement, and in general Shillard focused her own art on portraits. So not only was the timing of the painting for Edison interesting, but the subject matter itself was out of character and something of a one-off. Together, that seemed to suggest it had a special purpose.

As she mulled the problem, Keiley decided she needed three more pieces of information. First, what the heck was Theosophy? Second, why was Shillard-Smith involved in it? Was this something artists simply did at the time? And third, again, what was Thomas Edison doing in 1914 that might have brought the two together?

Rummaging through a long-forgotten file he found in a lower desk drawer, Edison came across a note attached to a colorful old engraving.

From the Desk of Charles R. Flint

Edison

You will recall some years ago passing along a bit of a discovery for which you had no purpose in mind. I have found such a purpose as has allowed my latest combination. In gratitude, and should it ever have much value, I enclose one point of the enterprise – the same I have granted to the Directors.

Yours –

Flint

This will do nicely, he thought to himself. *And this as well*, he added, grabbing a newly acquired memento. *And this*, grabbing an old favorite. All would go into the cylinder, and thence into the ground. Someday all would become clear . . . and at the same time, nothing.

This was a lot easier when I was younger, he thought as he slowly worked his way down the hill toward the spot where he vaguely remembered having buried the array of Schott's cylinders. The effort simply reinforced for Edison the fact that he did not move nearly as well as he once had, especially in the darkness, on the slope, and with a glass cylinder in one hand and the auger, retrieved from the garage after a lengthy but stealthy search, in the other. He nearly slipped and wrenched his back slightly in the effort to right himself.

To his surprise, he found the spot easily. The rock markers he had set nearly fifteen years ago were still in place. Glancing around, he assured himself that no one was watching. From the diagram, which he had successfully retrieved from an old file in his study, he located the desired spot, created the tiny tunnel he needed, inserted the cylinder, and covered the work with dirt and leaves as before. Then, using the auger as a walking stick of sorts, he climbed the hill, and made his way back.

Mission accomplished.

———

People who go into cartography tend to have ordered, perhaps even linear, minds and Keiley was no exception. She had a list of three tasks, and she was determined to work each one to her satisfaction. First up: Theosophy. She'd never heard of it before this, and in today's world, she found that was the norm. But back in the day—that day being about a hundred to a hundred fifty years ago—well, it was evidently quite the thing. Theosophy turned out to be a mixture of ideas from various religions, mainly Eastern, philosophy, science, and what we would probably call parapsychology today. Peace, love, brotherhood, reincarnation—something like that, and all fairly open-minded, or perhaps open-ended. Their credo was "There is no religion higher than truth," which, she concluded, told you why adherents to the movement had run into some problems over the years with people who thought they were devil worshippers—or worse. They just ducked their heads, it seemed, and kept going. The movement, she learned, had been founded back in the 1870s by a mysterious woman named Madame Helene Blavatsky, and Keiley was surprised to discover that Theosophy is apparently still around today, though the peak of its influence seemed to have come back in the 1920s or so, at least in the U.S. There are places today, she read, where the movement still thrives.

Okay, thought Keiley, *that fits with Edison, who was known to have been agnostic on the question of religion, or at least to have held views that lay outside the mainstream of his times.* He seemed to take pride in being unconventional, and that would certainly describe this movement. Plus, it looked like he got hooked on Theosophy fairly early in its run, if his 1878 membership card was any indicator. Ever the innovator.

Check.

Next up, why did Shillard-Smith get into this group? Keiley realized she could never really answer that one at a personal level. The poor woman was long dead and gone. But maybe there was some social reason she could at least guess at. Was Theosophy a thing for the "in" crowd? Keiley decided to see what she could find out about the membership. And sure enough, there they were—a bunch of prominent painters: Gauguin, though a member, had been dead ten years when Shillard-Smith joined, but Kandinsky, Klee, Mondrian—they were all essentially her contemporaries. And sculptors like Borglum, composers like Mahler and Sibelius, and writers, philosophers, and you name it. In Shillard-Smith's time, the membership was a real Who's Who of intellectuals. Not only was the group respectable, but it was even a status symbol in certain circles. And between her artistic bent and her money, Shillard-Smith clearly ran in those circles. So that made sense. Then Keiley hit something of a jackpot. Shillard-Smith, she recalled, had studied with James Whistler. And guess which other painter had been a theosophist? *If you said James Whistler,* she mused, *score one for the home team.*

Check.

That left the Edison question. What was Edison doing between July 1914, when Shillard-Smith joined up with the theosophists, and the following New Year's Day, the date on her painting? Was this some sort of initiation rite?

As soon as she looked at the Edison timeline published by their new friends at Rutgers, she had the answer, or at least a plausible one. On December 9, 1914, there was an explosion in the Film Inspection Building at Edison's West Orange compound. It started a fire that destroyed or damaged more than half of the buildings. It wasn't Edison's first experience with such fires, nor would it be his last. But it must have dealt the man, by then in his sixties, a devastating blow. Could it be that simple? Shillard-Smith knows Edison—perhaps from Theosophy, though he hardly seemed to have been active in the movement at that point, or more likely through some New Jersey or Florida connection— she hears of the tragedy and feels great sympathy for her famous friend, she rushes to make a painting to cheer him up. Not her customary style, but somehow what the situation demands. A yellow glow in the distance. He brought Light into the world. Feel better! And given what Keiley had now learned about Theosophy, she thought it was unlikely that a gift between two adherents of that movement would include a Biblical reference. The "He" in question was almost surely Edison himself.

Check.

Keiley knew right away that she needed to take another, closer look at that painting.

"Andy," she said into the phone later that day. "I'm at my place. I think you might want to come over here."

"On my way," he said. And fifteen minutes later he was climbing the stairs with her to the studio that consumed the entire second floor of her house just outside Morristown.

"What have you got?"

Keiley explained to him what she had learned about the artist, her painting, and her possible tie to Edison. She followed with her theory that, whatever their connection, Shillard-Smith was trying to console the inventor over the loss of so much of his laboratory complex in the fire a few weeks earlier. "That," Keiley concluded, "is what got me taking a really close look at this piece.

"I think the artist's label on the painting is the key. 'He brought Light into the world.' It could be a religious reference, of course, but in the circumstances, I think it's a reference to Edison and a reminder of all the good things in his life, all of his accomplishments. Now, when you look at the picture itself, there's that building that we took to be a farmhouse, with one tiny pinpoint of yellow light. I don't think that's a farmhouse at all. I think that's Glenmont—again something Edison loved.

"There's this technique in painting called the vanishing point. When you're using it, you pick a point on the distant horizon of the picture, and then you build in some working guidelines that you can use in creating the rest of the image. The guidelines are all supposed to represent parallel elements of the image, but you draw them in such a way that they all converge on that pinpoint, the vanishing point. Then you adjust your horizontal and vertical scales as you work from the bottom of the painting toward the horizon. So if you plan to include fairly small objects in your picture, you might mark points along the bottom at, say, half an inch apart. But if you plan to show only bigger objects, you could increase the spacing to an inch or two. Then you draw lines from each mark to the vanishing point, and you treat those lines as if they were parallel to one another. The result is that objects in the distance come out much smaller in proportion than in real life, and those in the foreground much larger.

"So, for instance, say you wanted to paint a perfect square. In the picture, the near edge would look wider than the far edge, and the left and right sides would appear to converge toward one another, so it would look like a trapezoid. More specifically, like an isosceles trapezoid."

"A what? Then," Andy inserted, "how would you know it was a square?"

"Because the two sides would be the same length and running along the guidelines. I think that could only happen with a perfect square," Keiley replied.

"Okay," rejoined Andy. "You have lost me completely."

"Didn't you ever take geometry in school?" she asked.

"I did. In fact, it was my favorite class. I sat behind Eva Butterworth in that class. She was this blond girl with great legs, and she had this way of—"

"Let me rephrase, *Counselor*!" Keiley said with more than a little emphasis. "Didn't you *learn* anything in geometry?"

"Well, not really," Andy said. "I was too distracted most of the time. Eva Butterworth had this—"

"Arrghh!" Keiley exclaimed. "Okay, let me see if I can put this in a way you might understand. You remember how fashionable ladies of, say, a hundred years ago used to carry around those fold-out paper fans to use in case they got too warm or felt they were about to experience the vapors, whatever those were?"

"Yes," was all Andy could offer.

"Okay. So picture one of those fans. You know how they made those? They took a relatively long piece of fairly stiff paper and they pleated it like it was a pleated skirt. Or in guy talk, so it looked like an accordion. Then they glued two flat sticks to the paper, one at either end, squeezed the thing together, and put a pin through the sticks and the paper at one end. Then, if you wanted to open the fan, all you had to do was rotate the sticks and voila.

"Try to stay with me here," she said with more than a hint of condescension in her voice. "If you think about the end with the pin as the business end of the fan and the other end as the open end, when it's spread out and you look at it from the open end, you're looking at a lot of folds that converge at the business end. We know that, in reality, those folds are parallel, because we folded the paper that way, but they no longer look like they are. Instead, they get closer together as they get closer to the pin at the other end.

"That's exactly how the vanishing point works.

"Now, if I'm right about this, then that building with the point of light on the horizon is actually a great big house—Glenmont. The trees you see are actually much more prominent than they appear. And the thing we've been calling a field in the foreground is a particular perspective on that house that, in real life, would be proportionately smaller than it appears. You with me?"

"So far. It's all so . . . scientific. I'm impressed. I thought you artistic types just sat down and slapped paint on some cloth."

That earned Andy a pinch.

"Just for that, I may not tell you the rest," Keiley said as she paused.

"Okay, okay! You win. Where are you headed with this?"

"Right here," she said, pointing to a wide, dark patch at the bottom center of the painting. "Think in terms of perspective. Does this remind you of anything? Remember, if two lines are parallel and equal in length, they'll appear to be slanted toward one another at an angle that suggests they'd meet at the vanishing point."

Andy took a moment to recalibrate his view of the picture. Then he stared at the dark patch for a moment. "Oh my God," was all he could muster. "Is that what I think it is?"

"If you're thinking it looks a lot like the business end of a rock shaped more or less like a home plate in baseball, then yes, I'd say so. I don't see the other two rocks from Edison's drawing, which could mean anything. Maybe they're off in some other direction. Or the artist dismissed them as unimportant to her composition. Or even that they may not have been there at the time she was painting. The fact that the painting used this particular perspective could have been a pure coincidence, and Edison could have chosen this location independently sometime later and added the other two markers when he did. Honestly, I don't know what to make of that. But I think we have found the starting point for the map.

"Here," Keiley continued, passing a copy of an old photo to Andy. "Look at this. I found it online at one of the National Park Service sites. You know, I assume, that Glenmont, the old Edison estate, is a National Park now."

Andy looked at the photo but didn't immediately see the point.

"That's the big lawn at one side of the house. It's taken from closer in and it was shot in 1960, but if you imagine away the younger trees in front of the house and squint your eyes to make everything smaller, you can . . ."

"See the house as a tiny image at the far end of a field of green grass with trees on either side. If it's not the same viewpoint as in the painting, it's sure a similar one."

"And there's something else. I found it earlier, but it didn't mean anything to me until now. I think that guy you talked with at Rutgers told you that Edison made the very first moving picture of a baseball game. That was back in 1898, and they have it online at the Library of Congress. So I watched it. The thing was filmed at a ball field, probably in Newark, quite possibly at Olympic Park, and it lasts less than a minute. If it wasn't the first of something, it wouldn't be special. But

it turns out that Edison actually made *two* baseball films, that one and another one the very next year. You remember *Casey at the Bat*, the Ernest Thayer poem? That was written in 1888, and it was a pretty big smash as poems go. Well, in 1899, Edison made another super short film, and it was named after and based on the Thayer poem. Some poor umpire makes a call the famous Casey doesn't like, so Casey trips him and then everybody from the bench runs over and piles on. I guess stuff like that actually happened back then. But the interesting thing about it is where the movie was made—in Edison's yard at Glenmont."

"I've got to call Sam with this," Andy said as he planted a big kiss on the cheek of his favorite cartographer.

Inside the Park

"Okay," Andy said, opening the conversation with Keiley. "Let me do a little thinking out loud. We have the diagram or map of these rocks—at least that's what we think they are—and all these hexagons. And we have a belief that this piece of paper was attached to the back of a painting—hidden there, really—by Thomas Edison. And we have a theory of what the hexagons might represent—a collection of glass cylinders—and an educated guess as to what might be in them. And we have a suspicion that whatever they are, they were buried at some time in the past, probably around 1915, more or less, by Thomas Edison. And we have the possibility that whatever Edison buried is still there, wherever 'there' is. And we have the painting itself that seems to suggest that the whole thing—rocks, cylinders, and anything else—could be buried on the grounds of Edison's old house, Glenmont. Of course, we could be overinterpreting or misinterpreting any one of these elements.

"The thing we absolutely don't know—and it's a big one—is how Thomas Edison made his way into this little conundrum in the first place. Thanks to your work and the appraisers', we can connect Edison to the *stuff*—the painting, the Tiffany lamps, the ring—but that only gets us so far. The only link we have from *Frank* to Edison is that his father, John Culbertson, once worked for the man. From what I've been reading—and I confess that it's mainly the Morris biography you told me to look at, and it wasn't a close reading—the guy was something of a curmudgeon when it came to dealing with his rank-and-file employees. So either this Culbertson fellow was more than that, or the connection doesn't make much sense. I mean, it's still possible that Culbertson simply stole all of these items.

"The one thing we know for sure is that Sam, our client, has inherited the entire puzzle along with a few other intriguing artifacts. It's time to find some actual facts. Because if we can't do that, all that Sam has inherited is a mysterious piece of paper. I think we need to take a run over to the old Edison place and see what we can see. Grab your umbrella. It's supposed to rain later."

Ten minutes later, they were in the Lexus and headed for West Orange.

"This is kind of exciting," Keiley said as they began their short journey. "I didn't grow up around here, and I've never been to Menlo Park."

"Rookie mistake," Andy chided. "Menlo Park was where Edison had his first big lab complex and where he did all of the lighting R&D that made him so rich and famous. That's further south. Actually not very far from the Rutgers campus I was at. But after his first wife died and he remarried, he shut that down and moved over to West Orange. That's where we're headed."

Andy had been to Edison's old works, now formally known as the Thomas Edison National Historical Park, not once but twice on class trips while he was in school. It was a big and fairly well-preserved complex of industrial buildings filled with fascinating displays. But neither he, nor his classmates, nor apparently the wise elders of the Morris County School District, who had overseen his education from kindergarten through high school, manifested any interest in Glenmont, the Edison manse. All of their focus had been directed to the laboratory and manufacturing complex in the middle of town. As far as Glenmont was concerned, he and Keiley were both first-timers.

So when the pair wound their way through Morristown, up to Parsippany to pick up the Essex Freeway, then down Mount Pleasant Avenue to Main, then left on Park Avenue to . . . Whoa! They discovered, to their dismay, that you can't get there from here. They found Llewellyn Park, Edison's old neighborhood, just fine. What they had not counted on was the gatehouse. The residents of Llewellyn Park, it turned out, did not cotton to strangers. In fact, they went to some rather elaborate lengths to keep them out. The guard was polite but firm. There was no way they would get in.

Andy had no choice but to turn their chariot around and head back to Mendham.

"We need a Plan B," was all he could think to say.

"Rookie mistake," Keiley said with just the faintest whiff of irony.

Back at the office in Mendham, Andy and Keiley regrouped. That is to say, they did a bit of due diligence that, had they thought to do it before, would have saved them a wasted trip to West Orange. They discovered two things.

First, they learned something they had already discovered. Llewellyn Park, the in-town suburb where Glenmont is located, is a gated community that is all but entirely closed to the public. Gates. Security guards. Llewellyn Park had the whole nine yards. Those people really valued their privacy. And yet, ironically, there was part of a national park, Glenmont, right there in their midst. So there had to be a way in.

That led to the second discovery. The way into Glenmont passed through the other part of that same national park, the Thomas Edison National Historical Park—the lab complex on Main Street in West Orange. Would-be visitors to Glenmont were required to visit the lab complex first to obtain a special yellow pass that would get them through the gate at Llewellyn Park and, using a designated route, to the parking lot adjacent to Glenmont. The pass itself stated the rules clearly: "NO PASS — NO ACCESS — NO EXCEPTIONS."

And there were added wrinkles.

House tours at Glenmont were only available on weekends, and only with advanced reservations. Andy thought that might be a cost-saving move, reducing the time demands on Park Service staff or volunteer docents. But then he read on and discovered that even the grounds at Glenmont were restricted. One could walk around outside the house more or less freely, but only on Thursdays through Sundays. And to reinforce the point, even the main part of the park with the laboratory buildings was open to the public only on those same four days of the week.

So it came to pass that, on the following Thursday morning, Andy and Keiley set out once again for West Orange, this time aiming for the Edison lab complex on Main Street. They worked their way through Morristown in the morning traffic, then up Mills to Speedwell Avenue, which eventually dumped them onto the interstates—80 and 280—off at the Montclair exit, then left onto Mount Pleasant and left again onto Main. From there it was just a few blocks to the Edison complex. Andy turned left into the small Park Service parking lot, and they walked across the street to the park entrance. Their timing had been almost perfect, as they arrived just a few minutes after the facility opened at ten.

The duo paused for a moment before entering. The complex gave every appearance of being the retired industrial site it was. Age-darkened red brick buildings surrounded by a black chain-link fence topped by barbed wire, likely a latter-day addition. In the distance and dominating the scene, a gray water tower perhaps fifty feet high. *It's hard to believe,* thought Andy, *that the modern age began here.* Then they joined the trickle of visitors passing through the tall iron gates, now opened to the world, past the faded message board listing the companies that were once headquartered there, under the balustraded brick arch, and, as instructed by a small white sign, left into the visitor center to register their presence. They paid their way into the park, making sure to collect the item of greatest interest that day, the half-page yellow parking pass that would admit them to the hideaway community that was Llewellyn Park.

For Andy, the experience brought a rush of schoolboy memories. Back then, the place had seemed much larger and somehow grander. He could not decide which the intervening years had aged more, himself or the workshop complex. Probably a bit of both. But for Keiley, with her greater interest in things technical, the complex retained its magic.

"Let's stay here a while and take a look around," she said.

Andy, trying not to show his impatience to begin the real task at hand, offered a begrudging, "Okay. But not too long. We don't know how long we'll need at Glenmont."

Most visitors, it seemed, began their tour at the end of Building 5 nearest the Main Street gate, directly opposite the Visitors Center, which houses Edison's wood-paneled multilevel library. But Andy and Keiley decided to do theirs in reverse, so the pair began with the more distant chemistry laboratory, then the machine shops, with their massive Victorian-era machines, and the spacious third-floor Music Room where so many of Edison's recordings were made. Scattered throughout were exhibits that included period photos and a variety of Edison's inventions. At one point they came to a collection of old storage batteries, including one that was encased in heavy glass, and a photo display centered on Edison's factory for manufacturing them. The photographs showed an operation on a far larger scale than either Andy or Keiley had imagined. One featured complex, belt-driven machines like those they had just seen, but in this case dedicated to creating the principal components of the batteries. Another showed a long assembly hall lined with numerous workstations, with some tasks clearly reserved for men and others assigned primarily to women. One photo in particular captured their attention, not only because it showed the elaborate preparation of one critical component of the batteries—nickel—but because it bore a handwritten date of January 15, 1915. This was what the operation looked like in the precise time period that seemed to be central to their research.

Eventually the pair headed down the final stairway at the front of Building 5 and took the left turn into Edison's library, with its prominent painting of the inventor, its massive wooden clock, its collection of patent and other literature, and even its oversized cot, tucked into one of the corners at Mina's direction so many years earlier. Had Andy known more of the real family history of his client, he might have paused to consider whether that might have been the scene of . . . whatever had happened nearly a hundred years earlier. But he did not, so he did not. And as he and Keiley wrapped up their tour, he was relieved at last to be heading back to the car. It was time to get to work.

As it turned out, the parking pass came with some very specific directions, first, for reaching the Llewellyn Park gatehouse—already familiar to Andy and Keiley—and then for traversing the approved route, and the *only* approved route, from the gatehouse to the parking lot for Glenmont. Straight ahead on Park Way, right on Glen Avenue, left on Honeysuckle, past Edison's garage on the left and his greenhouse on the right, and then right into the small, heavily shaded parking lot. Go to Jail, Go Directly to Jail. Do Not Pass Go, Do Not Collect $200. Finding about half of the available fifteen spaces vacant, Andy parked the car under one of the trees, and they walked across the narrow street and up toward the house, which, from this angle, completely dominated the surroundings.

At the end of the gravel walkway up toward the building, they came to a large circular driveway paved in chip seal—basically a coating of asphalt that was overlaid with chipped rock—that gave it a dark gray color. The driveway passed under a porte-cochère in front of the house, then framed an oval that was almost large enough to contain a soccer field. It being a Thursday, the house itself was not open to the public, but since they were far more interested in the grounds, this was not an impediment. They decided to begin their search by walking the full circumference of the oval to gain some perspective. At this point, Andy knew he must rely on Keiley's artistic eye to find what they were looking for.

"Okay, my dear," he said. "I need you to play clairvoyant now and see if you can channel the esteemed Georgine Shillard-Smith. What did she see? And more to the point, where did she see it from?"

Circling the driveway counterclockwise, since that was the way they were heading, they passed a footpath leading off to the gravesite of the famed inventor and his wife, then Keiley paused for a moment and looked off to the west toward Park Way. Another pause a few feet later, after which they passed an extension of the gravel drive that ran off to their right and down toward the same road. The next bend brought them to the side of the oval directly opposite the house, and here Keiley paused for a longer time, noting the lawn leading south to Glen Avenue at a point they had passed as they had driven in. Finally, they progressed through the remainder of the driveway, which was heavily shaded and offered no panoramic views in either direction—toward or away from the house. Finding a wrought iron bench on the nearby lawn—probably painted green at one time but blackened with age, with an open geometric pattern for its seat, and arms and back formed by a leafy metallic grape arbor—they sat in silence for two or three minutes.

"When you realize," Keiley began, "that even the oldest trees here would have been much smaller at the beginning of the last century, maybe even just saplings if they were here at all, you have to imagine away a lot of this landscaping. Of course, there could have been other older trees anywhere here that died and were cut down over the years, but let's assume not. In that case, there are only three places Edison could have planted his little experiment. One is that clearing area between that road," she said, pointing toward Park Way, "and the side of the house. It's wide enough, and it might have the correct angle. Plus, your view of the house does not include the driveway, which does not seem to be present in the painting. But even using a vanishing point, the distance there doesn't strike me as long enough to create the view in the painting. The second is that wider clearing running the same way toward the road from about a quarter of the way around the driveway. That one might be long enough, but the angle is wrong. Not only is the driveway centered in the view, but you're looking along it rather than across it. And the last one is the long stretch opposite the front of the house that's a straight shot to Glen Avenue. It's long enough, but it looks across the driveway twice and then has a full frontal view of the house.

"Here's the thing. None of the three is exactly right. At least I don't think so. Of course, it's kind of hard to be sure, because the house wasn't much more than a dot at the vanishing point in the painting, so everything would be distorted, though in a systematic kind of way. And that painting did not seem to account for the driveway, though surely that was there from long before. So taking all of that into account, here's what I think.

"I think we can all but eliminate that middle view, the one that runs along the driveway toward the front corner of the house. I just don't think it has artistic appeal, and as boring as the view in that painting is, we have to remember that Shillard-Smith was a true artist with serious training. I don't think she would have chosen that perspective. That leaves two choices: one that seems to be long enough, and one that might have the right angle. I think that our painter used a little artistic license. I think she combined the length of the front lawn, the one that runs down to Glen Avenue, with the angle of the side view. And that's what she painted.

"That leaves the question, then, of which place Edison actually used to bury his glass cylinders, or what we're assuming were his glass cylinders. I don't think the painting tells us that with any certainty."

"That may be true," Andy said, deciding it was time for him to hold up his end of the conversation. "But we have some more data to consider. First, one of those two areas is much more secluded than the other, and fundamentally more private. Assuming we're out at the far end somewhere, the Glen Avenue location is wide open to public view. If Edison was out there digging holes, or even if he did that at night and covered them up with dirt afterward, it's the sort of location that might attract the prying eyes of nosy neighbors. Maybe even some surreptitious digging by a neighbor or worker when Edison was away, just to see what he'd buried. At a minimum, I'd be willing to bet that, in this neighborhood, something like that would attract attention. Maybe even a visit from your friendly homeowners association. But the Park Way location is much more secluded.

"Plus, Edison was many things, but I don't recall anyone describing him as having an artistic bent. Shillard-Smith might have visualized in her mind's eye some kind of amalgam of the two views like you suggest—and by the way, I think that's a brilliant insight—but the chances that Edison grasped what would have been a rather fine artistic point? I don't think that would have been likely. So when he chose the painting as the messenger to carry that map to some unspecified point of future discovery, I don't see that as being top of mind. Of course, Shillard-Smith wasn't trying to capture some point where Edison had buried his experiment. No, it was Edison who saw the picture and must have been reminded of that experiment. And the fact that he used that array as the basis for our map or drawing? Well, that says to me that those glass cylinders, or whatever they are, are still in the ground somewhere.

"But here's the clincher for me. Think about the map again. There's some kind of a line curving around alongside the experiment. If you look over there at Glen Avenue, it runs straight as an arrow along that side of the property. But if you look down that side view toward Park Way, the road curves around pretty much like Edison drew it. I think we ought to walk over there and see what the ground looks like once you get away from the house."

"That's no fair," Keiley responded. "You told me to channel the artist. Now you get to channel the cartographer? That's my job!"

They had a good laugh, and after resting for another minute or two, rose from the bench, completed the circumnavigation of the driveway, and continued on to the point where the footpath ran down toward the gravesite. After the first few feet, they left the path and headed left and down the hill toward the road.

"I guess we can't go that far," Andy said, "but there's a streambed just on the other side of the road down here. And it pretty much mimics the curve of the road, so unless we see—"

Andy never finished his sentence. As they neared the road, the area known as the Ramble came into view on the other side. It was heavily wooded, and the area nearest them had a relatively steep slope down toward where Andy knew Wigwam Brook ran. Just across the road and near the top of the slope, they both saw it—a large angular boulder that seemed to point their way. Was this home plate rock, as they'd come to think of it? Without crossing into territory beyond the boundary of the national park, they could not be sure. But it was, at the very least, a stimulant to their imaginations.

Andy decided to have a closer look. He glanced back toward the house and did not notice anyone in a ranger uniform paying them any mind. But just as he was about to venture across the road, a Llewellyn Park security car rolled slowly by, then stopped a few feet short of the next bend. With a national park in their very midst, it was impossible for the residents to keep the prying eyes of the public out of their neighborhood completely. But it was, Andy guessed, unusual for tourists to wander down to this particular corner of the Glenmont grounds. So the guard was either curious or had chosen this particular spot for a break. Either way, the car had mirrors, and Andy didn't like his chances. Better to wait until he had a legal right to take a closer look.

As they started back up the hill toward the house, Keiley happened to look off to her right. "Andy," she said. "Do you see that?" She pointed off to the side of the clearing, then started to wander in that direction. Andy followed, and as he got closer, he saw what had caught her eye. It was not especially large, and it lay at least half buried in the lawn. But there it was. A rounded boulder only a fraction of the size of the one across the road. First base?

Andy and Keiley looked at one another, and then, as one, they turned around and, getting their bearings, began to walk in a straight line away from the rock while keeping the larger roadside boulder off their left shoulders. Passing the centerline of the unmarked track, they stared ahead, hoping to see a mate. But look as they might, none was evident.

"I guess if we could, we'd leave no stone unturned," Andy said shamelessly. "But there are no stones here." He knew this one would earn him one of Keiley's now famous knuckles to the arm, but he couldn't help himself.

Neither could she.

Leaving Glenmont, the specified route took them to the right from the parking lot onto Honeysuckle, a narrow one-way road, then left onto Park Way and back toward the gatehouse. Andy noticed that the security guard had moved on, and he stopped the car momentarily at the point where they had been considering a brief foray down to the brook. But he decided not to tempt the fates, and drove on.

The remainder of the trip back to Mendham was a little slower than anticipated. The police, it seemed, had pulled over a pair of drivers onto the left shoulder on the other side of the highway near the top of I-280, and though the lanes were open, the rubberneckers were slowing things down as they always did. But Andy and Keiley barely noticed the delay. Their heads were filled with what they'd found at Glenmont.

"Anything could have happened," he said as they worked their way toward the crunch point. "We could have the wrong home plate. That should be the first thing we check when we can get in there legitimately. I mean, from the little we could see, that slope down to the brook looked pretty steep. Edison would have been in his sixties, I think, when he decided to bury those cylinders, and if that soil over there is rocky, which it looked like it might be, well, that would have been some pretty hard digging. Of course, he could have hired someone to do that for him. No telling. But then, why would he bury something on common land? We'll have to take a close look at the property lines in that area. Or who knows? Maybe he didn't know where the property line was, or he thought his land ran all the way to the brook, or maybe he just didn't give a damn. I mean, who would argue with the guy? Still, home plate could be further down the slope and nearer to the water. That would certainly offer a stiffer test of durability."

"And if that boulder is home plate," said Keiley, picking up the thread, "and if that other rock we found was a second location marker, then anything could have happened to the third marker. It could have been moved in some landscaping adventure years later. It could have come loose and rolled down the hill. It could be completely buried. Or it could be someplace else, maybe further over than we were looking, or further up or down the hill. I mean, we're kind of assuming a particular relationship among those marker stones, and if you think about it, the only reason for that is that somebody suggested Edison liked baseball, and then one of us—and I won't point fingers here—thought that the big rock in the painting resembled home plate."

"Won't point fingers?" Andy rejoined. "Won't point fingers? If memory serves, that 'somebody' was you!"

"Be that as it may," she replied in a futile effort to regain the initiative. The two of them broke out laughing.

"Okay," Andy said in an effort to get the conversation back on track. "Whatever the case is, I think we have found ourselves a starting point for a search for those cylinders, and, hopefully, enough suggestive on-site evidence to get someone interested in letting us conduct that search. We just have to find the right somebody."

Just then they passed the remnants of the police chase and the traffic opened up before them. The remainder of the drive was uneventful.

———

Once he was back at his desk, Andy decided he needed some sort of contemporary map of the Glenmont area, something he could use both to figure out the various boundaries in question and to show anyone he might contact the specific area(s) he thought needed examining. And he also needed a document that would indicate the property lines back around the time when Edison would have been burying his experimental cylinders, so sometime around 1915. Fortunately, he had a professional cartographer in the next office. It was only a couple of hours later that Keiley plopped herself down in one of his client chairs and laid two maps on Andy's desk.

"What have you got?" he asked, glancing at first one and then the other of the maps.

"Couple of things. See if these will do. The first one," she said while pointing to a black-and-white street map, "shows all of the properties and property owners in Llewellyn Park, and it's dated 1913. I don't think you'll find anything closer to the middle of that decade, and in any event, it shows the Edison property very clearly. You can see it down there in the lower-left quadrant, right where there's a big bend in Park Way. The map itself doesn't show the legal details, like the specific boundary markers, but I think it's pretty clear. Glenmont was bounded by the three roads we saw—Park, Glen, and Honeysuckle—and that area of common land they call the Ramble seems to start immediately across Park Way, just like we thought. However—and I think I should get an honorary law degree for tracking this down—the block and lot information for Glenmont, which seems to cover several tracts of land, is 91/1; 101A/19; 101A/6B;

and 101A/22. All I can say is: Don't ask me what that means! But it does include the garage and greenhouse that we saw there."

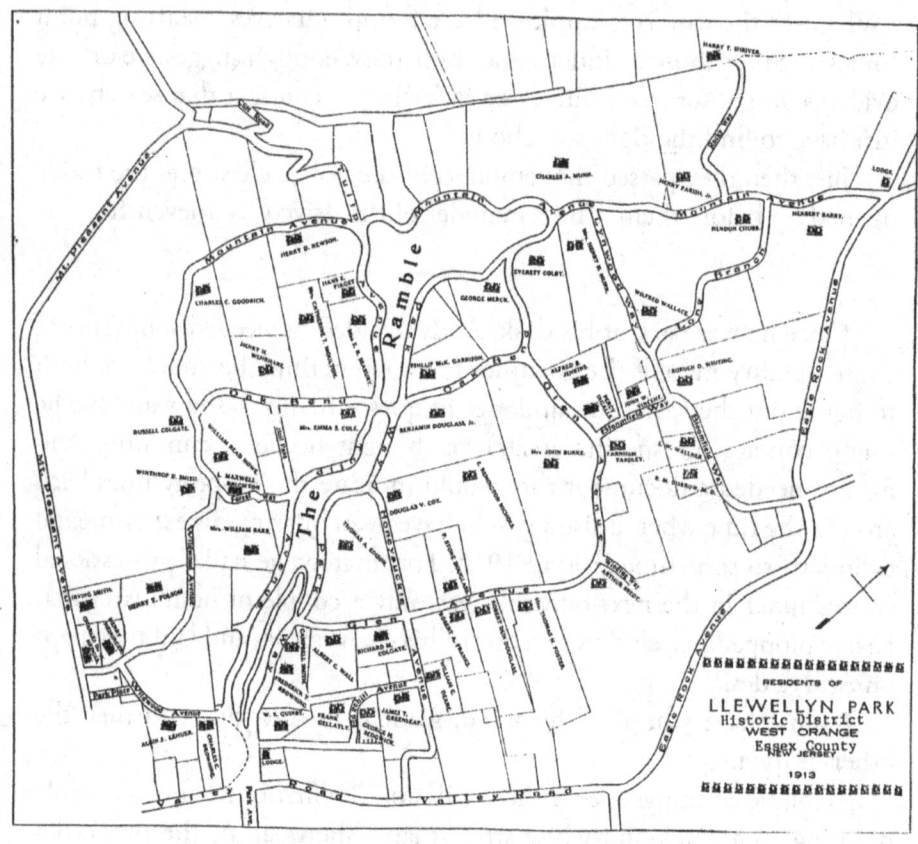

"That," Andy replied, "is pretty amazing for a girl." He knew he was safe for the simple reason that Keiley couldn't reach across the desk. But he did get *the look*.

"Do you want the rest of this?" she asked with an implied threat in her voice but a sly smile on her face.

"Yes," came the tentative reply.

"Then you'd best behave yourself, Lawyer Man. And see if you can wrap your clearly challenged intellect around this second map. This one is from the National Wetlands Inventory. That's a database that's put together by the Fish and Wildlife Service using geospatial data. That means satellites. You know, those big shiny things they're always sticking on top of rockets and launching into space? Like Sputnik?"

"Okay," he said, laughing. "I deserved that."

"Well," Keiley continued, having made her point, "Fish and Wildlife takes all these satellite images and puts them all together in some way in this tool they call a 'Wetlands Mapper' that lets people like us go online and pull up images of any wetland area in the country. And they have a pretty inclusive definition of a wetland. In this case, there's that brook running alongside Park Way across from Glenmont, and sure enough, it's in their database. So I pulled this image for you. Two things about it. First, Wigwam Brook shows up here as a wide line running through those trees. It's not anywhere near that wide in reality. It's just the FWS's way of locating the stream. But remember, their purpose is not to map the stream, but to map the wetland. And that's the area represented by the line. So there's a boundary of sorts there and we probably want to pay attention to it, because if memory serves, there are all sorts of special regulations when it comes to actual wetlands.

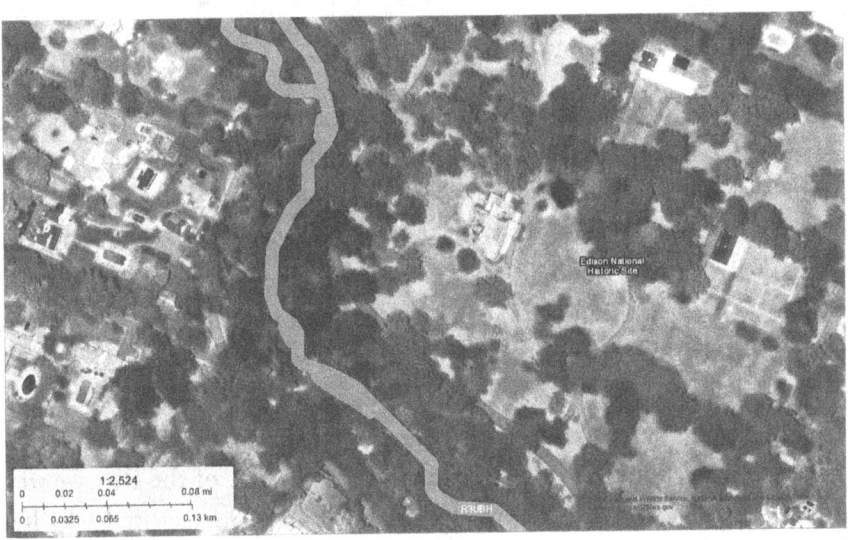

"Now, get ready to be really impressed. Back in 2011, the Park Service put together something they called a Cultural Landscapes Inventory for Glenmont. And as part of that, they mapped out all of the major vegetation on the property at that time. Keep in mind, of course, that this is like a hundred years after the period we're focused on, but still. Here's their landscape site plan," she said, passing yet another piece of paper across the desk.

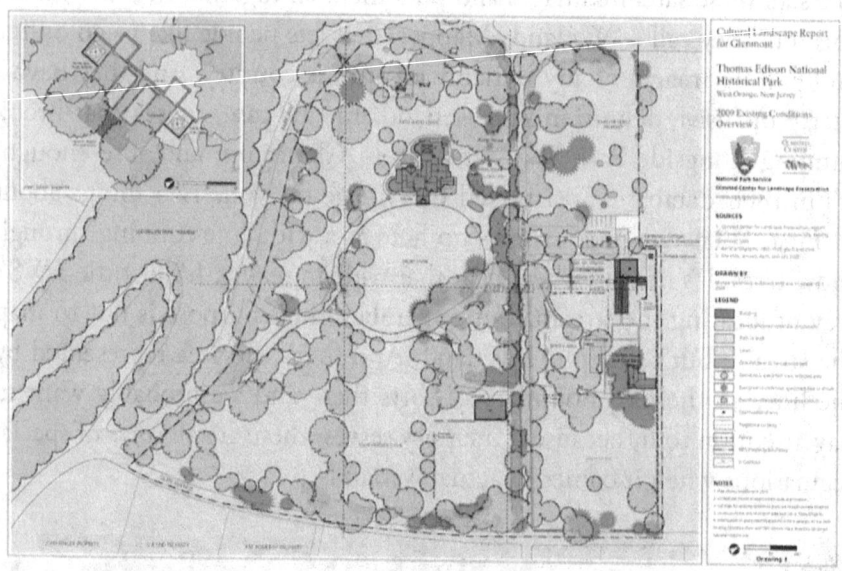

"What's really neat here is that the plan shows the same three points of view toward the house that we were looking at. If you think of the house as being twelve o'clock, at six o'clock off the oval you can see the long lawn that runs across the driveway down to Glen Avenue. At eight o'clock you can see the view that runs along the driveway and over to Park Way. And at about ten o'clock is the line of sight we were working on over toward the brook. So this is something you could use when you try to explain all of this to people who haven't been there.

"But let me add a couple of things. First, if you look closely, there appears to be a boundary line marking the perimeter of the Park Service property. And unfortunately for us, if that line is correct, it looks like there is a right-of-way along Park Way, which is another way of saying that the old Edison property may not have reached all the way to the road. That could simply be an easement, or it could mean that the land along the road is part of the common land. It might actually belong to the community. And that might be why that security guard was so interested in us. So, maybe not a good thing."

"Damn," said Andy. "But easy enough to find out."

"But it's not all bad news. Remember, I said there were a couple of things here. The other is that the map makes pretty clear how prominent the driveway would have had to be if eight o'clock was the viewpoint Shillard-Smith had selected. In fact, here's something else from the Park Service report. And you're not going to believe it." Keiley laid a copy of an old photo on the desk.

"This is a picture of the house taken from almost the exact eight-o'clock viewpoint that we were looking at and rejected. And if you look at it, there's no way you could paint that without including the driveway. Given the elevation, which is almost the same as the house, it's just too prominent. So I think we can be pretty sure we were right. She didn't use this angle at all."

"Okay, no fooling," Andy said when Keiley had finished. "This is just amazing. *You* are just amazing. These maps and the rest are exactly what we need to get started. The next thing I need to do is start pulling together whatever legal documents I can to figure out who the players are in this particular game and how we ought to go about getting what we need to pursue Sam's claim."

"What?" Keiley said, feigning some petulance. "You think I'm done?"

"There's more?" said Andy with a tone of incredulity.

"There's more," she replied. "Nothing quite so dramatic, but some interesting little facts I found in that same report that might be useful at some point. Park Way is paved now, but we were thinking at one point that, if the road was still gravel back in the day, Edison might have been able to put some or all of his experimental cylinders under the road. Not an obvious place, to say the least. But depending on the gravel and the road base, if he could have dug the holes, they would have been a cinch to cover back up with the surface gravel. All he'd need would have been a rake, and the vehicles passing by on the road afterward would have taken care of the rest. And the advantage would have been that it was a level surface that was still subject to weather and whatever other conditions he was trying to test. According to the Park Service report, that's not super likely, but we can't rule it out. The roads in Llewellyn Park were converted from dirt to gravel, and then paved over a period of almost sixty years. And they didn't finish until 1924. But we don't know which roads were paved when. Still, you'd think that Park Way, as the main entrance road, would have been paved early on.

"There was one exception. Honeysuckle, the road where the parking lot is now, was originally developed as a service road, and it was never paved until the Park Service did the job in 2001, 2002, and 2003. Of course, that's on the opposite side of the property to where we're looking, so I guess it's irrelevant. The Park Service also paved the driveways at Glenmont in 1962 and again in 1975. But then they changed their minds and restored them to chip sealing in 1985, which is what we found when we were over there. But here's an interesting note. Up until Edison's wife Mina died in 1947, there were apparently a bunch of walking paths on the west lawn, which is the lawn that runs down toward that big boulder. But after she died, and apparently before the Park Service took over the property, all of those paths were removed. So when Edison was alive, he would have had dirt walking paths leading down toward Park Road, not just a big expanse of lawn. Not sure if you noticed, but there was a set of concrete steps going down to the road near that bend that seemed to be there for no apparent reason. I'm guessing that one of the old paths ran to those steps.

"Here's another fun fact, and this one won't surprise you. Back in 1971, when they were still developing the property as a park, the Park Service wanted to build a walking trail from the lab complex on Main Street over to Glenmont, but the community resistance was pretty fierce. So they withdrew the proposal. Wrong backyards, I guess. But really, who could blame them?"

When Keiley paused to catch her breath, Andy waited a moment and then asked, "Is that all?"

"Actually," she replied, "there's one more thing that might come in handy. Back in 2011, when the Park Service was putting this cultural report together, there was another report being done by a private archeology contractor called The Louis Berger Group. Their findings aren't included in the document I found, but I think they must be on file with Essex County or some other state or local agency. But the point for us, I think, might be the simple fact that an archeological study was permitted on the property back then. Maybe that's some sort of, what's the word, precedent you can use."

"And you found all of this within, what, two or three hours?" Andy said once she had clearly finished reporting. "I think I should be the one working for you. This is like a jewelry store's worth of documentary gems, and I can already see ways to put some of this information to use. Amazing!" Andy stood up, walked around the desk, and planted a big kiss on Keiley's lips. "I'll have to find a way to thank you for all this," he said with a grin.

"Damn straight you will," she replied. "And I have a few ideas about that."

Chalking the Diamond

"Sam, thanks for coming in," said Andy, opening the meeting with Keiley and his client. "As you know, this matter of your uncle's estate has taken us to some places we never would have anticipated. What I'd like to do this morning is review where we are and start planning our next steps. We're pretty sure at this point that the document we have is a map, and we're pretty sure that it points us toward an area in Llewellyn Park that's either on the grounds of Glenmont or just off them on the HOA's common land. I think the time has come to take off our treasure-hunter hats for a while and get down to the business of framing a legal strategy so we can get you access to whatever it is that might be buried there that you might have a claim to. Unfortunately, it's becoming clear this will not be either simple or straightforward.

"For starters, we're going to have to convince somebody—a federal or state bureaucrat, a judge, or maybe someone else—that we're not just blowing smoke here . . . or smoking something. We need to frame an argument showing as strong a connection as we can between John Culbertson and Thomas Edison. If we can't do that, we're pretty much out of the game.

"So far, Keiley hasn't found anything definitive through her search of the genealogical record. The family names were just too common to allow for any certainty as to who was who, when, and where. So we have to find a back-door approach. And that's at least a two-parter. First, can we establish that the various artifacts we have in hand once belonged to Edison? Second, can we account for their coming into the possession of Frank's family?

"We have the document and the painting, of course, and we also have the ring and the lamps. The document has what appears to be Edison's signature, though I'm sure that could be faked. We'll need to see if we can get that authenticated, but it's such a stylized script and so widely available that it could be easily copied. My guess is that we'll need as much backup evidence as we can muster to lend that credibility. The ring has his initials, but again, there are doubtless many people with the same initials. Plus, there's no real way to date a simple piece of jewelry like that. Still, it does link him to the Theosophy movement, which he shared in common with Shillard-Smith, the artist who made the painting, and we do have good information on that. We've even got a copy of Edison's membership card, and we can show that she was a major donor of art and money to the Theosophy Society. Both spent much of their time in New Jersey and Florida, and it's reasonable to think they were acquainted, especially based on the date and the inscription on the back of the painting. It's all circumstantial, of course, in the context of this particular case, which is all it can likely ever be.

"That said, when it comes to the lamps, I think we have a less convincing argument. We don't know if Edison and Tiffany ever met or if Tiffany had any reason to send what we believe to have been prototype lamps to Edison. Keiley, I think that would be a good place for you to focus a little energy as a next step."

"I agree," she said. "I'm on it."

"Our second problem is a really difficult one. We don't yet know who we're dealing with or who we need to convince to let us search the grounds. Even though we know, or think we know, what the map represents and approximately where these glass cylinders, if that's what they prove to be, are buried, we don't have a clear picture of who controls that space. It could be the Llewellyn Park Committee of Managers. Or the National Park Service. Or the state of New Jersey. Or even, God forbid, the Army Corps of Engineers. It's pretty high ground there, so probably not technically a wetland. But we could also end up pretty close to that stream that runs through the area. Fish and Wildlife might try to get into the act, or the EPA. And there's probably a dozen historical preservation groups who'd oppose any sort of digging. We need some way to determine who's in this game and who's not. Then we need to identify the proper court of jurisdiction. Could be the probate court, but probably not. Could be state or federal. Hopefully it's not more than one of them.

"Once we can sort that out, we have to know what we're asking for. There's a real hierarchy of options here, and we need to give it some thought. We should probably have several approaches in mind short of randomly punching holes in the ground, because that is not likely to go over well. One thing we probably can't make much use of would be metal detectors, since we don't know that there's any metal involved. If we can find a promising area, then maybe we'll have to come up with something more invasive. And eventually we might be at a point where we need to do some serious excavating. I hope we never get there, because that could be a real can of worms. And I don't mean the ones we'd be digging up.

"As I'm talking this through, I'm starting to realize we'd be wise to find an anthropologist or an archeologist to advise us, maybe supervise the testing and digging. It would be a way to show that we want to act responsibly, and it might give us a good argument for whatever next steps we need. Either of you know anybody like that?"

Andy's question was met with silence.

"Okay, I'll work that angle, see if I can find someone.

"All of this so far just, hopefully, gets us to the cylinders, if they're still there. Then it'll be a question of what's in them. And this might be the place where we can make a deal. If these things are there, they could have some real historical value. And the fact is, you have no claim on most of them, and I would assume no real interest in their contents. It's only that one outlier cylinder that we're after. Thing is, we're the ones with the map. So maybe we can strike a deal—access to the map in return for the contents of the outlier cylinder if, and it's a big if, there is something in there that could arguably be ours and be unconnected with the rest of the grouping. In fact, once we figure out who we have to deal with, that might be a way to find a partner in this little enterprise rather than an adversary.

"Now, as you can probably tell, Keiley and I have been spending a good deal of time on all of this research. I have to say I find this to be a curious set of circumstances, and I'd like to keep following up on it until we reach a point where we either resolve the unknowns or it seems point-less to continue. But that is starting to cost some serious money, and I know you were concerned about that at the beginning. If it's agreeable to you, I'm willing to stake us a bit further down this path, but we'd need to have an understanding that if we find anything of real value at the end, something that fundamentally impacts the value of the estate, we'll be able to cover our costs through a contingency arrangement. The standard rate for that is thirty percent of the proceeds in exchange for covering all of the costs, and I think that's fair. Will that work for you? Or would you like us to draw a line here and file the estate?"

"Andy," said Sam with a broad smile as his attorney wrapped up his soliloquy. "Do you remember when I first came to see you and you told me this would be quick, simple, and easy?"

"That," said Andy, "was before I met your family."

After Sam left, Andy motioned to Keiley to grab a chair.

"As I said before," Andy began, "I think we'd be wise to come up with a range of search options that start out with things that don't involve digging or disturbing the ground in any way. We ought to be able to get permission at the very least to do some sort of visual inspection of the site—maybe even over on the community's side of wherever the property line actually lies. It's hard to see how they would object to that. And on the Park Service side, well, we've all but done that already. Basically, we just need to confirm our assumption that the boulder we saw is likely to be home plate rock or, if not, see if we can locate an alternative. And we ought to see just how steep and rocky the land is when you get across the road and down by that brook.

"Maybe the place to start would be using ground-penetrating radar."

"You know about GPR?" Keiley said in disbelief. "Isn't that kind of technological for you? Where'd you learn about that?"

"Hey," Andy responded. "I watch the History Channel! All those shows about hunting for alien bases underground, lost gold mines, cach-es of art stolen by the Nazis? They all use—what'd you call it?—GPR. Where did you learn about it?"

"Well," she said, "back when I was fresh out of school and I got that job with the mapping company in the City, they had this project up in Van Courtland Park. Ever heard of it?"

"Not really," Andy replied.

"It's actually pretty historic. Back in the 1870s, Frederick Law Olmstead, the guy who designed Central Park, did a survey in The Bronx and recommended using a particular site for a park. Eventually, that's what they did. So it goes back a long way. I think it's one of the three or four largest parks in the City. Anyway, at some point in the past they had electrified the park, you know, for the street lights and buildings and such. And to do that, since it was a park, they put all of this electrical cabling underground. Somebody doubtlessly mapped all of that when they did it, but sometime in the century and more after that, somebody else lost the map. Nobody was sure where the old electrical lines ran, or even if any of them were still hot. And they needed to do some heavy-duty maintenance in the park. So they hired my company to locate and map those old lines. Kind of like Miss Utility on steroids. We subcontracted part of the work to a firm that specialized in GPR, and somebody had to go out there with them day after day to make sure they were fulfilling the assignment. It wasn't the kind of job anybody with any seniority wanted, so guess who they sent. I watched those guys lay out their grids and walk back and forth with some pretty awkward equipment for weeks. Boring as hell. But on the plus side, at the end of each day I got to see the preliminary images they captured, and then later I got to see the results when they plotted them on a map of the park."

"How did that work?" Andy asked. "I mean, could they really see underground with that gear?"

"Yes and no. Basically, they were broadcasting radar signals down into the ground and reading the returns—just like the way they track planes or weather. They would generate these images of the ground, and they could identify places where the dirt had been disturbed at any time in the past. After a while, I even got the hang of doing that. Not as well as they did, of course. And then, within the disturbed areas, they'd get a different kind of signal for pipes or cables or old concrete structures or whatever. And they could tell what was what. Back then, they had to strap the gear to some guy's back and he'd just walk back and forth carrying it. But these days they have these units that look almost like lawnmowers, and they just push them around."

"Well, I guess I can see how they would get the feedback from the ground and it might give different images. But how do they map the site from that? Seems like that would be pretty complicated."

"That's the easy part. The radar gear includes a very precise GPS receiver. And when they capture the ground image at any particular place, they also capture the exact GPS coordinates. Part of the same data point, and since they're rolling the equipment around like that, the data are all continuous and identifiable, basically, to the specific piece of dirt under the sensor. So then they can go to a computer and match the GPS location markers to the radar returns and essentially weave all the data points together, and that's where the maps come from. That's when they bring in the heavy equipment and start digging."

"So," said Andy, getting to the main point, "do you think this radar equipment could find a bunch of buried glass cylinders?"

"I would need to ask somebody in the business to be sure," Keiley replied, "but I think so. It would surely locate the holes, because that would be disturbed ground. Beyond that, it might depend on what, if anything, is in those cylinders. But I would think so. And since we have a known burial pattern we're looking for, chances are pretty good we could find the holes even if the radar didn't pick out the cylinders."

"That's encouraging," Andy said. "I suppose if we could find a bunch of the holes, we could do something like poke a metal test rod into the ground at those spots and see if we hit anything. That's not especially intrusive, and it might also tell us how deeply buried these things are. Probably not very, is my guess."

Once she got back to her own desk, Keiley turned her attention to the question of how Uncle Frank might have come into possession of a nearly matched pair of Tiffany lamps. She was pretty sure the common link would be Edison, so she set about finding some connection between the inventor and Louis Comfort Tiffany. Finding it did not take long.

According to a letter Keiley found in the Rutgers archive, Edison was first approached by Tiffany & Company in 1882 as a prospective customer for one of its special pieces—a bronze and marble clock that had been christened "The Genius of Electricity" in his honor. She was never able to determine whether the "Genius"—a word he despised—had made the purchase.

It was a couple years later, in 1884, that Edison and Tiffany had first met in person when both were commissioned to decorate the Lyceum Theater on Broadway in New York City. Edison was brought in by theatrical innovator Steele MacKay to fill the building with the incandescent lights he had invented five years earlier. Tiffany, who was designing stained-glass windows at the time, was charged with embellishing those same lights with decorative glass. Born within a year of one another, the two entrepreneurs had become fast friends. In the course of that assignment, Edison appears to have inspired Tiffany to begin designing stained-glass lamps and other lighting fixtures. The following year, 1885, he established a new company, the Tiffany Glass Company, that manufactured stained glass using two then-revolutionary techniques, opaline and Favrile lenses, which soon cemented his status as designer and manufacturer. Some of his early prototype lamps were exhibited at the 1893 World's Fair in Chicago, and the company began selling the commercial versions in 1898.

Toward the end of her search, Keiley came across one more intriguing clue in the form of a program or brochure or guidebook from an older event, the 1889 Paris Exhibition, another of the expositions that were popular at the time as a means of enticing the public with the latest technological wonders.

The cover was rather tattered, but the pages inside offered a thorough description of the innovators on hand and their accomplishments. According to the brochure, Edison's exhibit occupied nine thousand square feet, or a full third of the space afforded the United States in the machinery hall. His exhibit featured many of his most important inventions to that date, but was dominated—as, indeed, was the entire hall—by a massive globe in the form of an incandescent lamp covered with thirteen thousand Edison light bulbs. Keiley found an old photo of Edison's display that showed clearly the extent to which it dominated the hall. Another prominent exhibitor in the American industrial section? Tiffany and Company, which featured a glittering array of precious stones and jewelry designs, its specialty at the time. Edison showed up for the exhibition in July, and doubtless spent quality time with his by-then good friend, Louis Comfort Tiffany.

Connection established.

Andy decided that his best starting point for parsing the legalities of the real estate in the vicinity of what he had come to think of as the cylinder experiment was with the land itself—the deed establishing the community, any zoning or development maps, or anything else he could find in the legal record. While searching for the original Deed of Trust that established ownership of the property in 1857, prior to its residential development, Andy came across a number of interesting documents.

The first and most important, as far as he was concerned, was a fundamental amendment to the deed itself that was adopted in June of 2000. While likely not as detailed as the original would have been, this document provided an up-to-date agreement as to the governance of the community. It set up (or in fact, simply continued) three separate governing bodies, including three so-called trustees, who would serve as the de facto "owners" of the common lands in the area; a nine-member Committee of Managers, who would be responsible for overseeing the day-to-day operations of the Park as well as setting and implementing its policies; and a nine-member advisory committee to keep an eye on the managers. Membership of these groups could not overlap. All of these positions were elected, and only property owners could serve in them. The document listed one hundred seventy-two property owners, so it looked like a fairly democratic place, with more than one in ten of the owners holding some leadership position at any given time. Reading down a bit in the document, though, Andy saw that votes were apportioned not by ownership alone but based on the acreage each owner held. Rather than one person, one vote, then, Llewellyn Park ran on the principle of one acre, one vote.

A good part of the document, and a section that particularly interested Andy, pertained to the common areas, including the area known as the Ramble, which included the undeveloped area along the stream that bordered Glenmont. It provided that:

> the Rambles shall be preserved as undeveloped lands in perpetuity and that neither the trustees nor the Committee of Managers shall suffer or permit any use of the Rambles inconsistent with this restriction . . . the clear intent and force of this restriction

being to preserve and conserve the Rambles forever green and undeveloped. . . .

This language could certainly be interpreted in a highly restrictive way, but Andy thought he saw a potential workaround if he needed it.

Beyond that, the amendment to the deed went on at some length about the powers of taxation, which were fairly broad in scope and entirely at the discretion of the managers committee. There was a passing reference to a baseline tax rate of ten dollars per acre, but that was a number Andy had seen in one of the histories of the Park, and he knew it was a reference to the tax rate set in the original Deed of Trust. The language here made clear that it was a meaningless specification. In yet another nod to the Park's history, the document established a "Ladies Association" to work on beautification projects. The president of this association could attend as an observer the meetings of the Committee of Managers, which was empowered to assign to the ladies their tasks. In recognition of the anachronistic nature of this particular provision, the document did note that membership in the Ladies Association was open to men and women alike.

Following upon these various structural and procedural points, there was a provision indemnifying the elected leaders of the community against any legal actions, which Andy knew was standard boilerplate in documents like this. Otherwise, in this litigious age, who would serve? Finally, there were two additional and potentially useful pieces of information. The first was a listing of the names and addresses of all of the property owners within the Park as of 2000, which might well come in handy as matters developed. Of more immediate interest, though, was the fact that the document was filed in the Chancery Division of the Superior Court of New Jersey, and, more specifically, in the Probate Part for Essex County. Should the questions he had surrounding Sam's claim end up requiring resolution at the state level, Andy now had at least one court of jurisdiction where he might file.

It would be an unusual choice, to be sure, and it took Andy back to a lecture on legal history he'd heard in law school. If he remembered correctly—*I will need to do some reading to be sure*, he thought—while other courts dealt with the letter of the law, chancery courts dealt with equity, or the fairness of the law. But they were still courts that rendered judicial decisions, and he could see that such an argument might emerge as his best course. New Jersey was one of the few states that had retained this sort of court, which had jurisdiction over property disputes, though in 1948, the chancery *court* was replaced by the chancery *division* of the state superior court. But the filing of the amended deed in that court, and maybe even the dates of Edison's actions, might open this legal pathway.

The next document Andy found was a judgment from an 1873 lawsuit, *Haskell and others v. Wright*, which would have been only sixteen years or so after Llewellyn Haskell established his new community. It was not especially revealing except in one regard. A fellow by the name of Wright had apparently started some sort of quarry or stone-crushing operation on his property, which adjoined Llewellyn Park, and used the roads in the Park to move the crushed stone out to the nearest main road. But Wright was only the most recent owner of the land, which had been conveyed by Haskell himself and subject to the same covenants he imposed on purchasers of land within his planned "recreational" community. One of those covenants held that "the grantee, his heirs and assigns, would not erect or permit upon the premises any hotel, livery stable, slaughter-house, smith shop, forge, furnace, steam engine, foundry, hat factory, tannery, brewery, distillery, or any other place or building for the accommodation of any other business dangerous or offensive to the neighboring inhabitants." In finding that Wright, the defendant in the case, was subject to the terms of the covenant and thus had no right to continue his stone-crushing business, the chancellor (the judge in a court of chancery—and there it was again) essentially locked into law strong restrictions on the use of Llewellyn Park land and infrastructure. *That, thought Andy, is sort of the ultimate NIMBY. Not in MY backyard, Sucker!* More to the point, with his on-site experimental activities at Glenmont, the workaholic Edison might already have been skating around the rules on commercial activity in the Park, and he would have known that being caught burying cylinders that might have been filled with industrial chemicals, when the whole point of the exercise might have been to determine the susceptibility of the cylinders to leaking, could have caused a genuine uproar. So if he did it, as Andy believed he had, then Edison surely would have done it late at night, probably in an area that was shrouded in darkness if not sheltered from prying eyes.

Next his search turned up another gem, the "Preservation and Maintenance Master Plan" that had been developed for the Committee of Managers in 2001. This one came accompanied by a set of maps detailing the proposed actions. A great deal of the detail here was given over to specific types of vegetation in various areas of the Park, of which there were nearly four dozen, including eight different categories of oak trees alone. It was easy for Andy to pick out Edison's old property near the corner of Park and Glen Avenues, and it appeared that little renovation was contemplated for the landscape of the common land in that vicinity, which raised the possibility that the area today might be largely as it was in Edison's time but for the growth and maturation of the plantings. That impression was reinforced by the master plan itself, which included a number of illustrations from the early years of the Park. At least one of these, dated 1906, seemed to show roads that were unpaved—not the case today—a fact that, as they had recognized, might impact their search. That possibility was brought home in another photo, apparently dating to the years when the Edisons were in residence, which showed the edge of a roadway, likely Park Avenue, adjacent to Glenmont. The road appeared to have comprised compacted dirt with a stone or concrete curb. All of this, of course, was of a piece with the information Keiley had turned up in that Park Service cultural inventory, and between the two, if needed—and Andy sincerely hoped it would not be—they might be able to figure out specific changes that had been made. The need for that would all depend on where the buried cylinders turned up.

For all of its detail regarding vegetation and the like, there was a single photo in the Master Plan that grabbed Andy's attention. Taken in 1906, it showed how Wigwam Brook, the stream that ran through Llewellyn Park, had been lined with dry-laid stone. What caught his eye, however, was a large boulder, clearly naturally occurring and not a landscaper's addition. It was not, to be sure, shaped like home plate. But it was big enough and near enough to Glenmont to support Keiley's supposition about the significance of the Shillard-Smith painting. If there was one large pre-development boulder in the area, there would surely have been more. That might provide a pedigree of sorts for the rock they had found opposite the west lawn.

The fourth document Andy reviewed didn't surprise him, but it gave him heartburn nonetheless. It was a lengthy National Park Service form dated 1968, nominating Llewellyn Park for the National Register of Historic Places—the same one Keiley had used to find the property map and legal description for Glenmont. Andy had known all along he would need to deal in some way with the National Park Service. After all, Glenmont was part of a proper national park. But the extraordinary amount of detail in this form—the extensive descriptions of the areas and even each house, the summary of the architecture, the history of the community, the landscape design, the cultural impact, and much more— brought home to him how difficult that negotiation might be given that listing on the Register effectively doubled down on the likely resistance to any request to disturb the grounds. At the same time, though, it might provide an opportunity to argue that finding a lost Edison experiment on the grounds of Glenmont could enhance the historical significance of the place. *Be a lawyer*, thought Andy. *Find an angle!*

Sometimes, of course, angles find you. It wasn't anything law-related in this case. But when he came across it, Andy was reminded that legal contests are not always won in the courtroom; sometimes they're won in the media. In his own recent case, he recalled vividly, he'd been able to leverage some embarrassing news about Major League Baseball into a de facto settlement he had thought was slipping away.

In the course of tracking down case law and regulatory documents, he came across an online posting from a group called Strong Towns that briefly summarized the history of setbacks, which are requirements established by zoning laws or neighborhood covenants that require certain specified distances between a home or other structure and the nearest street or boundary line. The effect of these rules is to set minimum lot sizes (say, an acre) and to prohibit commercial activity (for example, being too great a distance from the nearest street to engage with customers). In the process, setbacks serve to limit the residents of a given area to those able to afford relatively large lots. Llewellyn Park, he learned, was one of the very first neighborhoods to employ setbacks in this way.

More interesting, though, was what Andy learned when he skimmed one of the books cited in the posting, a study of urban sprawl by Benjamin Ross published in 2015. Over several pages early in his book, Ross offered some interesting insights into the community's early history. Some of what he read did not surprise Andy, though it was useful to know. Llewellyn Park, Ross argued, was built for the upper middle class rather than for the wealthy. The retention of the native forest rather than the introduction of formal landscaping, for instance, held down the costs of maintenance, and the minimum lot size of one acre was within reach of the target group but not sufficient to suit the truly well-off. True to form, the covenants in the Deed of Trust, as Andy already knew, mandated the minimum lot size and the setbacks, banned commercial enterprises, created the association of property owners, and set a fee structure to support the association. As if to confirm the point, Andy came across an 1887 newspaper clipping from the *Kansas City Star* that set out the special, and somewhat exclusive, character of the neighborhood, not to mention the Edisons' special place in it.

ORANGE, N. Y., Sept. 10.—Yesterday a correspondent of THE STAR visited the famous Llewellyn park, the history of which was told and the management described in a previous letter.

Mr. John W. Vincent, secretary of the association, accompanied the writer. To write of all that is of interest in the park would make a magazine, instead of a newspaper, article. Only American houses, not kingly palaces, nor yet lordly castles, are to be found here. Plain, substantial dwellings for the most part, nestling, and in some instances almost retiring, amid trees, shrubbery and flowers, with the ground gradually rising and ascending the southern slope of Orange mountain, with here and there a more pretentious edifice lifting its walls and variegated roofs and mixed cornices and towers above the tree tops, are the general features of the scene. Near at hand the birds are flying and singing from tree to tree, and occasionally a squirrel runs lightly along the road or skims up a tree in a manner so leisurely as to carry the assurance that neither dog nor gun have liberty to vex and worry on these favored grounds. To the busy and restless business man of the great city, a home in Llewellyn park must be an elysium of peace, existing within a whirlpool of strife and contention.

A number of notable people reside here. Chief among these is Thomas A. Edison, electrician and inventor. His home is the most elaborate and expensive building within the park, and at the same time so free from ostentation that it would be taken for the home of some retired banker, rather than the workshop and study of a man whose brain and hands are constantly at work. This Edison mansion has a

But that's when the fun stuff, as he immediately thought of it, came into the narrative. One of the early residents, for instance, was magazine editor Theodore Tilton, who, according to Ross, wrote a piece about the Paris Commune in 1871 in which he said, "the central idea of communism is the same that George Washington spent seven years in killing his fellow countrymen to achieve. . . ." Tilton was apparently not alone in seeing the early years of the Park as an experiment in communal living akin to socialism. As he had put it a few years earlier, in 1864, each Llewellyn Park property owner "possesses the whole park in common, so that the fortunate purchaser of two or three acres becomes a virtual owner of the whole five hundred." Framed in this way, Llewellyn Park could be seen as a radical social experiment in communal living for the near wealthy. Nor was it merely a socio-economic experiment. Apparently, it was also a center of sexual experimentation.

Ross quoted a newspaper of the time reporting on a May Day celebration in the Park: "In the center of the green, the May Pole was erected. It was a tall tulip tree, stripped of the bark, and the top of it was clasped by a garland of flowers and ribands, as in the old heathen days, when Priapus was a god, and all the people did him reverence. . . ." Ross went on to wonder just how it was that the residents of Llewellyn Park went about honoring the ancient Greek god of the phallus. But, he concluded, this early radicalism survived barely a generation. By the late 1880s, when the Edisons were in residence, the Park had cast off its aura of extremism, even as it retained its essential communal character.

Andy smiled to himself as he thought about how much fun a well-primed reporter could have playing with this obscure piece of history in the context of contemporary social mores and sensitivities. An arrow for the quiver.

———

Though he had not been born back in the seventies when Watergate was the scandal de jour, Andy had recently read a book about the subject—one written after the secret *Washington Post* source known as Deep Throat had been revealed as a former number two at the FBI—and then he'd tracked down and watched that old movie *All the President's Men.*

And one key takeaway from that incident that stuck with Andy was Deep Throat's advice to reporters Bob Woodward and Carl Bernstein: "Follow the money." He thought that might apply here as well, so he started digging into Llewellyn Park's finances.

He knew the original Deed of Trust had set an annual fee of ten dollars per acre to pay for infrastructure, and that, presumably symbolically, that number had carried forward into the amended deed he had found. But surely that was not enough to operate such an extensive and heavily landscaped property. Sure enough, one of the first finance documents he found was Edison's copy of a 1916 letter from the Llewellyn Park Trustees to the residents that, among other things, stated that the mandatory ten-dollar fee was insufficient and calling on each one to make additional voluntary contributions, something they were apparently doing each year. Interestingly, the projected budget for that year totaled eighty-six hundred dollars, an increase of about nine hundred from the year before. Edison's ten acres would have produced a mandatory payment of one hundred dollars; in the event he instructed his secretary to pay an additional one hundred eighty. The letter, which included a call to attend the community's annual meeting, also proclaimed the value of oiling the roads to better withstand storms, announced a plan to add more electric lamps in dark areas, which would surely have pleased at least one prominent resident, and, interestingly, decried the absence of adequate police protection. The latter could be read as the initiation point of what later became the dedicated Llewellyn Park security force, which, as Andy now knew, kept a particularly watchful eye on things.

At that point he also came across another letter from the community that had little to do with finance but much to do with Edison and, in particular, illustrated the kid gloves with which his neighbors treated him. This one was from December 1918. It seems that Edison had electric wires that ran underground from his factory on Main Street to his home, and he had asked permission to cut open Glen Avenue so that he might make some needed repairs to the line. When Andy got to the fourth paragraph of the letter, he had to laugh.

Tom, thought Andy, *move your damn junction box already!* The chairman of the Committee of Managers went on to say that of course he

HOWE & DAVIS
COUNSELLORS AT LAW
ORANGE, N.J.
WILLIAM READ HOWE
THOMAS A.DAVIS

NATIONAL BANK BUILDING
CABLE ADDRESS.HOWEBLAKE
TELEPHONE 332 ORANGE

Dec. 18, 1918.

Mr. Thomas A. Edison,
    Llewellyn Park,
      West Orange, N. J.

Dear Mr. Edison:-

        I am informed that you desire to open Glen
Avenue to make repairs to the electric wires, which run from
your factory to your residence.

        If I remember correctly, there is a junction
box about the centre of Glen Avenue, through which the line of
wires pass, and this box is located slightly under the surface
of the roadway, and covered with the macadamed surface. This
makes it a little different from the ordinary manhole, from
which the cover may be removed and replaced without disturbing
the surface of the road.

        My recollection is that this box has been un-
covered a good many times, and it has been suggested that perhaps it would be more to your advantage, as well as to the Park,
that the box should be removed from the centre of Glen Avenue to
some place within your property line, so as to avoid the frequent
opening on Glen Avenue.

        This is merely a suggestion and I hope you will
not consider it a criticism.

        I enclose the usual form of application, which
if you will remember the Park have adopted for many years, whenever it becomes necessary to open the roads.

        I have already started the papers for the con-
sent of the Trustees to do the work, and the permit of the Road
Master, which I expect will be received within twenty-four hours.

        If you will kindly sign the enclosed application,
and send it back to me with the usual $5. charge for preparing
the papers in accordance with the regulations, I will see that
the permit is sent to you at once.

            Yours very truly,

Enc. 1.

Wm Read Howe
Chairman Bd Managers

would grant Edison the permit to dig as soon as he filled out the requisite
form and paid the five-dollar fee. Though it was good for a chuckle, the
letter also provided some useful information. If Glen Avenue was paved
by that point in time, chances were pretty good that Park Way was paved
as well. And though he was clearly prepared to do so, digging up the
paved roads required a permit, something Edison likely would not have
sought to bury an experiment. That would seem to narrow the search

area in an important way, and also make any subsequent digging much less intrusive in its own right.

In 1984, Andy learned, the Llewellyn Park Trustees had gotten into a dispute with the Township of West Orange over the question of whether the township could impose a tax on the thirty-five acres that were set aside as parkland, which is to say, the Ramble, over and above the taxes assessed on the individual residential properties. The case got deep into the weeds of New Jersey tax law and the differences between Llewellyn Park, as a trust, and the typical homeowners association, but in the end, it was decided on what amounted to a technicality. An appeals court ruled in 1988 that, because the Park had not specified a dollar amount of the claimed double taxation, it failed to meet the burden of proof for its case. It looked to Andy like some sloppy lawyering, something he was secretly pleased to see, even from half a century ago.

Much more recently, in 2017, the township had completed an upgrade of the sewer system in and around the Park, at which point it sent around a notice of assessment to the various property owners. Pretty routine stuff, though Andy was sure it had not come as good news to those who would spend the next fifteen years paying off their respective shares of the $3.75 million project. But for Andy, the letter contained one more interesting fact: The total assessed value of properties within Llewellyn Park as of that date, which was just over $164 million. And that got him thinking about what the annual budget of the community might be. It had to cost a bundle to maintain and operate a place like that, and sure enough, it did. Since the Committee of Managers operated, he knew, as a 501(c)(4) organization—one of the nonprofit classifications set out in the tax code—the group was required to file an IRS Form 990, essentially a non-taxable tax return, each year, and these forms are part of the public record. The latest filing he could find showed the community had sixteen paid employees (the managers and trustees worked as volunteers) and an annual budget of just over a million and a quarter dollars. Of that, it had paid $115,000 to a management company for the day-to-day, and only about twelve hundred dollars for legal work. So it was not a place that was, as a rule, heavily lawyered up.

Andy didn't expect to get into any sort of legal battle with the community. In fact, that was something he very much wanted to avoid. But if it came to that, even this rudimentary understanding of its finances and some of the internal dynamics of the place might come in handy.

Loading the Bases

The time had arrived, Andy decided, to come up with a plan. And that had to begin with a list of the parties that he'd need to work with, or through, to find out if Sam's hidden legacy was real, if it was still in the place Edison had put it, if he could somehow gain access to it against an array of institutions and policies whose purpose was, in a sense, to prevent that very thing, and, ultimately, if there really was anything in that cylinder to which Sam might have a claim.

The first step in all of this had to be eyeballing the area of the Ramble between Edison's property line at the end of the so-called west lawn and Wigwam Brook. Was the slope too steep, or the ground too rocky or irregular, for Edison to have dug dozens of holes that were more or less neatly aligned on two dimensions? Probably, but he knew he couldn't assume such an outcome without having a first-hand look. Perhaps more importantly, did that boulder near the road at the top of that slope at all resemble a home plate in baseball as Keiley had guessed and he had bought in on? And if not, was there some other boulder nearby that better fit that description? There was only one legally defensible avenue to finding those answers, and it ran through the Llewellyn Park Committee of Managers. It was time to write them a letter, one that was respectful and reassuring of his limited purpose. He consulted Cause IQ, a database of nonprofit organization managers, to find the name of the committee's chair, James Cashman, then dispatched his letter:

Dear Mr. Cashman:

I am an attorney representing the Estate of Francis Culbertson.
Included in the estate is a document indicating that, circa
1915, a former resident of Llewellyn Park, Thomas A. Edison,
buried on or near his property, known as Glenmont, a series
of objects which we believe to be glass cylinders related to
his development of storage battery technology. We have
reason to believe these objects are still in place, though
their specific location is somewhat uncertain. According to
our documentation, discovery of the great majority of these
cylinders would be of primarily historic interest, and the Estate
makes no claim to them. One cylinder, however, appears to
have been buried with the intention of its being discovered by
Mr. Culbertson or his heirs.

I write to request the permission of the Committee of
Managers to examine the site we believe may contain either
one or more of these cylinders, or in the alternative, a clue
to their location elsewhere. That site lies between Park Way
and Wigwam Brook to the west of Glenmont. I do not request,
at this time, permission to disturb the area in any way, but
only to conduct a visual inspection and possibly a survey with
ground-penetrating radar, an entirely non-intrusive technique.

The personal representative of the Estate and I believe
that granting this permission would be consistent with the
historic nature of the Edison property and of Llewellyn Park,
while causing no disruption to the Park or its residents. I hope
you will agree.

This was followed by the requisite legal niceties and some extralegal bowing and scraping, along with a request for an early and favorable response.

Andy did hope for such a response, but given what he had learned about the sensitivities of the community, he didn't assign it a very high likelihood. Besides that, he knew that these things take time, and he also knew that chances were the field of cylinders lay not on the common land of the Park but on the grounds of Glenmont itself. And that put the matter squarely on the radar of the National Park Service—or would once he dispatched his second letter. But at this point, things became a little more complicated because he needed to figure out the proper contact point for his request. Before writing, he needed to study up on the Park Service and its relationship with the community surrounding Glenmont. He knew that Glenmont had been designated a National Historic Site back in 1955 and that the property had been donated to the federal government four years later. In 1962, Glenmont was merged with the laboratory complex, at the time a national monument, to form a combined Edison National Historic Site. And he knew from some of the materials Keiley had turned up that the house, like the laboratory complex, had been in pretty bad shape at that point, and the Park Service had done a lot of work to preserve them. The National Historical Park designation, which applied to both properties and represented a recognition of the extensive improvements made by the Park Service, hadn't come until Congress acted on the matter in 2005. All useful knowledge. But it did not get him to the starting line for the present purpose—getting access to the property for a bit of physical discovery and then perhaps something more intrusive.

But from his recent visit, he knew that there must have been some sort of agreement between the Park Service and the community over how that would work. On a hunch, he found it in the Park Service archives. Dated 1959, the document did not contain any real surprises, but the terms it set forth were nonetheless revealing. He pulled out a fresh legal pad and started making a list of bullet points he thought might come in handy later. He noted that the agreement:

- committed the Trustees to waiving certain restrictions in the deed that had earlier transferred the property to the McGraw-Edison Company, from which the Park Service had later acquired the property;
- committed the Park Service to staffing the facility adequately for its management, and to paying its share of the annual community assessments just like any other property owner;
- limited the number of days per week Glenmont could be open and the number of visitors allowed on any given day, all to be

controlled through the issuance of entry tickets at the Park headquarters on Main Street;

- limited the size of the vehicles that could bring visitors in (no buses), required the Park Service to stripe the road to indicate the only acceptable route for Glenmont visitors, specified the available parking for such vehicles, and characterized the limited signage that was acceptable; and
- ruled out picnicking, public address systems, and sales of refreshments or souvenirs on the property.

Essentially, the document committed the Park Service to honoring the norms of the community and the privacy of the residents insofar as possible. It set forth the rules of public access, right down to the stripe on the road and the sale of refreshments, that, as Andy knew, have endured to the present day. The only exception seemed to be the stripe, which he had not seen on his recent visit with Keiley.

That was a good start, but there remained an important loose end Andy wanted to tie up before he contacted the Park Service. He was about to ask for permission to dig holes in a national park, or at least he might be. *Probably a good idea*, he thought, *to find a consulting archeologist now rather than later.* It was not something he had ever looked into before, and he wasn't sure how to go about it. But then he remembered someone who'd already been helpful on this project—the chemistry department Chair at Rutgers, Hiram Burlmeister. Perhaps he would know someone at the university who might fit the role. Andy asked Betty to schedule a call with the professor as soon as he was available. As it turned out, Burlmeister was about to head to Chicago for a professional meeting, but he was available for a few minutes right when Betty called. Andy picked up the phone immediately.

"Professor, Andy Dennum. I'm the attorney who's working on that Thomas Edison project. Thanks so much for finding a few minutes to talk."

"Yes, I remember," said Burlmeister. "I'm about to head for the airport, but I can answer a question or two if they're brief. Otherwise—"

"I really only need a moment. We've made some progress, especially with your help. But we're now at a point where we need to bring in an expert of a different kind—an archeologist. Someone with really solid credentials, good enough to impress the National Park Service. Maybe even someone who's done some research either in the parks or somewhere here in New Jersey. Honestly, there aren't a lot of archeologists in the circles I run in, and I was hoping you might have a name or two to suggest. Maybe someone on the university faculty, though that's certainly not a requirement."

"Funny you should ask that," said the professor. "As it happens, I do know someone who fits that profile: well credentialed, has worked sites in the state, and has even done some work with the Park Service. That's the good news. The bad news is that she will be my traveling companion on the trip to Chicago and will be there for the better part of a week."

"Beg pardon?" Andy said.

Burlmeister had a good laugh. "She's my wife, Mr. Dennum. And she's also on the faculty here. Her name is Audrey Templeton. She already had an extensive professional reputation and kept her maiden name when we married a few years ago. I think she's just what you're looking for. But as I say, she'll be away for a few days. Why don't I connect the two of you by email, and you can judge for yourself. Perhaps set up a meeting for next week."

"It's a small world, professor," Andy replied. "That sounds like a great plan.

Audrey Templeton—Professor Templeton—was a woman Andy judged to be in her late forties, a lanky five-foot-ten or so, thin with hair that was beginning to gray, something she was clearly not at pains to hide. She had a pleasant smile and a direct manner and seemed completely at ease in her small office with its piles of books and papers and its shelves of artifacts and . . . were those bones? Andy liked her right away; the office he could take or leave.

"Thank you for seeing me," he opened. "I'm not sure how much your husband has told you about our little project, or for that matter how much I told him when we met a few weeks ago. Matters have developed a good deal since then.

"You know I'm an attorney out in Mendham. I represent the estate of a man named Francis Culbertson. Mr. Culbertson was nearly a hundred years old when he passed, and his father appears to have worked for Thomas Edison. Probably in the 1920s—we're not sure what he did. But in the estate, we've found a number of items that seem to trace back to Mr. Edison himself. In particular, there was a painting that was passed down to the current and sole heir of the estate, a fellow named Sam Patrick. Attached to the back of the painting was this document." Andy handed her a copy of the diagram or map.

"Your husband helped us to understand what this might be—an array of specialized glass cylinders that Edison might have buried as part of his search for improved housings for his storage batteries. That was probably sometime between about 1910 and 1915. Most of those cylinders, which is to say, the essential part of Edison's experiment, are not of any interest to us, though they might very well interest others. The only one we are really interested in is that one," he said, while pointing to the outlier cylinder at the top of the array. "We think that one holds something, and we don't know what, that Edison intended to pass along to the now deceased Mr. Culbertson. After some further research, we think we know where these cylinders might be buried—on or near the grounds of Edison's old home in West Orange. And we want to find and retrieve that one particular cylinder."

"You're talking about Glenmont?" she queried.

"Yes," replied Andy.

"And you know that's part of a national park?"

"Exactly. And that's why I'm here. I'm about to contact the Park Service to ask if we can get permission to scout around to see if we can find these cylinders, and I thought it might be a good idea to add an archeologist to the team to keep us in line and show that we plan to act responsibly. Your husband suggested you."

"Do you have any idea what you are about to set into motion?"

"Not really," Andy responded hesitantly. "It's not something I've dealt with before. Should I be worried?"

"That," replied Templeton, "depends on whether you bill by the hour, the month, or the year."

"I don't think I like the sound of that," said Andy. "I take it you've done this before. What's the story?"

"You might have noticed the gray in my hair," she said with a smile. "That's how it got there. The process is all intended for a good purpose, but it's incredibly convoluted. Back in 1966, Congress passed something called the National Historic Preservation Act, the purpose of which is to regulate, among other things, archeological activity in the national parks. It's still on the books. And it requires that you notify a whole slew of interested parties of what you want to do—the Park Service in this case, the state preservation people, the local governments, and anybody in the general public who might have some kind of interest in the project. And that's just for starters. Glenmont, as you probably know, is listed in the National Register of Historic Places, and there are special regulations applying there as well, so that means involving the Advisory Council on Historic Preservation, the group that maintains the Register. You'll need to look at a couple of documents before you do anything else. One of those is NPS-28. That's the rulebook for managing cultural resources in the parks, and there's a chapter, six, I think, that lays everything out in excruciating detail. You have to remember, these are federal bureaucrats writing this stuff. Hold on. . . ."

She reached over to one of the stacks of paper on a nearby credenza, and handed a thick, soft-covered, blue-and-white book to Andy. It was the very guide she had been describing a moment ago. "We have to make sure our undergrad majors and grad students understand all of these rules before they go out the door, so I keep a few copies of this one on hand. The other place you need to go is to the website of the advisory council itself. They have several ways of telling you how many hoops you need to jump through if you ever hope to have a project approved. And you can expect a lot of questions. What's the benefit of doing your project? Will it disturb the site? Does it fit with the objectives of the park and its management? Does it make significant demands on the staff? And not least, where is the money coming from for the project? It's certainly enough to keep you busy."

"They don't want people doing this kind of thing, do they?" Andy opined.

"Well, I wouldn't say that," replied the professor. "But they want to be sure the people who do it are serious people who go about it in a responsible way. And, of course, they want to be sure the project itself provides some public benefit. Tell you what. I've done a bunch of these things over the years. I've learned the buzzwords and gotten comfortable with the process. If you'd like me to, I can draft some talking points, maybe frame out an argument. And I might even have an idea or two about cutting some corners."

"That would be fantastic," said Andy.

"Give me about a week, and I'll be in touch."

———————

While he was waiting to hear back from Professor Templeton and the Llewellyn Park Committee of Managers—and he wasn't holding his breath for the latter—Andy decided he needed to line up a company that worked with ground-penetrating radar. He began by listing some of the criteria that should drive the selection: a national reputation, a service area that included West Orange, some sort of professional certification, equipment that could be . . . tuned? . . . to identify either the glass cylinders themselves or the void they created in the ground, experience with similar projects, availability. . . . When he went onto the internet to begin his search, he found that there were a number of contractors to choose from, and he had absolutely no idea how to select among them. So he decided on an alternate way of searching. *After all,* he thought, *what do I, a mere lawyer(!), know about this stuff? Less than zero. But there are a lot of people who know a lot. They work for the utilities that need these guys to map out underground impediments, just like Keiley's old mapping company did.* It was, in a way, just like that story about Edison and the volume of the light bulb. Find a shortcut that gives a better answer. So rather than cold-calling a bunch of radar services, he reached out to the local utility companies and agencies—water, power, sewer, cable companies, and anything else he could think of—asking in each instance to speak with a contracting executive. As expected, he got quite a few runarounds and dead ends, but within a couple of hours, he had his answer: Gallegos & Golden GPR. Of the four people who were willing to speak with him, three had settled on G&G as their contractor of choice, and all gave similar positive reviews. His next call was to the company's main office in Patterson, where he explained his need in general terms and set an appointment for two days hence.

Since Keiley had experience with GPR and knew the lingo, he made the wise decision to take her along to the meeting. The office was located in one of those nameless prefab-looking industrial parks that have come to dot the urban landscape. A modest sign over the door was the only indication they had arrived at the right place. They were greeted at the reception desk, a spartan affair, and directed to a conference room. Mr. Gallegos himself would be with them in a moment.

The conference room was on the small side, and the furnishings were consistent with the spartan feel of the entire office. *This*, thought Andy, *is a far cry from the fancy, or often the faux fancy, furnishings typical of my own profession. Different clientele, different function, different message.* Just then, a tall man with angular features walked into the room.

"Rudy?" said Keiley, clearly showing surprise.

The man looked at her for a moment, uncertain as to how she knew his name. Then an image flashed in his brain. "Kelly?" he replied.

"Keiley, but close. I sure didn't expect to see you here!"

"You can say that again," he replied. Then he turned to Andy. "I'm sorry. We haven't met. At least, I don't think so. Rudy Gallegos," he said, extending his hand.

"Andy Dennum," came the reply as Andy returned the gesture. "Am I missing something here?"

Keiley took the question. "Andy, remember I told you how I spent weeks when I took that mapping job in New York watching a GPR crew wander around Van Courtland Park? Well, Rudy here was the foreman of that crew. He was the guy who taught me how to read some of the returns on the computer." Then, turning to Gallegos, she added, "What a small world! This is your company?"

"Yeah," he said. "I got tired of working for somebody else, and tired of the City. So me and Golden—he was another supervisor, but I don't think you ever would have met him—anyway, we decided to go out on our own. We put together some money for the equipment, got ourselves some classy office space and some really impressive furniture, as you can tell, hired away the four best guys we had working for us over there, and set ourselves up here. We got lucky. The equipment we wanted was fairly cheap—we hit the very beginning of that construction boom a few years ago—and we haven't looked back. I'd knock on wood, but I don't think any of this stuff has wood in it."

Once the conversation got onto a more professional track, Andy learned that G&G was fully certified and had even won awards from its peers, that they had experience working on archeological projects, and that they could easily fit a small project into their schedule. Given Keiley's obvious enthusiasm, that left only one question, and it was the most important.

"Rudy, let me ask you about your equipment," he began. He passed a copy of the Edison diagram across the table, then continued. "This is what we're looking for. We think this drawing represents an array of glass cylinders of some sort that were buried by Thomas Edison over a hundred years ago. We're not sure what's in them, if anything, and we're not sure how big they are. But we think they're probably not buried very deeply, and we believe we know more or less where they're located. What we would need you to do is examine one or two locations to see if they're there. Is that something your equipment can do?"

Rudy thought for a moment. "I don't want to get too technical," he said, "but the simple answer is yes. Radar works using microwave frequencies. When the radar signal goes into the ground, it's either going to be more or less fully absorbed, in which case there wouldn't be any significant return, or it's going to bounce off some underground structure or layer or some other kind of irregularity. That produces what's called a Fresnel reflection coefficient, and that's part of what we read. Different materials and different shapes and different densities produce different coefficients. It's not sharp like a photograph, but it's precise as to location and indicative as to size and shape and, in some circumstances, the material that's encountered. In reality, it's a good bit more complex than that, but that's the idea.

"Now in your case, it sounds like there are four main factors in play. First, we're looking for something that's been buried. That means that the dirt around and above the targets will have been disturbed at some time in the past. Doesn't matter how long ago. GPR can distinguish between dirt that's been disturbed and dirt that hasn't. So that's a help. Second, you say that these cylinders are buried in shallow ground. That's a major plus, because being nearer to the surface, they're easy to sense. We can go quite deep when we need to, but shallow is always good. Third, they're made of glass. It's not the most reflective of materials when it comes to radar, and I can't say I recall a project where we've been looking for glass objects, but GPR can see PVC pipe underground, so it can certainly see glass. And since your cylinders have a distinct structure, they will produce a sharp boundary between the dirt above them and the cylinders. Those boundaries are precisely what we read with GPR. And the cylinders themselves are either empty, which will produce voids, or filled with some sort of material that might itself be reflective of our microwave signals. All of that should be visible.

"But it's the fourth point that really gives us a good shot at finding these things if they are where you think they are in this drawing. If this is accurate, or even reasonably representative, of what's under the ground, then when we pass the GPR signal over the area, we're going to see a systematic, repeated pattern of returns. We're going to see images that replicate this grid pattern. At the end of the day, GPR sees reflections of *something* under the ground, and we can often make highly educated guesses as to what that is. If you find an old lead utility cable at point A on a line and the same signal shows up at points B and C and so on, you can pretty well guess what that is. But you still have to interpret the signals as best you can, and then dig to be sure. Here, we might get a series of weak and ambiguous returns because it's glass or a very small void or for some other reason, but if we get . . . what is this, about three dozen? If we get three dozen ambiguous returns that are all ambiguous in the same way, and if they map out like this, then we know we've found what we're looking for.

"And to answer the question that started that monologue—and I apologize for going on so long—yes, we have the latest gear from Sensors & Software, one of the industry leaders, and we definitely have what we'd need to do this job."

"I think," said Andy, "we've come to the right place. We'll be in touch when we get to a point where we can, hopefully, schedule you guys onto the site."

Keiley and Rudy exchanged smiles and a quick hug, then she and Andy headed to the SUV.

"Should I be jealous?" Andy asked after starting the engine.

"Always," came the reply.

When Andy and Keiley got back to the office, there were two pieces of mail waiting: one from an address in Llewellyn Park and the other from Professor Templeton at Rutgers. Andy slit open the first envelope and scanned the letter. He looked up in surprise.

"Well, there's something unexpected," he said to Keiley. "They're going to let us walk around over there. Look at this." He handed her the letter, which was on plain stationery but signed by James Cashman, the chairman of the Committee of Managers.

"Andy, this is great news," said Keiley.

"It is, and it's kind of surprising. With all the defensive language in their documents, and the gate, and the guards, and the general aura of the place, I really didn't think they'd make it easy for us—we don't want to get ahead of ourselves—but this is a terrific way to start, and chances are, if that big rock turns out to be what we think it is, it's the only time we'll have to bother them.

"Now let's see what our archeologist has to say." Andy picked up the second envelope and cut it open. Inside, he found a brief cover note and a long list of suggested talking points for his initial contact with the Park Service. A second document contained a list of organizations the professor thought might be interested parties. In addition to the National Park Service, her list included, as expected, the Advisory Council on Historic Preservation, the National Trust for Historic Preservation, and the New Jersey Historical Commission. But there were also some surprises: the Smithsonian Institution, the West Orange Historic Preservation Commission, and even the Trustees of Llewellyn Park. Then there was something called Preservation New Jersey, which she described as a

Dear Mr. Dennum:

We are in receipt of your recent letter requesting access to a limited area of The Ramble for purposes of a visual inspection in search of possible historical artifacts. On the advice of our legal affairs committee, we hereby grant you permission for such an inspection subject to the following conditions:

1. You must be accompanied at all times by an official representative of the community, a role which I shall fulfill personally;

2. You must limit your search to areas of The Ramble that are directly adjacent to the Glenmont property;

3. In conducting your search, you may not employ any form of loud or otherwise disruptive equipment; and

4. In the course of your search, you may not disturb the ground in any way, as for example by digging a hole or moving rocks aside.

On first visit, you may not conduct tests using ground penetrating radar. However, it is not our intention at this time to rule out such use at a future date should you present an acceptable rationale and plan for doing so.

Nothing in this letter grants you permission to excavate any site located on the common land of Llewellyn Park, and nothing in this letter concedes ownership or legal control of any artifacts that may be discovered during this or any subsequent visit. If subsequent visits are required, each must be approved in advance by the Committee of Managers.

Please contact me at your convenience to arrange for your visual inspection visit.

James Cashman, Chair

Committee of Managers

private, nonprofit advocacy group that had been around since the 1970s. Audrey noted that as recently as 2020, the group had given Llewellyn Park a $150,000 grant to refurbish the gatehouse, which had apparently been falling apart. It was a good guess that they would take an interest. So in addition to taking on a slew of new bureaucracies, it looked to Andy as if he'd be seeing the Llewellyn Park folks on more than the one occasion he had just arranged. Clearly, he had his work cut out for him. Task one was now evident: to keep himself from being totally overwhelmed.

Most people think of lawyering as standing up in court in front of a judge and jury and arguing their case. That's what it looks like in crime novels; that's what it looks like on television and in movies; that's what it looks like in the news. But in reality, as Andy was coming to realize, that's not what it's like at all. Oh, sure, there are lawyers who specialize in that sort of thing. The profession calls them litigators, and their job is basically to look and act just like those fictional characters and TV actors, only in the real world. For those chosen few, lawyering is a form of drama, a morality play with real consequences, and many of them, he thought, are the professional equivalent of drama queens. But most lawyers are more like high-end, highly trained, back-office bureaucrats whose job is to figure out what the laws and regulations are with respect to any particular line of business or type of activity, then either to ensure that their clients comply with those requirements or to protect them insofar as possible when they do not. In this alternative world, lawyering is a test of one's intellect, of one's command of logic, language, logistics, and, occasionally, the law. Since there are literally hundreds of thousands of laws and regulations on the books—federal, state, local, and more—it can hardly be surprising that there are many thousands of lawyers to interpret and implement them. And in that professional ecosystem, it can hardly be surprising that so many of them end up working for (becoming, really) the governments themselves.

I've been a licensed attorney for more than two years now, thought Andy, *and while I have seen the inside of a courtroom, I haven't been anywhere near an actual trial. I'm not sure that dealing with this maze of agencies and regulations, other law firms, judicial back offices, and the like is what I had in mind when I chose this path. But it's where I am. Welcome to Life of a Lawyer 1.0.*

He couldn't say he was looking forward to crafting a series of separate yet interlocking strategies for navigating so many different sets of interests and requirements. People did dig holes in the ground in the national parks, so obviously it could be done. But as he thought about all of the work that would be involved, all of the challenges that would be faced, and all of the little disagreements that could add up to failure, he came to a decision.

Time to call Sam, he decided. *All of this will cost even more money and time, and it's not clear that it will really serve the guy's interest as Culbertson's heir. Best see what he wants me to do.*

Andy asked Betty to arrange a meeting with Sam for the following week. He thought that would probably be the end of the matter, or at least the beginning of the end. He could file a final report with the court, close out the estate, and let Sam take his lamps and his rugs and his ring and his painting and his strange diagram and go about the rest of his life. Selling the lamps and the rugs, if that's what he decided to do, should give him a nice little reserve for his youngest kid's college fund, his retirement nest egg, or whatever he chose to do with it.

Sometimes plans change unexpectedly.

The day before Andy's scheduled meeting with his client, he followed up with Professor Templeton. He had meant to call and thank her for the thoroughness of her recommendations, but that had been lost in the shuffle of other business—the run-of-the-mill real estate, divorce, business dispute, and other cases that kept a practice like his afloat. Now, he realized, he not only needed to thank her for her work (and apologize for his own lack of courtesy), but he had to get her invoice for that work, which he would need in order to close out the estate paperwork.

"Professor," he said when she came on the line, "I'm so sorry. I meant to get back to you after I received your materials, and I just got sidetracked. But I want to tell you that I really appreciated the thoroughness of your lists. They gave me a genuine appreciation of the complexity of this project we were considering. So please do send me your invoice, and I'll make sure it gets paid right away."

"Did I just hear you refer to this project in the past tense?" Templeton asked.

"Yes, I'm afraid so. I have a meeting scheduled with my client tomorrow morning, and we'll probably make a final decision. But given the timetable of, what, two years or more that you laid out and the number of parties involved, I'm afraid the estate is not big enough to justify the expense of all that. Plus, my client's just an everyday working stiff, and he doesn't have those kinds of resources. So I'm planning to recommend that we forgo any further pursuit of the Edison cylinders and just close things out."

"Well," she said, "I can certainly understand that. As I cautioned you at the outset, it's a pretty daunting process. But as I also mentioned, though it was not in my notes, I thought there might be a workaround that might make the whole thing less time-consuming and less onerous."

"I'm listening," replied Andy.

"Now, you said you thought this was probably some sort of battery-related experiment, correct?"

"Yes. And your husband was helpful in pointing us in that direction."

"Do you have any documentation or other kind of evidence to suggest that's what Edison was doing? Anything, for example, that describes the experiment?"

"Let me think. We don't have any piece of paper that relates directly to it. But the director of the Edison Papers Project at the university did point us to several contemporaneous letters or notebook pages—I'm trying to recall the specifics—that put everything into that frame. And there was a lot of history around that and trying to make improvements in the batteries for submarines around that time. So it fits into the history pretty well."

"So you've been working with Art Escalon at the Papers Project?"

"Well, I can't say 'working with,' but yes, he was one of the first people I consulted with. And for what it's worth, he was interested in obtaining the original of that map or diagram that I showed you last week. They were going to try to match it, I think, to Edison notes that they haven't yet gotten around to digitizing. I don't know if they've had a chance to finish looking at that or not."

"That," she replied, "is excellent on many levels. But before I get to that, let me ask you something else. In these battery experiments, and speaking more generally now because I know you can't say what is in these specific buried cylinders, but in these experiments, do you know what kind of chemicals that might involve?"

"It's funny you should ask me that, because that's sort of the same question I took to your husband. So he'd be a much better source on the specifics. But from what I've read and the little I know about the problems Edison was having, you could safely say they would have involved corrosive liquids, flammable gases, highly reactive metals. So dangerous stuff."

"And why was he playing around with different kinds of tubing materials, if that's what he was about here?"

"As I understand it, his batteries were subject to leakage. He was looking for a better way to keep all of these menacing components inside the batteries so they could work at full strength. Apparently, the stuff was pretty nasty, whatever it was, and at least in the case of the submarine batteries, the gases could explode and catch fire. There'd apparently been some bad burns, and even some deaths."

"Perfect," Templeton said.

"I beg your pardon?" Andy rejoined.

"Well, not perfect for Edison or those poor people who got burned or worse. But for us all these years later, maybe perfect. Let me tell you why."

———

When Sam was ushered into Andy's office the following afternoon, he was surprised to find another person already present, a woman he judged to be about forty-five with graying hair and a large briefcase on her lap.

"Sam, thanks for coming in. This is Audrey Templeton—Professor Audrey Templeton—from Rutgers. She's an archeologist I consulted about this issue of finding and digging up the glass cylinders. When I had Betty call you last week to arrange this meeting, I was getting ready to tell you that I thought we ought to give up the search. But then I spoke later with Professor Templeton here—"

"Please. Just Audrey," she inserted.

"With Audrey here," Andy continued with a nod and a smile, "and she gave me a whole new perspective on the problem. I invited her to join us today so you could hear what she has to say and we could plot out a path forward, whatever direction forward ends up being. Audrey, the floor is yours."

"Thanks, Andy," she said. Then she turned to Sam. "Sam, let me begin by summarizing for you some things I told Andy a couple of weeks ago that will almost certainly explain his first instinct to walk away from this situation. What you have in this map of yours is a very interesting document, but an extremely ambiguous one. I have the sense that neither of you is sure what this offset hexagon represents, where it is, or even if whatever it is is still wherever it was. So it's not at all clear if there is any figurative gold at the end of this particular rainbow. I am also given to understand that the resources available to chase this thing down are very limited. But let's suppose, for the sake of argument, that what you have is a map of a lost experiment by Thomas Edison—and some sort of secondary object that is more personally meaningful to you—which you believe is located on or near the Glenmont property. The experiment is of potentially significant historical importance, but the property happens to be owned by the federal government, operated by the National Park Service, monitored by the New Jersey historical preservation agency, adjacent to a rigorously private residential community, listed on the National Register of Historic Places, and potentially in or slightly upslope from a wetland area that may be regulated by the Environmental Protection Agency, the Fish and Wildlife Service, or even the Army Corps of Engineers. Within that matrix of interests, if we can call it that, there are some unobtrusive ways in which you can conduct a search that might let you rule out the location in question or determine that your objective might be buried there. You can eyeball the site—and it sounds like the community is amenable to taking the first step of that process by visually inspecting the pertinent area of their common land—and chances are the Park Service would also permit that, as well as an assessment using ground-penetrating radar." She paused and asked, "Are you familiar with that technology?"

"I think so," Sam said. "They just send radar signals down into the ground and try to interpret the signals that bounce back. Same as tracking an airplane or a storm, except they point the thing down rather than up. Beyond that, like how they figure out what's there, is all way beyond me."

Templeton resumed her narrative. "That's basically correct, and the main idea is that they can determine, to some degree, what's underground, if anything is, and exactly where it is, all without turning over any dirt. Since that methodology is also unobtrusive and has no impact on the site, they'd probably let you do that. Now, if you do all of this and find nothing, then you know you're in the wrong place and you can sit down and rethink your approach, or even whether you want to proceed. But if the visual or radar inspections seem to confirm your theory, then you need a giant opener for the can of worms you are about to let loose. Things can very quickly get very complicated and very expensive.

"When you want to dig up the ground in search of what you believe to be important historical artifacts—and a lost Edison experiment would certainly qualify—you need an archeologist, someone like me, to control the dig so that everything is done systematically, nothing of importance is lost, and any finds are recorded *in situ*—where they are found—extracted safely, preserved, recorded, and interpreted. You can't just go digging things up. And when you want to do that digging on a site that you don't own or control and which is overseen by layers and layers of watchful eyes like this one, once you mention the word 'archeology' you open a virtual Pandora's box of regulatory requirements and processes. Let me give you just one example.

"Because Glenmont is a registered historic place, it is governed by a federal law, the National Historic Preservation Act, and more specifically by the part of that law we call Section 106. Administration of that law is under the purview of something called the Advisory Council on Historic Preservation. That commission has several members who are either experts in the field or are there to represent the general public, along with half a dozen cabinet members—and we're talking the president's cabinet here—like the Secretary of the Interior and the Chair of the Council on Environmental Quality, plus a governor, a mayor, and a member of a Native American tribe, and representatives of some major preservationist organizations. Now of course, most of those people will staff out attendance at meetings and such, but the point is that it's a whole-of-government deal, and fairly high-powered.

"Basically, Section 106 requires that all of the potentially interested federal agencies be given the chance to weigh in on your request to dig a hole, and each of those agencies has to give the public a chance to be heard on the matter. In addition to those agencies, you have to solicit input from private groups like the National Trust for Historic Preservation. And that's just the federal law. Because Glenmont is in New Jersey and is listed in the state's Register of Historic Places, it is also subject to the New Jersey Register of Historic Places Act, which requires a review by the Historic Preservation Office, or HPO, part of the state's Department of Environmental Protection, which will also likely receive comments or recommendations from private groups like Preservation New Jersey. The HPO is run by a commissioner over in Trenton who gets advice from an eleven-member Historic Sites Council appointed by the governor. The commissioner can become either your advocate and facilitator or your worst enemy. Then there are the local government folks. Back in 1990, for example, the West Orange Township Council passed its own historic preservation ordinance. That one aligns with the state guidelines, and it can't supersede anything at the federal level, but it does add yet another layer of bureaucratic review. At each step along the way, the decision-makers would likely hear from the Llewellyn Park folks, probably through their Llewellyn Park Preservation Foundation, who have a clear interest in this, and also by the West Orange Historic Preservation Commission, which has its own set of concerns that may or may not overlap those of the immediate neighbors.

"Now I'm going to pause to catch my breath," she said, "while you silently whisper to yourself, 'Oh my God!'"

"To hell with silence," Sam responded. "Oh my God!"

"Precisely," the professor continued. "But there's more. Suppose that you find the right location, get everyone's permission to proceed, dig the holes, and find exactly what you're looking for. All of a sudden, you're into a whole new set of legal issues surrounding ownership. Who owns what you've found? I'm sure Andy can say a lot more about this, but basically, you've now discovered a previously unknown Edison artifact on public land in a community where, dollars to doughnuts, Edison's burying it there was a violation of some protocol or covenant to which he had legally committed himself by virtue of purchasing the property. You can expect claimants to come out of the woodwork for a piece of that action. Every state has what's known colloquially as a 'finders-keepers law,' and New Jersey is no exception. But the number of ambiguities here as to who is the legal finder and how the law would apply when set against other kinds of claims will be huge. If Andy is good at his job, you might prevail. But even if he is exceptional at his job, you might not."

As she layered issue upon issue, Templeton could see Sam sinking lower and lower into his chair. But she had one more blow to deliver before turning the conversation in a more positive direction.

"When all is said and done, Sam, you can expect the permitting process alone to take at least two years, and that's if everything goes smoothly. If you start running into objections, it can take much longer, not least because every accommodation you make at one level or to one set of interests is then subject to re-review by all of the other parties. As I said to Andy, it's not that all of these guardians—and that's truly what they are and how they view themselves—it's not that they don't want anyone doing this archeology. After all, if there is unknown history to be uncovered through a dig, it is entirely compatible with their interests to find it. But they want to be sure everyone involved is serious and every aspect of the project is done right and properly supervised. Along the way, though, there are a great many opportunities to be frustrated, whether it's by the slow pace of the review or as a result of some requirement imposed by one or another of these agencies.

"Now, before you go searching for a bottle of valium or a stiff drink, let me tell you why I'm really here. All of these laws and regulations and policies and agencies are in place for good and valid reasons. And generally, this is how we go about these things. But there is a loophole, and I think there is a way we can take advantage of it in this case."

⸺◈◈⸺

At the end of her meeting with Andy and Sam, Professor Templeton had offered to take the initiative in exploring the possibility she had laid before the two. While she did that, and with her concurrence, Andy had asked Betty to contact Mr. Cashman at Llewellyn Park to arrange a meeting and a visual exploration of the area of interest.

It was just a few days later when he and Keiley found themselves at the gatehouse to the Park, where, after being waved through the gate and parking in the small lot just behind the gatehouse, they were met by a nattily dressed and slightly balding gentleman of an advanced age who identified himself as their host.

"Mr. Cashman, I'm Andy Dennum," he said, reaching out to shake hands, "and this is my mapping consultant, Keiley Barefoot. Thank you so much for agreeing to let us have a look at this area of interest."

"It's a pleasure to meet you, Mr. Dennum, Ms. Barefoot. As you know, our neighbors in this community prize their privacy, so we're very careful about whom we allow into the Park. But we are also a community of history lovers, and of course, we realize that we have a national treasure in our midst. So your request, though unusual, did resonate with our committee. But as I said in my letter, I must caution you. The only request to which we have acceded is to allow today's visual inspection. Anything more than that would require a step-by-step further review, and I will say to you bluntly that we are likely to resist something along the lines of an excavation in the Ramble. Although, resist is perhaps too mild a word."

"Mr. Cashman, I understand completely where you're coming from. I guess we'll know more in just a few minutes. But I will tell you that our expectation is that what we find in today's observation is likely to redirect our attention to the Glenmont property itself. And if anything is to come of that, it would almost surely be subject to some level of review by the Park Service. My understanding is—and you will likely be more familiar with this than I am—but as I understand it, any sort of archeological research project," Andy continued, choosing his words with particular care here, "would be subject to a comprehensive review with built-in opportunities for your community's participation."

"Good," said Cashman. "So we understand one another. Shall we begin?"

Cashman nodded to a security guard who had been among those standing behind a desk in the gatehouse. The guard led the threesome to a waiting Jeep. He pointed Andy and Keiley toward the rear bench, then climbed into the driver's seat while Cashman took the other front seat.

The guy is bringing security along, Andy thought. *What does he think we're going to do? Mug him and then start turning over rocks?*

The ride to a spot on Park Way opposite the west lawn of Glenmont took less than a minute, with Andy guiding the driver to the spot of greatest interest. The guard remained in the Jeep while the others clambered out and walked across the road to the area known as the Ramble. It was basically a densely wooded gash that ran along a stream, Wigwam Brook, for the length of the community, and it was the principal feature that gave the area its park-like character. Andy knew from studying satellite views online that the Ramble was lined with walking paths and spotted with gazebos, benches, and other features. But here, across from Glenmont, the Ramble was little more than a steep slope leading down to the waterway, which had been lined in a much earlier age by the placement of small flat rocks that defined and preserved its course.

Andy and Keiley turned their attention to the large boulder near the road, the one they hoped might be the hypothesized home plate rock. They saw at once that the top of the rock, when viewed from above—a perspective that was hidden in all of the available satellite views by the dense overhead foliage—was at the very least a viable candidate. It could not be described as a perfect linear match for the five-sided baseball hearthstone—the focal point of the game's heat and light—but then, with only a few exceptions that generally pertain to crystalline structures, natural features are seldom truly linear. With a little imagination, though, and not that much, the boulder fit the bill. The two explorers shared a glance at one another.

At that point, it was Keiley who began moving closer to the slope.

"Careful!" cautioned Andy. "What are you doing?"

"I want to look at the perspective from further down," came her reply. "I want to see what the artist saw, see if it fits the painting."

"Painting?" asked Cashman. "Is there some painting of this area?"

"Ah," replied Andy as Keiley reconsidered her descent. She was coming to the conclusion that the climb down to the brook she had anticipated making would be impossible without ropes and rappelling gear.

"Yes," Andy was continuing, "one of the items in the estate I represent is an old painting. It's kind of plain, to tell you the truth. But while we're here, we thought we'd see if we could figure out where the artist might have been standing when she made it. We'll just be another minute or two."

In the event, Keiley had made it about three or four feet down the slope, which was already further than she judged safe, secured her balance, turned her eyes back toward the rock, the road, and the Glenmont estate beyond, taken in the scene, imagined what she would be seeing as if there were a true vanishing point to match the one Shillard-Smith had employed, then eased her way back up to Park Way. Now reassembled, the group rejoined the security guard in the Jeep and made their way back to the gatehouse.

"This was really helpful," Andy said to Cashman. "Thank you very much for letting us do this."

"My pleasure," replied the chairman of the Committee of Managers. "I hope you found what you needed."

Andy and Keiley nodded without responding, then made their way back to Andy's SUV and headed for home.

"What do you think?" Andy queried as they turned onto Main Street.

"Three things," came the reply. "First, I think that is almost certainly our home plate rock. The shape is pretty close, and of course, it didn't matter whether Shillard-Smith thought of it that way or not. All that matters is the degree to which it seems to match the rock she painted. Second, there's no way Edison was digging holes on that slope. Not if he valued his life. Way too steep. I don't think I'd call that a stream bed; I'd call it a gorge. And the soil is pretty rocky, too. So we're not looking down there. And third, when I was down there even that short way and looking back, I could see the rock, but at that angle, it didn't look like a home plate shape. It just looked like a rock that had a couple of more or less straight sides and then a point. And that is, in fact, what she painted. The other thing, and it was the one I was most concerned about, was the road. There's not a hint of the road in that painting. And you remember that we rejected one of the other possible locations because the driveway would have been so prominent in the painting. Unavoidable, really. And the road is certainly wider than that driveway. But the thing is, from even that short distance down there, the ground is so steep that you don't even see the road. You see the rock, and then you see beyond it the lawn and the house. It's only when you get to the very top that you realize the road is there.

"Bottom line? I'm more convinced than ever that we have this right. That's the rock, Glenmont is the house at the vanishing point, and you know what? From across the road, the length of the west lawn is accentuated. It looks longer than it is. So Shillard-Smith *might* have drawn some inspiration from the length of the south lawn that runs from the front of the house to Glen Avenue, but it's not essential to the painting that she did. It could simply be an artist's eye kind of thing. After all, she was already doing some shape-shifting with the perspective to set that light in the distance. What's a little more fudging between friends? Plus, let's remember that she was trained less in landscape painting than as a portraitist. Maybe she just got it a little wrong."

"Hmm," mused Andy. "Well, be that as it may, and of course we can never resolve that one, it does seem that we have a starting point for our search. And as importantly, we have a touchpoint for making our case if Audrey Templeton can make the arrangements she mentioned. All in all, I'd say this was a day well spent."

"Lunch and a beer?" she asked.

"I was thinking something at Dante's and a glass of wine," he replied.

"Better still. But drive faster. I'm hungry."

Squeeze Play

It was just starting to rain lightly as the group gathered outside the gate of the Thomas Edison National Historical Park; more specifically, the laboratory and industrial complex on Main Street. Audrey Templeton, who had arranged this meeting, was there along with her husband, Hiram Burlmeister, Chair of the chemistry department at Rutgers; Art Escalon, director of the Edison Papers Project at the university; Keiley; Andy; and Andy's client, Sam Patrick, who was the last to arrive. Everyone had come prepared to review the pending request from his or her perspective, and most had brought with them some relevant documentation. It was a Wednesday, and the park wasn't open to the public, which made this the perfect time to meet. At ten thirty on the dot, a tall African American man in a ranger's uniform, complete with Smokey hat, emerged from behind a brick wall and approached the gate.

"Good morning, everyone," he said as he came closer.

"Ephraim," Audrey Templeton exclaimed. "Let us in. It's getting wet out here!"

"Sorry, Audrey," he said with a smile as he worked the lock and swung open the gate. "That's why we wear these hats, you know. Come on in, folks. Is everyone here?"

"We are," said Audrey. "But let's get out of the rain before we make introductions." *Clearly*, thought Andy, *Audrey does not like the rain. Odd for an archeologist.*

Following the ranger, the group moved quickly into the park, past the entrance to the Visitors Center, and then into a nearby doorway on the left under a sign that read "Building 11." Once inside, they found themselves in a smallish room with a lectern at the far end and a pair of Edison phonographs in wooden cabinets along the left-hand wall. A shelf above them held a variety of phonographic horns. Toward the rear of the room was a tinfoil phonograph model and a display case showing the internal workings of an Edison disc phonograph. The display was rounded out by a large video screen that was obviously used for presentations. Finally, to their right was a folding table, about eight feet long, surrounded by some old wooden chairs. Everyone claimed a seat around the table, leaving the chair at one end open for the ranger, while Audrey made a point of claiming the one at the opposite end. The professor knew how to control a meeting.

"That's better," said Audrey. "Everyone, I'd like you to meet Ephraim Cook. Ephraim is the superintendent of the park. He's a lifer in the Park Service, and he's been in this position for, what, six years now?"

"Seven, actually," replied the ranger.

"I stand corrected. And he is not only an effective steward of the park, but an all-around good guy."

"Thank you, Audrey," said Ephraim. "And welcome to our obviously very formal conference room. Of course I know Hi and Art very well. Morning, fellas. But perhaps, Audrey, you could introduce the rest of your group?"

"Sure. The gentleman on your immediate left is Sam Patrick." Sam raised his hand slightly in greeting. "He's the heir to the Francis Culbertson estate and ultimately the reason that we are all here this morning. Just to his left is his attorney, Andy Dennum." Andy nodded. "And just to my left is his associate, Keiley Barefoot." Keiley smiled. "Basically, we have all of the principals and relevant disciplines here— Hi for chemistry, Art for Edison and history, Keiley for cartography, Andy for legal, and Sam because he, or really his late uncle, is the one we are all here to serve."

"Thanks, Audrey," said Ephraim. "Sounds like a pretty good group. As half of you know, and the other half are about to find out, I detest long meetings and I like to cut to the chase as quickly as possible. In this instance, Audrey has filled me in on some background information, and she's made an unusual suggestion. The reason I asked to have you all visit today is so that I can gather some information that will help me process her suggestion and decide whether and how I can let this thing move forward. Mr. Patrick, let me begin with you. Can you tell me a little bit about your uncle and about what it is that he left you that has caused all of this ruckus?"

Sam offered a thumbnail sketch of his Uncle Frank, and also of his grandfather, John Culbertson, and his grandmother, Jennie. He ended by describing the items Frank had left him, particularly the Tiffany Lamps, the ring, and the painting.

Ephraim then turned to Andy, who told of the discovery of the diagram by the appraisers when they were evaluating the painting. He told of how that discovery, with its Edison signature, had led to further inquiries into any possible relationship between Edison and Culbertson, including their undocumented belief that Culbertson had been a long-time Edison Company employee. Andy brought Keiley into the discussion to summarize her findings regarding the friendship between Edison and Tiffany and Edison's little-known membership in the Theosophy Society, which she then tied to the ring. Finally, she made the connection between Edison and the painter, Shillard-Smith, again through Theosophy.

At this point the superintendent reasserted himself in the conversation. "So, Ms. Barefoot, I understand you are a cartographer. What do you make of this diagram. Is it a map or something else?"

"I do believe it's a map. Not a map of some large geographic area, but a map of a very localized area intended to show the placement of a set of objects represented by these three dozen hexagons. I can't say that the objects themselves are hexagonal. But the thing about hexagons used this way is that they are easily drawn and easily equalized. In other words, it's not difficult to make them all the same size and organize them in straight lines, and to use those regularities to represent scale or spacing. Whatever is there, the place to look would likely be at the center point of each hexagon. And, of course, you have the landmarks—the large boulder at the base and the two lesser boulders marking the lateral extremes."

"And you think that Edison buried these objects, then commissioned the painting to help him remember where?"

Andy stepped in to answer the question. "Actually, no. Once I'd had a chance to consult with Art and Hi here and we understood more of the history and what Edison might have been doing, we came to pretty much the opposite conclusion. We believe, and I'll yield to Art on this, that back around 1910 or 1912, Edison was trying to solve problems with his storage battery designs, and that these objects, which, thanks to Hi, we have come to understand as most likely glass cylinders of some specialized type, were part of that. Edison was looking for ways to minimize leakage of the flammable gases or other components of his batteries." At the mention of leakage, Ephraim Cook looked up from his eyes-down listening pose.

Andy continued. "We think that he buried these experimental cylinders on the grounds at Glenmont for some reason—privacy, security, test conditions, we really can't say. Anyway, he drew this map, except for one element, at that time. The painting is dated later, at the beginning of 1915, which was right after there had been an explosion and fire right here at West Orange. We think the painting was a gift meant to cheer him up. It has a very uplifting message: He brought Light into the world."

"And this is a painting of Glenmont?"

"Yes and no." It was Keiley's turn again. "The point of the painting, given its title, is to focus the eye on a bright point of light in the center distance. To accomplish that, the artist used a technique known as a vanishing point, which makes objects in the foreground look bigger and those in the distance smaller, all angling in toward a central point, in this case the light. It was when we spent some time walking around the grounds at Glenmont that we became convinced the scene was a stylized depiction of the grounds, with the house situated very near the vanishing point. If we're correct, then Edison had the painting in hand early in 1915. But we don't think he gave it to John Culbertson at that time. We're speculating now, but we think he might have given it to Culbertson as a wedding gift, which would have made that around 1928, according to Sam here. And we think the very last of those hexagons—the one at the top of the array there—represents a cylinder that was buried at that later time. We think that Edison used the painting to indicate the general location, attached the map to the back of the painting to make the connection, and then covered the back of the canvas with brown craft paper to hide the map. Now, why he would have done that, we can't say."

"Goodness," said the superintendent. "That's quite a tale. So what we have is a great deal of speculation based on what I will confess are some rather intriguing clues. Art, anything to add here?"

"Only that, as Andy has suggested, we looked at a number of documents in our collection—notebooks, letters, and so forth. We were able to confirm that Edison was devoting a great deal of attention to solving some basic problems with his battery designs at just that time period. And we found some pages that referenced working with cylinders as containers and with glass cylinders in particular, though we have not yet tied the glass cylinders precisely to the battery work at that moment in time. Of course, if I recall, you have an example of an Edison battery in a glass container just across the way there in Building 5, don't you?"

The superintendent smiled and nodded in the affirmative.

Escalon resumed his narrative. "We haven't yet found a single page that describes the experiment Andy and Keiley are talking about, but as you know very well, there are thousands of pages in the microfilm record that we haven't yet been able to digitize and index. So it's a difficult search. One other thing, though, is the signature on the diagram. Edison had about ten different ways of signing things, and this one is close to his most formal signature, with the large arc across the top. But I think if someone had set out to forge that signature, it would be much closer to perfection than what we have. I've seen this variation on a couple of other documents. I think of it as kind of his rushed version of the formal autograph. And I think it's very likely authentic."

"Okay then," said Ephraim. "I guess that leaves you, Hi. Anything you'd like to contribute? What are all those markings on some of the hexagons?"

"That's a really interesting question, Ephraim, and it goes right to the heart of the matter. Edison was a good bench chemist, as you know, and of course he had a lot of experience with making glass. Around the time in question, there was a new type of glass being rolled out, if you'll pardon the pun. It was called borosilicate glass, made by adding boron and some other elements to the mix, and it was all the rage in industrial and scientific uses because it gave the glass more strength, better optical properties, and more. Those markings on the headers for the rows of hexagons are, in fact, different formulas for borosilicate glass, and the way these things are arrayed is a strong indicator that this was, in fact, some kind of comparison experiment across the different formulations."

"And if these were tests of containers for batteries," Superintendent Cook said as he picked up the thread, "what would have been in them?"

"Well," Burlmeister replied, "without the lab notes, it's impossible to be sure. But typically we'd be dealing with acids, explosive gases, and just a lot of caustic chemicals in general. That's just the nature of storage batteries. And it was kind of the point. I think Edison was trying to find out whether any of these different types of glass cylinders was up to the task of containing them."

"So," asked Ephraim, "do I take it that they might or might not have been effective containment vessels? They might have leaked?"

"Leaked? Sure," replied the chemist. "Or even simply broken. After all, we are talking about glass cylinders that have been buried in the ground for over a hundred years. Who knows what might have happened."

"And what about this outlier cylinder, the one with the strange diagram on top? Any idea what that is?"

"Well, I can tell you about the marking. But it's almost certain that's not what is, or was, in the cylinder. The diagram there represents a borate ion called orthoborate. It's a strong base, and the stronger a base is, the more caustic it is. Just like a strong acid. Now, if you looked at a chart that ranked such things, you'd find that this borate ion is actually in second place on the base end of that list. Really caustic. But the thing is, unless Edison had found something no one else has then or since, the stuff doesn't exist in isolation—only as a component of various compounds. So it couldn't be in that cylinder on its own. There must have been some other reason for that label. For example, it could have been a warning to just keep away, kind of like the way we use a warning sign everyone recognizes where there's radiation danger. Matter of fact, it kind of resembles that sign a little bit. But it would take a chemist to even recognize this marking, let alone interpret it properly. The reason the radiation signage works is because people have had decades of messaging to learn its meaning. That's not the case here. So that's a mystery."

"If I can jump in here," Andy inserted, "it's that last cylinder that we're mainly interested in. We believe we've uncovered a lost Edison experiment, and we see the historical value of doing some archeology on that discovery, assuming that we can nail down the location. But at the end of the day, Sam here is interested only in that outlier cylinder. We believe that was added to the diagram, and presumably to the in-ground array, at a later date. The ink is different, the symbol is different, and the cylinder stands off on its own. We believe there is something in that cylinder that was meant for John Culbertson but that he never discovered because he never had any reason to uncover the back of the canvas. Nor did his son Frank, Sam's uncle. It was only when we had to have the painting appraised in the course of valuing Frank's estate that the drawing was discovered. And as to the marking, obviously it's a cautionary note of some kind."

"I'm afraid I need to bring this discussion to a conclusion," said the superintendent, "as I have another obligation. But this has been tremendously helpful, and I think I understand why Audrey has made the suggestion she has. I have a great deal to think about before deciding whether and how to proceed with some sort of archeological dig. But in the meantime, let me suggest this. There is enough substance here that it would probably be worthwhile to see if you can isolate a likely location for such a project. So I'm going to authorize you to do a noninvasive site survey, including using the GPR, to see if you are even on the right track. I'll assign one of my rangers to work with you on that, and I'll want him or her on-site with you when you're doing the work. Audrey, I'll be in touch as soon as I make that assignment. In the meantime, Mr. Dennum, your request to do that survey is granted, and you can go ahead and schedule the work. Thanks everyone for coming in today."

As Cook rose to end the meeting, everyone in the group expressed their appreciation to him. He then led the group back to the gate, which he opened for them, then relocked when they had filed out.

Once on the sidewalk, Andy turned to Audrey. "I don't know what you said to Superintendent Cook or what exactly you have in mind, but it has certainly gotten things rolling. I assume you'll want to be there when we roll out the radar?"

"Wouldn't miss it for the world," she replied.

And with that, the group broke up and, in ones and twos, went their separate ways.

<hr />

The weather was cooperating as the team from Gallegos & Golden parked their van along the side of Park Way the Tuesday following the meeting with Ephraim Cook. In general, the Park discouraged parking along its roads, especially its main roads, like Park Way. But under the circumstances, the Committee of Managers had made an exception, and the crew took care to set out a line of orange cones, warning passing motorists of this unexpected obstruction. Keiley had hoped Rudy Gallegos himself might make an appearance, but the short notice and small scale of the job did not warrant his leaving the large utility project he was overseeing a few miles to the south. In his stead, though, Rudy had convinced his co-owner, Stanley Golden, to tag along and be helpful.

Waiting at the site for the G&G crew were Andy and Keiley; archeologist Audrey Templeton; James Cashman, the Chair of the Llewellyn Park Committee of Managers who, when asked about the parking, had invited himself along as an observer; and one new face, that of Peggy Morse, or more correctly, Ranger Peggy Morse, who was there to represent the national park and its superintendent. Sam had hoped to participate but had been called away to deal with a crisis at his work. Stanley Golden stepped down from the passenger side of the van and introduced himself and his technician assistant, Ray Cordova, who had also joined the group. Everyone agreed to address one another on a first-name basis, and the others agreed that this informality should not apply to Ranger Morse. These niceties accounted for, the G&G duo got down to business.

"Andy, Keiley," Stan Golden said for openers, "we have a copy of this diagram you showed to Rudy. Why don't you show us the general area you'd like us to survey and we can get started."

Andy suggested that they begin just uphill from the road at a spot aligned with the boulder on the other side and the house in the distance, and survey a square of perhaps fifty feet on a side. They might, he noted, need to extend further up toward the house or even outward on one or both sides, but that was undetermined for the moment. Stan and Ray returned to their van and retrieved a number of metal stakes and a healthy length of heavy twine. They proceeded to measure and stake out the outer boundaries of the indicated area. Next they worked up the hill on the left side of the square, placing a stake in the ground every four feet, a procedure they replicated down the opposite, right side of the square. Finally, using the twine, they connected each pair of opposing stakes with twine, which they laid on the ground. At this point, they were ready to conduct a grid search of the area.

Back at the van once more, the radar team extracted a device that resembled a large lawn mower, just as Keiley had said. But rather than a motor and the other mechanical components of a mower, this one featured a flat yellow box on its base, which Stan explained was the radar transmitter and sensor, a saucer-shaped appendage in the front that housed a GPS unit, a touch-screen display resting atop the handle, and a battery on the fiberglass frame that powered the device. The screen display seemed to offer several optional views, the selection controlled by a row of ten buttons located just below it. There was a USB port on one side of the display panel and, as Stan explained, a Wi-Fi antenna built in. The entire device looked to weigh about seventy-five pounds, and traveled freely on four eight-inch rubber tires with plastic hubs. Andy noticed that none of the structural components of the unit seemed to have metal parts which, upon reflection, made perfect sense.

"You can see," Stan was saying, "that this is a pretty compact unit. But it's more than we need to get the job done here. We've marked off a search pattern that's two feet wide in each pass, which is a good deal less than the width capacity of the unit, so we'll get lots of overlapping signals to reinforce whatever results we find. And we'll be able to look down about three feet into the ground as we go, which, from what you've said, should be all we need. Everybody ready? Let's do this."

Ray Cordova started up the unit, which amounted to pressing a switch on the control pad and waiting until the various status lights were lit, and began the methodical process of moving gradually up the hill, rolling from one side to the other while keeping the wheels on the left side of the unit in contact with the guide string on each pass. At the same time, he kept one eye on the screen, watching for anomalies. On the seventh pass, about four feet in from the side marker, he paused and signaled to Stan to join him. The pair conferred, then Stan placed a small white landscaper's flag in the ground. Ray resumed his search but moved only a foot or so before he again motioned to Stan. Again, Stan placed a white flag in the ground. Again. Again. Again. Again. Again. Again. But suddenly the radar anomalies ceased as Ray completed that line of the grid. He made the customary one-hundred-and-eighty-degree turn, lined up his left wheels, and began the next pass two feet higher up on the hill. When he reached the spot just above what would then have been the last lower-down marker, he paused again to share the screen view with Stan. Another flag went into the ground. And in this manner the flags multiplied and took form: four parallel rows of eight flags each, tightly organized in an obvious rectangular pattern.

When Ray turned once again and began what would be the eleventh pass over the test area, he was surprised by what he did *not* see. When he reached the now customary point just above the first flag in the previous rank, there was no anomaly. Only Andy and Keiley, whose shared excitement was by this time palpable, realized what this might mean. Both held their breath as Ray pushed the radar onward until . . . Stop. Consult. Flag. Not in line with those that had already been planted, but midway between the first and second flags instead. Push. Stop. Consult. Flag. Not midway between the second and third ranks of flags, but between the third and fourth. By now, they had no doubt. They had found the site of Edison's experiment. The flags made it clear; they were a perfect match for the diagram. And by now, everyone else had caught on to the significance of the radar returns. It was not an X that marked the spot, but rather a field of flags. All that remained for today was to identify the location of the last cylinder, the one Andy and Keiley were convinced was added later and meant, at the time, for John Culbertson.

Ray made the next turn and a full pass without stopping. Then he made the next turn, and the next, and the next, all without result. There was no sign of the outlier cylinder. Stan turned to Andy and opened his palms in a gesture that said, "What now, chief?"

Andy returned the gesture by raising his hands, palms forward. "Let's take a break for a few minutes and give this some thought."

Ray, who had, after all, been the one doing all of the physical labor, switched off the radar device and walked off to one side of the grid, where he'd noticed a rock that seemed big enough to sit on. He plopped himself down and took off the G&G baseball cap he'd been wearing for shade, or perhaps because it was a required part of his uniform. In the meantime, Andy, Keiley, and Audrey Templeton put their heads together in search of a plan, while the rest of the group gathered for some idle chitchat.

It was three or four minutes later when Andy happened to glance over at Ray, who by then was stretched out on the grass, using the rock as something of a pillow. Then he glanced back in the direction of the road. He was lost in thought for a moment, then said, "I think I know where the missing cylinder might be."

Keiley and Audrey gave him their full attention.

"Audrey," he said, "do you remember when we were in that big meeting last week and Ephraim Cook asked your husband what might be in that last cylinder, and the pair of them got into a discussion of boron and ions and such?"

"Yes, vaguely," she replied.

"And as Hi was explaining acids and bases and various caustic chemicals, he said something that rang a bell, something I'd heard before. He told Cook that that formula on the last cylinder was for . . . borate, I think, or something like that, and that it was a very strong base. So strong, in fact, that if you looked at a table of acids and bases ranked by their strength, it would be the second strongest base on that list. And when I heard that, I remembered that, back when we first talked, he had told me the very same thing. It would be the second strongest base on that list. *The second strongest base.*

"Now, I think it was Art Escalon at the Papers Project who first noticed the odd shape of that big boulder that we now know is across the street there, that it looked like a home plate in baseball, and he told us

157

that Edison was a huge baseball fan. And Keiley, you did some amazing research into Edison and baseball—sponsoring teams, throwing out game balls, hitting against Ty Cobb, and even playing fanboy to the A's when they were training in Florida. And when we looked back at the diagram in that light, why, it appeared that Edison had placed marker stones that looked like they represented first and third base relative to home plate rock, and he put his experiment right between them.

"Well, we found home plate rock, and it's pretty obvious now that was exactly the marker we imagined. And when Keiley and I were first checking out this location, we found first base. Ray is over there trying to sleep on it. When we looked, we didn't find third base, even though we thought we knew where to look. But a lot of things can happen to a rock over the course of a hundred years. We should look again with the radar. If we find it, or even if we don't, I think Edison has already told us where to find the missing cylinder."

One beat. Two beats. "Second base!" shouted Keiley, loud enough to draw the attention of the entire group. Even Ray stirred and looked her way. "It's wherever second base would be!"

"Stan, Ray," shouted Andy, "time to go back to work. We're looking for two things. I guess you could call them a rock and a soft place.

"First, if you guys could lay out a search line that starts at that rock, where Ray's been catching Z's, and runs perpendicular to the center line from the boulder over there up to the house, and continues on an equal distance, or maybe a little further on the other side. We're looking for a rock, probably about the same size as Ray's pillow, that might be only slightly buried over on that other side."

Stan and Ray laid out a twine search line, then Ray cranked up the radar unit and followed the line. The first twenty feet or so showed nothing but general background clutter. After that, Ray found himself skirting the array of flags they had already mapped out, again without significant new result. But when he had gone another twenty feet or so beyond the flag array, just before he reached the end of the twine, he stopped and, repeating his routine, called Stan over to consult.

"We've got something here," Stan said to the others. "It's different from what we saw before. Those were all pretty small returns—disturbed dirt and some sort of hard, regular, round objects reflecting back. Almost certainly manmade. This is different—hard but very irregular, oddly shaped. And no loose cover. A return like this almost always traces to a rock, and if that's what this is, it's only an inch or two down and it's maybe a foot and a half or two feet across. Probably about the same size as that other one across the way." He pointed toward the rock that everyone had begun to think of as Ray's pillow.

Andy gave Audrey a knowing glance, then the two of them walked over to Ranger Morse. "I'm aware," said Andy, "that we're not allowed to do any digging here today. But do you think it would be all right if we were to poke a few very small holes in the ground over there just to see if we could figure out the size of that buried rock?"

Morse, who'd been caught up in the moment herself, simply winked at Andy and Audrey, then busied herself walking over to the G&G van and inspecting the inside, which, it turned out, held even more equipment in which she took a sudden interest.

"Give me one of your flags, would you?" Audrey said, addressing the question to Stan. He complied.

Rather than planting the flag to mark the location of the rock, Audrey bent low and began pushing the metal flag stick into the ground, here and there, here and there, until she had defined its boundaries. After a minute or two, she planted the flag in the center of what was now a rough circle of tiny holes.

"Rock," she said. "Shallow, about that shape. We're a little further down the hill on this side. Probably just got buried by a hundred years of erosion, leaf waste, overgrowth. And without measuring, I'd say if you projected the lines, you'd find it makes pretty close to a right angle with Ray's pillow down there at the home plate rock. I think we've found third base."

It was just what Andy was hoping to hear. "I think we actually need to have these guys do that with their twine, trace those lines down to the rock across the road, mark the string where they meet at a right angle, presumably at the boulder, then flip the string over and walk it up the hill. Wherever that right angle ends up on the upslope, that's where we're going to find second base. I need to go talk with Cashman."

"Mr. Cashman," he said loudly as he approached the Llewellyn Park observer. "I need to ask a small favor."

Andy explained his request, and as it became entirely clear that this project was not likely to impinge any further on the Ramble or any other part of the community's common land, Cashman readily granted his permission. At that point, Stan and Ray proceeded to lay down a line from Ray's pillow, henceforth known to the group as first base rock, across Park Way to the nearest point on home plate rock, then onward to the flag marking the newly discovered third base rock. Returning across the road, they then measured the angle formed by the two lines, concluding that it was very nearly ninety degrees. *This*, thought Andy, *is getting good*. Then, as prescribed, they secured the ends of the twine and, firmly grasping the midpoint, Stan proceeded back across Park Way once more, stepping carefully through the array of flags, and continued up the hill until the string once again became taut. He placed the twine on the ground and held it steady while Ray measured the angle. They made some minor adjustments to the position of the string, then Stan secured it to the ground using another one of his flags.

"Second base, Andy," he said.

"Excellent," came the reply. "Now, if you guys would run the radar over that spot and in that general area, let's see if we get any sort of interesting return."

———————

Superintendent Ephraim Cook pulled Andy aside as he arrived for the meeting Cook had called at the lab complex. "I wanted to pass along some news before we get started," he said. "I asked my archivist to do a little research on that fellow, John Culbertson, you thought had been an Edison employee. A lot of Edison's papers are over at the university, but we still have some here at the Park as well. And among our papers is a collection of all of the payroll records from the various Edison enterprises that were based here. It turns out that a John Culbertson was indeed employed in the laboratory as some sort of handyman or mechanic. He started work not long after World War I, and he stayed on the staff until the mid-1930s, a couple of years after Edison's death. My guy then took a little initiative and dug a bit deeper in the public records beyond our own archive, basically in Essex

County, and he found a wedding license for a John Culbertson and a woman named Jennifer O'Connor in 1928, and a birth record for a Francis Culbertson that same year. I guess his curiosity was up, because then he went back into our archive, into some otherwise unconnected notes and drawings that never made it over to Rutgers. And he found a scribbled note from Edison to 'WHM'—that would have been William Henry Meadowcroft, his private secretary at the time—to send a spray of flowers to a local church for the Culbertsons' wedding. We don't have any more than that, or any idea why he would have sent flowers to that wedding in particular, which was unusual for him. But I thought I'd pass this along in case it's helpful."

"That's unbelievable that you could, or that you *would*, track that down. It really makes the connection we've just been guessing at."

"Again, it wasn't me. It was our archivist. But I thought you might find it interesting."

"I'm going to need the name of that archivist. I've got to thank that fellow personally."

"Shall we go on in?" the superintendent asked. And he followed Andy into the occasional conference room that was Building 11. This time, Andy noticed, a second portable table had been added, along with more chairs.

"If you'll forgive me," the superintendent said to begin the discussion, "I'd like to open this meeting by reading the mission statement of the Thomas Edison National Historical Park. Relax, it's brief. But I think it sets the context for the discussion we are about to have. It reads: 'Our mission is to promote an international understanding and appreciation of the life and extraordinary achievements of Thomas Alva Edison by preserving, protecting, and interpreting the park's extensive historic artifact and archive collections at the Laboratory Complex and Glenmont, the Edison family estate.' In our discussions today and going forward, I'd like us to be guided by that clear objective."

The group this time included all of the participants at the gathering a couple of weeks earlier, but also some new faces. Cook may have been the only one in the room who knew everyone, and he proceeded to make the introductions.

"Now, let me save some time," he said, "by going around the table and introducing everyone." The superintendent started with those who'd been at the previous meeting, then moved on to the newcomers. "Next," he said, "is James Cashman. Mr. Cashman is the Chair of the Committee of Managers for the Llewellyn Park community where Glenmont is located. Ed McVay is a regional representative of the Environmental Protection Agency. Maggie Harmon is here representing the New Jersey Historic Preservation Office, and to her left is Jackson Drummond from the West Orange Historic Preservation Commission. Next to Jackson is Doris Mayo from Preservation New Jersey. Finally, on my immediate right, is Anne Driscoll Smith, representing the secretary of of Interior. As you all know, the National Park Service is a part of the Interior Department, which makes Anne here my boss a couple of levels up. The Park Service has a memorandum of agreement with the Army Corps of Engineers to make sure the two agencies are not stepping on one another's toes, so I went ahead and contacted my liaison with the Corps, and I also touched base with the Fish and Wildlife Service, but as I described the issue to them they both indicated that their participation in this meeting would be either premature or unnecessary.

"In sum, we have at the table not only an amazing array of talented individuals, but all the decision-makers we'll need to address today's agenda.

"It goes without saying that under Section 106, everyone here will have an opportunity to comment on the project that we are about to discuss, and that is sure to be an ongoing process. But there is another dimension to the problem, and I hope we can get that one resolved today.

"If you've had a chance to visit the Glenmont property before coming over this afternoon, you will have seen an area of the west lawn that's covered by some rows of white flags. That's the area we are discussing today. Andy, would you mind filling everyone in on what you believe that area represents?"

"Sure," Andy replied. He took nearly fifteen minutes to summarize the aspects of the estate that tied it to Thomas Edison, and passed around copies of the original map for each attendee. Then he summarized the returns from the GPR survey of the area, and distributed copies of the site map that Gallegos & Golden had prepared in the interim. Finally, he circled in on the single outlier cylinder.

"We are pleased," he concluded, "to have been able to locate an area at Glenmont where the radar returns seem to align with the pattern indicated on our map, and I imagine the prospect of finding an unknown experiment of this type would interest many people around this table. But for us, the real item of interest is that isolated site at the very top of the array of flags. Because that portion of the diagram appears to have been added well after the rest, and because the diagram itself was secreted behind a painting that we believe to have been a gift from Edison to Frank Culbertson's father, John, we think that one cylinder was intended for the Culbertson family. Superintendent Cook informed me just before the meeting that John Culbertson was a long-time employee here at the Edison Works, and also that Edison seems to have instructed his private secretary to send flowers to Culbertson's wedding. One might speculate, then, that the painting, along with several other artifacts in the estate, could even have served as a wedding gift. Why Edison would have passed along such a map to Culbertson, I could not begin to speculate, but that does not mean he did not do precisely that. Taking all of that together, it is our position that the contents of that single cylinder, meant for John Culbertson, should pass to his heirs, of whom, at this time, my client here, Sam Patrick, is the lone survivor."

"It's pretty clear," said Ephraim Cook, picking up the conversation, "that any lost and buried Edison experiment would be of great interest. So one way or another, we'll want to conduct some serious archeology at that site. And Section 106 lays out the process for pursuing that. As you know, it can take a couple of years or more to jump through all the hoops provided in the law, and that might even be a bit optimistic. To be clear, we are not here to cut that corner today. And I hope there will be a working group that forms itself after this meeting to begin that effort. But there is another aspect to this situation that was brought to my attention by Hi Burlmeister here, and it's the reason I have asked Anne to join us from Washington. It is just possible that what we have here is a buried chemical hazard."

This revelation caused a hubbub around the table and, in particular, grabbed the attention of James Cashman, whose constituents, he quickly realized, might be the ones most endangered by whatever this was.

"Hi," Cook continued. "Would you walk us through that issue?"

"Sure, Ephraim. When Mr. Dennum here came to me with a request to interpret the chemical compounds that are shown on the labels of these hexagons on the drawing, I realized that Edison was likely experimenting with glass cylinders he was hoping to use as containment vessels, as we would say today, for his batteries or their components. He was involved at that time in developing large-scale rechargeable storage batteries for use in Navy submarines, and his early designs were suffering from leakage. There was one instance of a terrible explosion and fire on a submarine being fitted out at the Brooklyn Navy Yard. Several men died, and the blast was laid to the Edison Batteries. So he was desperate to find a solution. Now, why he might have buried a bunch of experimental glass cylinders at Glenmont, that I can't say. But he was certainly known to do experimentation at home, so he may not even have thought twice about it."

"Hi," said Ephraim Cook. "Don't bury the lede. What would have been in those cylinders?"

"Ah," said Burlmeister. "That's the problem. If Edison was testing containment cylinders for batteries, then the contents would most likely have been all sorts of potentially caustic chemicals—acids, bases, noxious gases, certain metals. And if these chemicals were placed in glass containers and left buried in the ground for over a hundred years, there is no guarantee that one or more of those containers has not cracked, or simply leaked, allowing its contents to enter the soil on that hillside. Plus, there is that outlier cylinder, the one Mr. Dennum here said was of particular interest to his client. We have no idea what might be in that cylinder. But the marking on the top is for a chemical called orthoborate, which is an extremely strong base, and therefore quite caustic. We can't rule out the possibility that that one, as well, may contain—or once have contained—toxic chemicals."

"Thank you, Hi," the superintendent said. "I trust that has gotten everyone's attention, and it explains in particular why I asked the EPA to send a representative to our little meeting. And it gets us to what I hope will be our decision point for today.

"It is true, as noted, that Section 106 governs the conduct of archeological digs in the national parks. However, there is an exception. In the event of a designated emergency, the superintendent of any park, after consultation with his or her superiors, has the authority to waive the Section 106 review for work that could mitigate such an emergency. I suggest to you—and I know Anne will back me up on this—that the potential for leakage of caustic toxic chemicals from this site, lying as it does above and near to Wigwam Brook, a tributary waterway in the heart of a residential community, constitutes such an emergency. Accordingly, and subject to your general concurrence today, I propose that we divide the site into two separate projects. In the main, the array of anomalous sites defined on the GPR map Andy distributed a few minutes ago will be considered for a traditional archeological investigation to determine whether it does, in fact, constitute a lost Edison experiment and, if so, what that experiment might have been. This search can be coordinated with the Rutgers papers archive to see if there may be previously undiscovered or misinterpreted notebook entries or other documents tied to the site. In that"—he turned to address Sam—"it might be very productive were the park or the university to come into possession of the original of this diagram of yours."

Sam nodded.

"All of that work," Cook continued, "would be conducted pursuant to Section 106. However, to address the potential danger of ground and groundwater pollution, I propose two limited and tightly controlled digs on the site for the authorization of which I would exercise my discretionary authority. The first would be a trench, perhaps three feet deep, running the length of the lowest rank of indicated locations on the hillside and six to eighteen inches from the apparent bottom of the array. Audrey, I would ask you to oversee that dig to be sure that it follows all of the standard archeological protocols. And Ed, I would especially want the advice of EPA on the depth and placement of that trench. The objective would be to detect any indication that one or more of these cylinders has leaked its contents and that such leakage has extended beyond the array itself. If there is a problem, this will give us a chance to assess and then mitigate it as needed, and that would take priority over any potential research dig.

"The second dig would be in the area of the outlier cylinder. Because that cylinder, unlike the others, is marked with a symbol of what could be a particularly toxic payload, and because the cylinder, if it's there, is generally isolated, I propose that we dig out and remove that entire cylinder, taking the necessary precautions as we proceed. Audrey, I hope you can help us with that, especially since this was originally your idea. If the cylinder is intact, we can then open it up to see if it offers any clues to what lies buried in the larger number of containers further down the hill. We can also determine if the contents are of a personal nature, as Mr. Dennum has suggested, as opposed to being more directly connected to the larger experimental array or other Edison interests. To be clear, whatever is in that cylinder will be treated initially as the property of the government through the Park Service, though it may be that some other appropriate disposition presents itself at that time."

Andy couldn't believe what he was hearing. Superintendent Cook had just cleared the way for Sam to obtain whatever personal items might be buried in the outlier cylinder without having to wait out, and quite likely pay for, a full archeological exploration of the area. For his part, Sam wore a quizzical look and seemed lost in all of the jargon. Seeing that, Andy passed him a brief note.

I think we just won big time. I'll explain later.

Digging in at the Plate

It was a Wednesday morning, so the Glenmont parking lot was empty but for those in the excavation party, and there were no tourists in sight. A few curiosity seekers from Llewellyn Park, alerted by their community leaders, had set up lawn chairs along the roadway at the bottom of the west lawn hill to watch the proceedings. Overnight rain had softened the ground without turning it into a muddy quagmire, but by the time everyone who needed to be present had arrived on site, the skies had cleared and the sun was beginning to dry things out.

Audrey Templeton took charge of the dig, once again under the watchful eye of Ranger Morse. Using string and small metal stakes, she delineated the boundaries of the main dig just below the array of flags as had been agreed. After outlining a trench two feet across running the length of the array, she moved another three feet or so down the hill, where she and Morse used wooden stakes and black plastic to construct a barrier to prevent any movement of the spoil further toward the road and the brook. James Cashman nodded his approval. Then Audrey led the small crew of graduate assistants she had brought along back to their university van, from which they extracted a sorting screen assembly, which they then set up between the trench site and the plastic barrier. As was customary in archeological digs, all of the soil removed from the trench would be sorted to be sure no artifacts were present, then the spoil, that which had sifted through the screen as well as the larger pieces that remained on top of it, would be added to a pile. In truth, Audrey did not expect to find any such artifacts. The point of this limited dig was simply to determine whether any chemicals had leaked from what was still only presumed to be a collection of buried glass cylinders.

Audrey instructed her crew to carefully cut away and stack the sod that covered the designated area, then she and the students began working their way down to a depth of approximately three feet. The best guess arrived at by her husband, Hi, and Art Escalon, based on their knowledge of Edison, his glass works, and his batteries, was that the cylinders probably did not extend beyond eighteen inches plus whatever amount of dirt he had piled on top of the them, which they judged to be not more than three or four inches. So a three-foot dig should put them both downhill from and well below the bottom of the suspected array of cylinders, deep enough to detect any signs of pollution. Ed McVay, the EPA representative, though not present for the dig itself, had indicated he was comfortable with this assessment.

Even though they did not expect to find anything on the way down, the dig needed to be executed with due care, and it was well past two in the afternoon before the job was finished. As everyone looked down into the trench, the result was clear: there was no evidence of an underground chemical spill. The excavation of the main array of cylinders could be deferred pending the standard review and approval processes set out in Section 106. And as an added benefit of today's activity, Audrey could prepare a brief report detailing the nature of the soil any subsequent dig would encounter.

After a short rest break, Audrey took some photographs, then assigned two of her students to refill the trench with the spoil, tamp it down, and then cover the dig with the sod that they had removed earlier. She figured it would take about a year, depending on the rainfall patterns, to eliminate the slight residual mounding that their work would have produced, and after conferring, she, Ranger Morse, and Cashman decided they should leave the plastic erosion barrier in place for at least a few weeks or until no more loose dirt was visible at the site. Then Audrey and her remaining student headed up the hill to the vicinity of the suspected outlier cylinder, where they repeated their setup procedures, creating a plastic erosion barrier and marking the area of the planned dig, which this time incorporated just four square feet of ground surrounding the anomaly detected by the GPR sweep. This dig would require considerably more care since, they hoped, their tools would shortly be encountering a hundred-year-old glass cylinder.

In the circumstances, Audrey altered her methodology. After carefully removing and stacking the covering sod, as before, she took a foot-long jerry-rigged device that was part auger handle and part steel rod and gently poked it into the ground. She began in the center of the square, and immediately had a result. The test rod struck a solid object at a depth of about four inches. Moving very gingerly, she determined that the object, whatever it was, was likely circular with a diameter of six to eight inches. Extending her testing outward to the edges of the square, she found no other objects at any depth up to the length of the rod. Next, Audrey carefully removed the dirt covering the object she had detected. Four inches down, she uncovered exactly what she by then expected: the top of a glass cylinder. Then she and the student began their excavation, working from the outer edge of the cylinder to the edges of the dig site. In this way they made sure not to strike, and possibly crack or break, the cylinder as they moved the dirt out of the area. An hour into the process, little remained except to brush the covering soil off of the object and carefully remove it from the hole. As the pair began this process, Ranger Morse took out her cell phone and called Ephraim Cook.

"Super," she said, shortening his title, "you might want to come on over here. They found something."

By now, Andy had become used to the superintendent's meeting routine. These gatherings were always held in the conference room at the park, and usually on Wednesdays when the facility was closed to the public, but the staff were all on hand, answering phones and emails, completing clerical tasks, and doing all the other unseen tasks that kept such a complex enterprise humming. Andy knew this was perhaps the most important meeting of all on this case, but he had come alone this time. Keiley was consumed with catching up on her own work that she had been putting off—two sets of charts for her genealogical clients and a mapping project she'd landed with Morris County. And Sam, who really should be here for this one, was on his way to Florida and points west taking his youngest son on a tour of prospective colleges. The trip had been planned for months, including interviews with various admissions officers, and there was no way he could, or would, reschedule it. Andy had tried to move the meeting back a couple of weeks, but several of the critical participants, not least among them Superintendent Cook, had overlapping conflicts that would have meant a delay of over a month. So Andy was on his own.

Andy aside, the cast of characters had continued to evolve. Since this was not a meeting about future excavations or the like, EPA saw no reason to attend. Hi Burlmeister was standing by in his office at the university just in case there was some chemical question or, heaven forbid, emergency. But Audrey Templeton was on hand to explain the extraction of the cylinder, and Art Escalon was there, as much out of curiosity as anything else. James Cashman was unable to attend the meeting, and so far, no designated substitute had appeared, though Cook had made provision to have a representative of Llewellyn Park admitted should one show up. Both the state and local historical preservation interests were represented, and Anne Driscoll Smith from Interior was present as well. And there were three newcomers—Tina Winston, a property specialist with the Park Service; Barley Acres, an attorney with the New Jersey attorney general's office; and Ross Rubin from the General Services Administration, the federal office that managed government property. As the participant list suggested, the purpose of the meeting was to unseal the glass cylinder that Andy thought of as second base, and to agree insofar as possible upon a proper disposition of whatever would be found therein. To Andy's surprise, it was Anne Driscoll Smith who claimed the chair at the head of the table, and who opened the discussion.

"I want to thank everyone for taking the time to participate here today, especially those of you who had to travel some distance to be with us. As you can see, on the table before us is a sealed glass container. And as you will know, either because you were there when this item was dug up on the Glenmont property or from the briefing paper that Ephraim circulated a few days ago, this item was located with the assistance of—really, to be frank, strictly because of—a map that was found in the course of appraising the estate of a gentleman named Francis Culbertson and was brought to us by Andrew Dennum here, as attorney of record for the estate. Unfortunately, Andy's client, Sam Patrick, was unable to be here today because of a prior commitment, but Andy is fully authorized to act on his behalf. The cylinder itself was found separated from, but in physical association with, what we believe will prove to be a hitherto unknown experiment by Thomas Edison that was located on the grounds of Glenmont. It is Mr. Dennum's view that the content of this cylinder, whatever it may be, is unrelated to the contents of the numerous other cylinders that we believe to be buried on the grounds, and that it is of a more personal nature. He claims that, given the circumstances of their discovery, whatever is in here should properly convey with the estate to the sole surviving heir, Mr. Patrick. Basically, we're all here this morning to open this thing up, take a look at the contents, and see if we can come to some agreement as to what's fair, proper, and legal."

"Anne, could I jump in here?" It was Tina from the Park Service headquarters in Washington who spoke up. She was thin as a rail, with sharp facial features and longish brown hair that she had pulled tightly over to the left side of her head. "After we received the briefing materials and the roster for today's meeting, I set up a conference call with Barley and Ross here, and we agreed that it would be a good idea, at this point in the meeting, before we see what's inside this cylinder thing, to just lay out a few basic legal and procedural considerations when it comes to lost or abandoned property in a national park or on government property more generally." She held up a hand as Andy cleared his throat as if to speak, then continued. "I can guess that you are about to question whether this property was lost or abandoned in the usual sense."

Andy nodded.

"Obviously," Tina went on, "the circumstances here are rather . . . no, I think we can say highly unusual, which creates some room for interpretation, and I think I can speak for the three of us when I say we are cognizant of that and plan to be open-minded about it, albeit giving due consideration to the various parameters within which we work."

It's a good thing Sam isn't here, Andy thought. *About ten more seconds of this government jargon and he'd probably be out the door anyway.* Lost in that notion for a moment, he missed the first few words of Tina's next sentence.

". . . of the primary laws and regulations that apply. The top level of that hierarchy for our purposes is U.S. Code, Title 40, Subtitle I, Chapter 5, Subchapter iii, Section 552. And if you doubt for a moment," Tina said, smiling broadly, "that I am from the government and I am here to help you, perhaps that doubt has now been addressed. Anyway, Section 552 essentially provides for conditions under which an owner may file a claim to recover unclaimed property that has been abandoned on some government premises. And we're talking here, of course, about the federal government. If the claim is filed in a timely manner as provided in the statute, and if it's found to be valid, there are provisions for returning the property to the ostensible owner or, when that is no longer possible, providing compensation. Basically, the claimant owner has three years from the time of abandonment to seek return of the property. Now, in the present instance, this raises two issues. One is timeliness. Obviously this thing was buried well over three years ago. But it was discovered only recently. So the question is, which date starts the clock. The second consideration, and an obvious one, is ownership. The property in question here was abandoned, not by Mr. Patrick or Mr. Culbertson, but by Mr. Edison. So to establish ownership, there would have to be some evidence of direct descent, or at the very least, specific intent, in order to sustain any contemporary claim. And at the moment, we don't seem to have that.

"The second statute of relevance, or regulation really, is 36 CFR 2.22, which applies specifically to the Park Service and other properties managed by the Department of the Interior. That regulation starts out by stating that abandoning property in one of the parks is prohibited, which I acknowledge is not especially helpful here since Glenmont was not a national park, or even public property, at the time this property was believed to have been abandoned by Edison upon his death. This one, however, gives the owner of any such property only sixty days to file a claim, considerably less than three years, to say the least. But the really salient point, and the reason Barley is even here today, is in paragraph (c) (4), which provides that any unclaimed property in one of the parks that had been owned by a deceased person, as I think we can all agree would include Mr. Edison, gets disposed of under the laws of the state where the park is located. Barley, you want to pick it up from here?"

"Thanks, Tina," said the New Jersey Attorney General's representative. Acres was a rumpled man somewhere just to one side or the other of his midlife crisis. He was soft in the way of a man who had spent too many years in a sedentary profession, and wore glasses that seemed designed to draw attention away from his receding hairline. "And thanks also to Anne and Ephraim for including me in this meeting. As Tina said, the question before us today may well come down to how the State of New Jersey views the ownership of the property inside that cylinder on the table. And in general, I can tell you that we subscribe to the 2016 version of what is generally referred to as the Uniform Unclaimed Property Act. Technically our version is called Title 46 of the New Jersey Statutes, and more particularly Section 46:30C, the part dealing with property. A lot of this legislation has to do with financial instruments of various kinds—abandoned savings or checking accounts, traveler's checks, gift cards, and so forth—and, as Tina has pointed out, there's a distinction in the law between lost property and abandoned property that could well be germane here. There's also a lot of procedural stuff in there about who is supposed to contact whom and when and how. In the present case, one of the relevant requirements is that the holder of the property has an obligation to notify the owner of the property that the property in question is being held. That notification starts the clock ticking on abandonment and the state's claim. Plus, the state is supposed to engage in a good-faith effort to locate the owner. The thing is, all of this gets very complicated in the present situation since, one could argue and I would imagine Mr. Dennum here will do so, that the clock does not start ticking until we open this cylinder and see what's inside. That is an argument that can be made, but only on behalf of a bona fide owner. Which gets us to the very same place where Tina left us a moment ago. At this instant, even Mr. Dennum would be hard-pressed to argue that there is clear and convincing evidence of ownership by the Culbertson estate, and hence by Mr. Patrick. So from the State of New Jersey's perspective, we'll need to find something pretty definitive of Edison's lineage or intent in the next few minutes."

At this point, Andy felt that he ought to speak up. "Since the last couple of speakers have spoken so well for me, I hesitate to jump in here. But I do just want to note a couple of things. First, the only reason we are here today is because my client, Sam Patrick, inherited a map that, with the help of Art and Audrey and others, we were able to apply to a particular location at Glenmont, which we subsequently validated using ground-penetrating radar and some good archeology by Audrey. Second, we feel that the discoveries so far have validated the map, which could only have come down from Edison himself, though I would concede that we do not know the reason he would have entrusted this to Frank Culbertson's father, John Culbertson. However, Superintendent Cook here has confirmed that John Culbertson was a long-time Edison employee and that Edison took at least some measure of interest in his personal life. And third, none of us know what's inside this cylinder on the table, and I hope we'll all keep an open mind as to its implications once we have something real to consider. That said, I agree entirely with the presentation of the relevant laws and regulations, and I sincerely appreciate the fact that everyone here is inclined to work toward a prompt and amicable resolution of the ownership question once we have these final facts."

And with that, the moment of truth had arrived.

Anne Driscoll Smith reclaimed control of what was, after all, her meeting.

"All right, here we go," she said with rising enthusiasm. "Audrey, you dug this thing up. Would you do the honors?"

"Of course," said the archeologist. "The first thing I think we ought to do is to rinse off the rest of this dirt. Ephraim, is there a handy source of water and maybe some paper towels nearby?"

The superintendent rose from his chair and walked to a nearby closet, which he proceeded to unlock with one of the several keys on the ring attached to his uniform belt. Using a utility sink in the closet, he filled a black plastic bucket part way, then grabbed a roll of towels and returned to the conference table. "Here you go," he said to Audrey, handing her the cleaning supplies.

Audrey carefully rinsed away the remaining dirt that had shrouded the cylinder ever since it had been removed from its burial place of a century or so. The disappointment was palpable as the assemblage saw that the glass itself was opaque, either by nature or as a result of its history, and it was still impossible to see the contents within. And if there had been any markings on the top of the cylinder, after a century in the ground, they were no longer evident.

Next Audrey took out a long metal ruler, that seemed to be calibrated with greater than the customary level of precision, and measured the length of the cylinder. She repeated the measurement at a different location. Though it was a bit awkward to use such a long ruler to do so, she then measured the thickness of the glass surrounding the removable top of the cylinder.

"That's interesting," she said. "The cylinder is approximately fifteen and three-quarters inches long. But it is exactly forty centimeters. It's approximately half an inch thick, but exactly twelve point five millimeters. Does anyone know if Edison was accustomed to using metric measurements?"

"I don't remember ever seeing anything in his notebooks that used metric," said Art Escalon.

"I don't remember coming across that either," added Ephraim Cook. "That might make this buried experiment interesting in itself. I wonder why he would have done that."

"I wonder if there was any European influence here," offered Ross Rubin from the GSA, the first time he had spoken a word at the meeting. "For example, I think Germany made metric mandatory way back in 1872." All the heads around the table turned his way. "What? I was a history of science major in college, okay?"

Everyone had a good laugh at his expense, Rubin included.

Returning to the task at hand, Audrey set the ruler aside and examined the top of the cylinder more closely, hoping to find either a protuberance or an indentation that she could use to grasp and twist the lid, but that would have been too easy. Her next option was to open the lid by pressing down on the top and turning it. She donned a pair of rubber gloves she had thought to bring along, pressed down, and tried to turn the lid, first counterclockwise then in the reverse direction. No joy.

"Okay. This thing has been in the ground for a long time, and there has probably been a good amount of dirt that's worked its way into the space between the lid and the cylinder proper. But maybe, just maybe, we're making this harder than it needs to be. I have been assuming this is a grooved lid that has been twisted tight. But it's equally possible, and perhaps even more so, that the lid is simply set into the cylinder and was being held in place by the combination of gravity and four inches of dirt on top of it, and probably also by a ground glass joint between the cylinder and the lid, which would have been a standard laboratory practice back then. In that case, the way to open it is basically to turn it upside down and, if needed, shake it. But that is not without risk, particularly if the contents shift as we do it, and most especially if, as is still possible, those contents pose a risk to health. And, of course, by trying such a physical process, we could always break something. We can probably mitigate some portion of the risk by moving outdoors before we turn it over. But that's not a perfect solution. Anne? Ephraim? Andy? What do you think?"

Andy was first to respond in the affirmative, and once he did, Anne, and then Ephraim, followed suit.

The meeting adjourned to the courtyard outside Building 11. Audrey had brought along the bucket and towels. Once outside, she emptied the water from the bucket onto the ground, then placed the bucket upside down atop the cylinder. She then turned the entire assembly over so that the bucket was right side up and the cylinder was inverted. As she performed this last maneuver, she could feel weights shifting within the cylinder, something she pointed out to the others. Then, slowly, wearing her rubber gloves for traction, she grasped the cylinder near its structural bottom, which at that point was up in the air, and pulled slowly. When that didn't work, she intensified her grip, then lifted the cylinder a couple of inches and shook it.

The Sweet Spot

"Keiley," Andy nearly shouted into the phone. "I'm back at the office, and you've got to get over here!"

Twenty minutes later, Andy got his wish.

As the two settled in on opposite sides of his desk, Andy filled Keiley in on the details of the meeting that had concluded just a couple of hours before. He knew that she'd want to get a sense of the meeting, but also that she probably didn't care about the way the various legal positions were staked out, so he fast-forwarded to Audrey's efforts to measure and open the cylinder, and then cut straight to the chase.

"So she starts to turn the thing over to see if she could get it open by gravity, I guess, or by the weight of whatever was inside pushing against the lid. After a shake or two, the lid did start to separate from the cylinder, so she stopped shaking and worked to slowly pry the two pieces apart. That took a minute or two, but off came the top. And the first thing that fell out was this." He placed an object on the desktop.

"What is that, like, a twenty-dollar gold piece?" she asked.

"That was my first thought as well. But Ephraim Cook knew exactly what it was. Back in May 1928, when Edison was about eighty, Andrew

Mellon, who was the Treasury Secretary under Coolidge, had written to Congress, pointing out that, although the inventor had been honored by nine foreign nations, including receiving the ribbon of the French Legion of Honor, and had received honorary degrees from more than twenty colleges, he had never been appropriately recognized by the United States, his native country. Apparently there are some things Congress can do quickly when it's so inclined, and this seems to have been one. A resolution to strike a congressional gold medal sailed through within a week and was signed by the president, and in October 1928, Mellon traveled to the laboratory in West Orange, the very spot where we were meeting, and presented it to Edison. And that was the last anyone ever saw of the thing. Until today. Cook almost levitated out of his chair when he saw what it was. But it was Tina Winston, the property lawyer from the National Park Service, who verbalized the significance. She announced in so many words that this pretty well sealed the deal as to who would end up owning the contents of the cylinder. Historical significance, importance to the collection, and blah blah blah."

"Shit," said Keiley. "So all of this work was for nothing, at least as far as Sam is concerned. I'm so sorry, Andy."

"Hang on," he replied, "because you haven't heard the rest of it. And the fact that this medal is sitting here on my desk should give you a little hint.

"There was still at least one more object moving around in the cylinder, so Audrey tilted it again very slowly, and this rolled out." Andy reached into the open desk drawer, where he had stored these treasures, and added to the desktop an old baseball bearing a dozen or more signatures.

"And this is?" queried Keiley.

"This, as you can see, is an old baseball. And honestly, there's nothing special about it. Just an old ball signed by a bunch of guys no one ever heard of and apparently presented to Edison. Or so we might surmise. But it turned out that the signatures were kind of interesting. Ephraim looked pretty closely at the ball, and then he called a timeout. He picked up the ball, said he'd be back but it might be a while, and disappeared. He rolled back in about forty-five minutes later, put the ball on the table, and announced that, on a hunch, he'd been visiting with the Park archivist, and together, they had pulled out some of the Edison Company payroll records from the early 1920s. And sure enough, they'd begun finding some of these same names on Edison's roster of employees. There had not been enough time to find them all, but every single name they had researched had been a winner. The two of them had concluded that this was a baseball that had been autographed as a memento by the members of one of Edison's industrial league baseball teams, and most likely presented to Edison as their sponsor. Maybe they won some tournament or something. I guess someone could research that. But regardless, we know he was a big fan of the game and sponsored quite a number of these semi-pro teams, so that would fit. Then he rolled the ball across the table to me, and he said, and I'm quoting here, 'Andy, I think you might find one of these names of particular interest. It's on the sweet spot.'"

Baseball again, thought Andy, as he'd reached out to pick up the ball. His short legal career seemed to be intertwined with the sport. It wasn't one that he had followed much as a youngster, but not long ago he had found himself immersed in the game. It was then that he had first heard about the sweet spot on a baseball. The stitching on a baseball makes a sort of loose figure eight, so there are basically four larger areas that resemble horseshoes, and two narrow bands where the horseshoes converge. One of these usually has a manufacturer's label or a league logo, and the other is known as the sweet spot. As Andy had learned, when a whole team signs a ball, there's a traditional protocol that reserves the sweet spot for the manager. But there are also times when that spot is reserved for, say, the most valuable player on the team or one who just had a special performance. Babe Ruth, for one, was always signing balls on their sweet spot.

But that was then, this is now.

"So I picked up the ball," Andy continued, "and rotated it so I could look, and there it was. The ball was signed by John Culbertson. I held it out so everyone could see, then I looked back over at that Winston woman, who was suddenly lost in thoughts of her own. Fifteen all, I thought, even though it's a mixed metaphor, and I don't even like tennis. It's just the thought that occurred to me.

"Next thing I knew, Audrey was turning the cylinder all the way onto its open end, but nothing else came rolling out. So she tilted the open end toward her and looked inside. She was still wearing those rubber gloves, which were the littlest bit tacky, and she reached in with a couple of fingers and pulled out this piece of paper." Andy moved a third item from his desk drawer to the desktop.

"A stock certificate?"

"Precisely. Apparently from 1911. I'd never heard of this company, this Computing-Tabulating-Recording Company, and neither had anybody else at the meeting, even Ephraim. But from the name, it sure looked like one of Edison's companies, and God knows he had a bunch of them—pretty much one for every line of business he was in. So the fact that nobody there recognized the name probably didn't mean a thing.

"Anyway, there it was. Some old stock certificate. No obvious value to it. But when Audrey turned the certificate over, things got interesting again. I don't know how much you know about stock certificates, and of course, these days you almost never come across them because shares tend to be held in electronic form by brokerage companies and the like, and almost all of the actual financial transactions are done by computers. So people never see them. But back in the day, all of the financial transactions were done on actual paper. In fact, you didn't even have to go through some broker to do it. And to facilitate that, every stock certificate had places on the back that you could fill out and sign to transfer ownership from one person to another. When the certificate changed hands a bunch of times and all those spaces were filled, well, I guess then you could exchange it with the company for a new one. But to get to the point, on the back of this particular certificate you could see that it had been transferred, and get this. It was transferred from Thomas Edison to Francis Culbertson. To Sam's Uncle Frank. Directly." Andy flipped the paper over so it lay on the desk face down.

"The date, as you can see, is in November 1928. That's just a few weeks after Edison would have received this congressional medal over here, and it must have been after Sam's Uncle Frank had been born. Or maybe he knew beforehand what they were going to call the baby. You know, Francis is a name that works for a boy or a girl. I wouldn't have put it past Edison to have suggested it. Well, at this point, Tina was looking a little devastated. Thirty-fifteen flashed through my head. The tennis analogy again. Because between the baseball and the stock certificate, we had just established a pretty strong link, not only between Edison and John Culbertson, Sam's grandfather, but a link that somehow extended even to his Uncle Frank. And that, as everyone around the table was beginning to realize, moved us into a whole new position with respect to the disposition of the contents of the cylinder. There is a downside, of course. Because except for the Edison medal, which obviously has some value, we had just established ownership of an old baseball and some worthless paper. But still."

"That's quite a story. You're making me wish I had been at that meeting."

"I know. But you do have your own business you need to take care of, and there was no way to know that this would turn out as it has."

"I guess. But as I'm looking at all this stuff on the desk, there's something that bothers me, that's not quite right. I can't put my finger on it right now, but I want to give it some thought. Can I take this stuff with me to my office to look at more closely? I promise I'll take good care of it. Besides, it's only one door down."

"Of course. Let me know if anything occurs to you. Because right now, I'd say things are looking pretty good for Sam. He has a gold medal to add to his Tiffany lamps. When he gets back, it looks like he'll have to decide whether to give it to the Edison National Park—and I know they'd love to have it—sell it at auction, or hold onto the thing. It'll be interesting to see which one he chooses."

Just then, Andy's cell phone rang. He looked at the screen, then said to Keiley, "Sorry, I need to take this."

She nodded in understanding and left his office. She didn't know what she was missing, but she would find out soon enough.

⚬

The following morning found Andy sitting through one of those divorce-case depositions that he was rapidly learning to despise, *Davis v. Davis*. This time, unfortunately, there were small children involved: a boy of seven and a girl of four. The trouble had started when the couple had returned home from dinner at a local boutique restaurant, and Davis, that being Richard, the husband, was driving the babysitter home afterward. At first glance, it was a classic scenario: a young husband and an impressionable babysitter have the hots for one another and act on their basest urges. But this one played out a little differently. The couple had had difficulty lining up a babysitter and, on the recommendation of a friend, had finally found a young woman at one of the local colleges who was willing to help out. The downside was that the college was forty-five minutes away and she did not have her own transportation. It was decided that one Davis, that being Maryanne, the wife, would make the hour-and-a-half roundtrip trek to pick up the babysitter while the other Davis would make the drive to take her home.

Things began to go off the rails when the young lady retrieved a message on her cell phone shortly after she and Richard Davis had departed. It seemed that some of her friends had gathered at a bar not far away from the Davis home and wanted her to join the party. She asked Davis if he could simply drop her at the bar, saying she could easily find a ride back to campus with one or another of her friends. Needless to say, he was more than happy to comply. He dropped her outside the bar and dutifully waited to be sure she got inside safely, then turned around and headed home.

Having made that long drive to the college and back herself, Maryanne Davis knew that her husband would be away for a while. So she pulled out her cell phone and placed a call to her next-door neighbor, one Victor Marshall, whose own wife, she knew—because he had made a point of telling her—was away for two weeks visiting her mother. She wondered, she said, if Victor would like to come over for a few minutes for a quick drink. Richard would not be back for an hour or more, she said, and she hated to drink alone.

When Richard arrived home unexpectedly, he found Maryanne and Victor doing something that they were probably ill-advised to have been doing, particularly since both were naked. Yet another case, thought Andy, of being caught in the act. This discovery caused a certain amount of consternation on the part of all three parties, but most especially for Richard. Still, things might have been resolved more or less amicably, or at least without violence, had not the seven-year-old chosen that moment to leave his bedroom unnoticed and walk to the kitchen to get himself a glass of water. It was on the way back that he happened to glance into the living room where the aforesaid drama was playing out, and, seeing that his parents had returned home from their dinner, gone in to ask them to come and tuck him back into bed. What he saw and heard was best left to the imagination, though, as attorney for the aggrieved husband, it was Andy's unfortunate duty to try to extract a description of same from the youngster in the presence of a temporary guardian who had been appointed by the county's Child Protective Services once the graphic nature of the dispute had become public. To her everlasting credit, Maryanne Davis, through her attorney, had halted the proceedings and conceded the related facts in the case that had previously been contested or left ambiguous.

The entire experience left Andy feeling as if he needed a hot shower, followed by a long bourbon. And the day was scarcely half over. Little did he realize that it was only starting to get interesting.

When he returned to the office to decompress, Keiley was waiting in ambush. "Come into *my* office," she said, implicitly making the point that she was always being invited into his when there were matters to discuss. And, she admitted to herself, at other, more pleasurable times as well. That was one of the benefits of sharing a workplace with your boyfriend.

"You remember how yesterday I said something about how that stuff from the glass cylinder didn't feel quite right?" she began.

"Yes," he replied.

"Well, I figured out why. You said that everybody agreed this Computer-Tabulating-Recording Company—I'm just going to call it CTRC—must have been just one more of Edison's many start-ups, and probably one that just didn't get anywhere. Which would have explained why none of you had ever heard of it. And that kind of made sense. But I looked more closely at that stock certificate, and I had to ask myself a question: If this was Edison's company, why did he have stock certificate number six, and not number one? And why did he have only a hundred shares? Of course, he could have owned all the certificates from number one up as high as they went, and there's no telling how many shares would have been issued in the first place. That's all true. But if that was the case, you'd think some of the other certificates would have turned up somewhere. Maybe he had them, or maybe he gave them out to all of his favorite employees. But with every certificate he had or gave out, you'd think the chances increased that at least one of them would have resurfaced during the century-plus since 1911, and then somebody at your meeting—certainly either Ephraim or Art—would have known about it. But they didn't. It was a curiosity. So I decided to see what I could find out about CTRC.

"It turns out that it wasn't Edison who formed that company, but a fellow named Charles Ranlett Flint."

"Never heard of him."

"Hold your horses. It's worth the wait. As I was saying before I was so rudely interrupted, this Flint guy started this company. And back then, he was pretty famous. Some would have said infamous. Remember, we're talking late 1800s, early 1900s. So the era of the big financial and industrial trusts. People always hear about Rockefeller and Carnegie and Morgan and some others, but it turns out that Flint ran in those same circles. He was the one who put together the U.S. Rubber trust to control the rubber market and a bunch of others. He was very prominent, and as time went on and the politics shifted against the trusts, more than a little controversial."

"Don't tell me," Andy interjected. "Good friend of Edison's."

"If you don't stop interrupting me, I'm going to stop telling you what I found. And believe me, you'll regret it. But to your point, I have no idea whether he knew Edison or not, though Edison certainly was at home in that fast and rich company. Now, Flint just loved to buy up companies and push them together into some new and larger, more dominating entity. And that's what he did here. He got control of four different companies, all of which had gotten started in the 1890s. There was one called Bundy Manufacturing. It was started by a couple of brothers, Willard and Harlow Bundy. Whatever happened to names like Willard and Harlow, anyway? Willard was apparently the guy who invented the first time clock—you know, the ones workers use to punch in and out—and they set up the company to manufacture those. But then a couple of years later, they decided to make adding machines instead, so they sold the time clock business to another company, International Time Recording Company, and funny thing. A few years later, when he was putting together CTRC, that was the second company Flint bought. The third one was called the Computing Scale Company of America. Similar kind of manufacturing company, but in this case, they made commercial scales. So they're all a bunch of nuts-and-bolts-type companies that were big on calibration and relatively delicate instruments that basically provided some of the management infrastructure—time clocks, scales, adding machines—for other companies.

"Now, if you know your history, the fourth company in this little amalgamation Flint was putting in play will give the game away. It was the Tabulating Machine Company, which sounds like more of the same, and kind of was. This was the company started by Herman Hollerith to make punch card data processing equipment. Hollerith was this guy who had studied the looms that were used over in Europe, where punch card instructions were used to feed different yarns or threads into the loom to make very complex patterns in woven fabrics or rugs, and to do it with exceptional efficiency. Fellow named Joseph Jacquard had invented that back in 1884. It really cut the cost of manufacturing fancy textiles by a lot. Then Hollerith focused his attention on the U.S. Census data from the 1880 and 1890 censuses and figured out a way to use those same punch cards to make the count more accurate and efficient. He started his company in 1896, and right away he got the government contract to do the count for the census in 1900. Pretty lucrative deal for a start-up, I'd say, and he was very successful. But because the census only came around every ten years, he had to find some other way to make a living in the interim, so he set about developing punch card control or counting operations for various industries, which he did right up until 1911 when our old friend Flint stepped up and bought him out for somewhere north of a million bucks."

"Hollerith," said Andy. "I know that name from somewhere."

"You should, because the guy was about to have a lot of influence, to change the world, really. But back to the story. The Tabulating Machine Company was the last one Flint needed to complete his deal. And once he had it, he created CTRC as a kind of holding company and moved all of the other companies under that umbrella. All in, there were about thirteen hundred employees, which made it a middle-sized company in its day. Our old friend Herman Hollerith worked for the company as a consulting engineer until he retired in 1921, and Flint stayed on the company's board of directors until he died in 1930, just the year before Edison passed. Now, why Thomas Edison would have had shares of that new holding company, let alone shares conveyed in a very low-numbered certificate, I could not tell you. But that's what he had."

"Okay," said Andy once it was clear that Keiley had wound down her tale. "That's a really fascinating story, and when the time comes, I'll let you tell Sam all about it, because I'll never remember all of those companies and what they did."

"Then you're going to be letting me tell Sam a piece of really good news," she said.

Andy raised his eyebrows but did not speak.

"Because there's one more piece to this story. In 1914, just shortly after he had put this thing together, Flint decided to hire a fellow who had just been convicted for antitrust violations based on his record of extortionate writings when he was an official with another company, National Cash Register. Big scandal around that one. So he didn't exactly have a reputation for honesty. Nevertheless, Flint wanted him to run the new company. But the other members of the CTRC board were distinctly uncomfortable with that, so they gave him the lower-ranking title of general manager. That's when Thomas J. Watson joined CTRC."

Andy looked shocked. "I know that name!" he said.

"I should hope so. And now you can see where this is headed. In 1924, George Fairchild, the fellow the board had kept at the helm of CTRC back in 1914 to block out Watson, passed away, and Watson got control of the company. And you know the first thing he did?"

"Changed the name?" Andy surmised.

"Changed the name," Keiley confirmed. "And do you know what the new name was that he chose?"

"International Business Machines."

"You got it, Lawyer Man. If this certificate is valid and still good, your client has just inherited a hundred shares of the company that is now IBM, and that's the number of shares back at the beginning. I'd wager he would have a few more now."

"Oh my God," was all that Andy could muster in response.

———

Once the shock and awe had passed, Andy realized he had at least two tasks to perform before he could fully internalize Keiley's news and share it with his client. First up: Find some sort of official documentation—anything, really—to establish the bona fides of her characterization of CTRC. He found that in an unexpected place—a report from 1936 from a hearing on the pooling of patents held by the House Committee on Patents. The report included documentation of the establishment of the holding company, CTRC, under the laws of New York State in 1911, including the component companies, the directors, and numerous other details. Of particular interest, though, was the paragraph summarizing the issuance of the company's capital stock, which was assigned an aggregate value of ten thousand dollars. Edison's shares amounted to one percent of the total capitalization.

That led quite naturally to the next important task, determining the value today of one hundred of the 1911 shares, or one percent, of CTRC, or better yet, IBM. For that, Andy needed some expert help.

Andy had never been much of an investor. It had taken all of his resources plus the salary from his day job as an insurance inspector for the state to cover the costs of his night school law degree—hard earned, then, in *two* ways from Mad Jeff's House of Torts, AKA Madison-Jefferson School of Law. And the salary from his one year of "Big Law" in the City, before he was summarily downsized, was all but consumed covering the sheer cost of living in the Big Apple. By the time he had limped home to northern New Jersey, chewed up, spit out, and downright dejected, he had little left other than his beat-up old Ford Escape. At least living in his parents' old house in Mendham provided him with a roof. Even the good fortune of entering a new partnership with Lou D'Antonio was short-lived; Lou passed away mere days after the newly renamed D'Antonio and Dennum got started, and Andy was left with the challenge of retaining Lou's old clients while prospecting for new ones.

Then, of course, everything had changed. His personal life took a decided turn for the better when he met Keiley Barefoot, with whom he had shared a program at a local life care community. And with Keiley's help and through an extraordinary series of coincidences, he had confronted his old City law firm, embarrassed the hell out of the partner who'd hired and then callously fired him, beaten a skilled and dangerous foe in the Commissioner of Baseball, and oh yes, found himself several million dollars richer, even after taxes. At that moment Andy was struck with the realization that he had no idea how to manage such a sum, or even a fraction of it. After consulting with his parents and some others around town, he'd made an appointment with Jim Grey, a broker with one of the more conservative investment firms, and the two had worked out an investment plan. They had also become good friends. So it was only natural that Andy would turn to Grey for help in tackling the current dilemma—the value today of one hundred shares of CRTC issued in 1911.

"Betty," he said, "would you please call over to Jim Grey's office and see if he's around? Ask if I can come over there with a question I need answered."

A few minutes later he was in the Lexus on his way along the few blocks down Main Street that separated their two offices. He found a parking spot right in front of the building that housed the brokerage, and when he arrived at the second-floor entrance to the office, he found his friend at the reception desk, awaiting his arrival. They shook hands and exchanged a couple of pleasantries, then Grey led Andy to his personal office.

"What's this big question my secretary tells me you've got?" Grey asked. "She said that Betty made it sound pretty mysterious."

"Not mysterious. Just something I think you can help me with. It's a client thing, so I can't really tell you why I need to know. But I need to figure out the value today of one hundred shares issued in 1911 in a company called the Computing-Tabulating-Recording Company. You probably never—"

"You're talking about IBM, right?" the broker interjected. "You're asking me the present value of one hundred shares of what's now IBM that was issued . . . when the company was founded? Before it was even called IBM? Do I remember my business history course correctly?"

"That's pretty impressive," said Andy with a smile on his face. "You actually studied that kind of thing? And you remember it? I'm lucky if I can remember what a tort is."

"What can I say? I have a brilliant financial mind! And even I know what a tort is. I like 'em loaded with chocolate."

"You never could spell, could you?" replied Andy.

They both laughed.

Then Andy picked up the thread of the conversation. "But yes. That's exactly what I need to know."

"Well," said Grey as he collected his thought, "I can't answer that one myself. But I can call the main office in St. Louis, and they'll be able to figure it out pretty quickly. How soon do you need the information?"

"Yesterday would have been great, except I didn't know I needed it until an hour or two ago. Tomorrow if you can do it."

"Shouldn't be a problem. I'll give you a call, probably around mid-morning."

"Thanks, man," said Andy. "I appreciate it."

"You bet. Of course, I'll be looking for your client with the IBM shares to be in the market for brilliant investment advice."

"Yeah. I'm sure. That's what Google is for, right?"

"Get the fuck out of my office," Grey replied, laughing. "I'll call you as soon as I hear back."

———

Andy was out of the office when Jim Grey called around nine thirty the following morning. He was trying to mediate a minor business dispute, this time between two of his own clients, and for the moment, it was not going well. To Andy, the matter seemed genuinely trivial, a difference of opinion over the discount rate that the first client, a butcher, should have applied to the order he filled for the second client, a restauranteur, for twenty pounds of ground beef. One said fifteen percent was appropriate, the other expected eighteen percent. The difference amounted to less than fifty dollars, but you'd have thought a gang war had broken out. Finally, in exasperation, Andy pointed out that the hour he had just spent as mediator in a dispute that somehow defied mediation would cost each of them about ten times more than the amount in dispute. And that did the trick. Both suddenly agreed that sixteen-and-a-half percent would work just fine.

Flush with this last-minute success, Andy walked into his office, where he was greeted by Betty. "Jim Grey called earlier. He said to tell you the answer was whatever the price is when you look online times 1,187,900 shares."

"That many?"

"That's what he said. What's the company? I can look it up on the outside internet system."

"IBM."

"I beg your pardon? Somebody you know owns more than a million shares of IBM?"

"Yep," replied Andy. "And the funny thing is, he doesn't even know it yet."

"I want to be in that room when you tell him," said Betty. "I guess I know the symbol. Let me look it up. . . .

"Let's see . . . Rounded off, right now a share of IBM is priced at $139. So 139 times 1,187,900 is . . . $165,132,000, and some loose change. How old is he? Is he cute? Married?"

Betty had a brutal sense of humor that she broke out every so often, and she and Andy had a good laugh—so good, in fact, that Keiley, who'd been closeted in her own office working on a project, came out to see what was so funny.

"It's Sam," said Andy, choking out the words between guffaws. "We just did the calculation of the current value of those CRTC shares from the cylinder. They're worth over $165 million. Of course, that assumes they're still valid shares. And God knows what the taxes will be."

"Wow. I can see why that's going to make Sam pretty happy when he finds out. But why was that so funny?"

"No," Andy replied. "It got funny when Betty started thinking about getting him to leave his wife for her."

"OMG, Betty!" said Keiley, joining in the mirth. "I always suspected you were a cradle robber! But a homewrecker on top of it?" Then, to Andy, "Are you going to call him and tell him the great news?"

"Nah. Let's wait until he's back. We can go through the whole inventory from the cylinder then. And besides, I'm like Betty. I want to see his face when we break this particular bit of news."

———

Sam and his son made it back to New Jersey early in the next week, but it wasn't until a few days later that he finally got around to returning Betty's calls.

"Betty, hey, it's Sam Patrick."

"You're a hard man to reach."

"Yeah, I know. And I'm sorry. I did get your messages and your texts. But after two weeks away and a long drive back, I needed to decompress. Plus, I was way behind at work. But here I am. What's up?"

"Andy wanted me to tell you," she said, "that there have been some major developments in the estate case. I think you know there was a big meeting over at the Edison labs ten or twelve days ago."

"Yeah," he said. "Andy wanted me to go, but that trip was important and I just couldn't change it."

"Yes, that's what Andy said. But apparently there were some big doings at that meeting, and he was hoping you could come by the office for an hour or so at your convenience so he could tell you about that in person. Can that work for you?"

"Of course," Sam replied. "Let me pull up my calendar . . . How about sometime next Monday afternoon? Maybe two or three?"

"Andy said to schedule this for any time you wanted, and we'd clear any conflicts. So yes, absolutely. Shall we say two o'clock on Monday?"

"Done," Sam agreed.

"You have a wonderful weekend," Betty said, knowing that, no matter what, the weekend would pale in comparison with the first day of next week.

"You, too. And don't forget that margarita!"

Oh, she thought, *we'll do better than that.*

***

The weekend was sunny and bright; Monday was gray and drizzly. On top of that, Sam had managed to come down with a head cold and the congestion was getting him down. But he'd put off Betty and Andy long enough, and he knew he had to keep this appointment. So he dragged himself to his car and sneezed himself through traffic, feeling somehow lucky that he was blowing his nose more than his horn. *If I get anything back from selling off those Tiffany lamps*, he thought, *I should buy stock in the company that makes Kleenex.* Over the course of his drive of twenty or so miles, he'd pretty well guaranteed them a profit for the year.

To make matters worse, by the time he got to Andy's office in the middle of Mendham, the lunchtime crowd had returned to work and, in the process, consumed most of the available nearby parking. He did the best he could, then grabbed his umbrella, thrust it out the car door as he opened it in the hopes of staying at least somewhat dry, and trudged the block-and-a-half to D'Antonio and Dennum. Once under the modest overhang outside the door, he closed his umbrella, shook it to disperse the bulk of the water, and opened the door. Betty looked up from her desk across the small lobby area and couldn't decide whether to cry for the poor man or laugh at him.

"My goodness," she exclaimed. "Is that you, Sam?"

"I think so," came the reply. "But to tell you the truth, I'm not sure. You know, years ago my kids had this book I used to read to them about a kid named Alexander who had a terrible, horrible, no good, very bad day. It was always funny to read that. But the way this day's going, I'm thinking of changing my name to Alexander."

Betty knew well that Sam's day was about to take a turn for the better, but it was not her place to deliver the news. So she feigned sympathy—unadulterated and deeply felt sympathy—even as she suppressed a smile. "Let me tell Andy you're here. And let's get you out of that wet raincoat."

Andy was out of his office in an instant. After he overcame the shock of seeing his client looking so bedraggled, he shook Sam's hand and guided him toward his office. As he did, he turned to Betty. "Ask Keiley to join us, will you?" And with that, he closed the door behind him. Keiley followed moments later, knocking on the door and then entering on her own. By pre-arrangement with Betty, and with Andy's prior consent, she closed the door softly, leaving it slightly ajar. Betty then rose from her own chair and ever so quietly busied herself neatening the set of book and display shelves that occupied the wall between the doors to the two offices. Legal ethics be damned; she was not going to miss this.

"God, Sam," Andy began. "You look awful!"

"I hab a code," replied his client, overdoing it a bit for effect, slouching and flashing a wan smile.

"Well," Andy replied, "let me see if I can find some cold medicine here." With that, he opened a drawer on his desk and rooted around a bit. Out came Thomas Edison's congressional medal, which he placed on the desk.

Sam sat bolt upright.

"Let me tell you about the meeting you missed. It was quite a gathering. We had the folks you'd expect—the superintendent, that woman from Interior, Art Escalon from the Papers Project, and Professor Templeton. But then there were a bunch of lawyers from the Park Service and the General Services Administration and even the state attorney general's office. Ephraim Cook did us a real favor there, because he really did set this up as a meeting where some decisions could be made. And right from the start, it was evident he had bought into Professor Templeton's plan. It was pretty clear after the dig over at Glenmont that there wasn't really any sort of environmental threat, but there could have been. And the way he'd arranged that so that the main archeological exploration of the Edison experiment would go through normal channels, however long that might take, but in the meantime she could dig up the outlier cylinder and give everyone a chance to see what was in it—well, that was just perfect for us. So we had the cylinder out on the table, still covered with dirt and grime, and all the government lawyers were there to claim ownership of the contents, as long as they didn't ooze out and poison us all.

"Audrey cleaned the cylinder up and took some precautions as she set about opening it up. That took a while, but eventually she got the top off and this little bauble on the desk here came tumbling out. According to people in that room who would know, this is an original medal given to Edison by Congress. There was some discussion of the backstory for that, and I'll be glad to share that with you later, because you should know it, but the salient point was that no one had seen the medal since Edison had received it. And there it was. That got the lawyers, and even Ephraim Cook, I think, all excited because it looked like the government could claim this cylinder was full of artifacts that would belong to the Park Service, which is to say, the government. What it really did, though, as it turned out, was date the cylinder to late 1928 at the earliest, because Edison didn't receive this medal until October of that year, right around the time John and Jennie Culbertson got married. And you remember how Ephraim had pulled me aside at the previous meeting and told me they had records showing your grandfather John was a long-time Edison employee *and* a handwritten instruction from Edison to his aide to buy flowers for John's wedding? So all that really did was tie together some loose ends."

"Wow," was all the response Sam could muster as he took all of this in.

"It only gets better. There was still something moving around inside the cylinder, so Audrey tipped it over and this rolled out." Andy put the baseball on the desk, then pointed. "If you look right there, you can see that one of the signatures was your grandfather's."

Sam picked up the ball and studied John Culbertson's signature.

"At this point, the lawyers started getting nervous. They could still argue that the contents of the cylinder were just government-owned artifacts, but because of the way we all came to search for the thing, all at our initiative using that map from the back of the painting that clearly had come down through your family, their argument was getting a little weaker.

"Then we struck gold, or you did. Audrey looked into the cylinder and pulled out a piece of paper that turned out to be this old stock certificate." Andy placed the elaborately engraved CTRC certificate on the desk. Keiley held her breath because she knew what was coming. And outside the door, Betty nearly fell over as she was leaning closer to the door, but fortunately caught herself on the bookcase, preventing both a noisy fall and the resultant embarrassment.

"This," Andy said, "is a certificate for shares in a company called CTRC for short, and as you can see, the certificate is made out to Mr. Edison and dated 1911, which is when that company was formed. But on the back,"—Andy flipped the certificate over as he spoke—"is a signed transfer of the shares, and look whom it's to. *Francis* Culbertson. So Edison not only sent flowers to your grandparents' wedding, but he must have known about your Uncle Frank being born, because this is made out to him. And that's kind of interesting in its own right. But as far as that meeting was concerned, it made it a deadlock certainty that the contents of that cylinder were personal in nature. And you could see the lawyers just sink back in their chairs. They could still have fought the whole thing out through the courts, but they could see they had a losing hand." Andy turned the certificate right side up.

"Now, let's talk about CTRC. You probably never heard of it. I know I hadn't. At first everybody at the meeting thought it was one of the many Edison companies, but that wasn't the case. CTRC, you will be pleased to learn, was renamed in 1924, and it's still around today. The new name has kind of stuck. It's now called International Business Machines. IBM."

"So I have a hundred shares of IBM stock?" Sam asked.

"Not exactly. You stand to inherit—and remember, none of this is yours yet, not until it clears probate—one hundred *1911* shares of IBM, which, given where and how we found this certificate, have almost surely never been redeemed. I did a little research on this, and that one hundred 1911 shares of IBM translate today into almost 1,200,000 shares."

"Say that again?" was Sam's response.

"When the estate clears probate, you will own 1,187,900 shares of IBM stock, to be precise. At today's price, the last time I looked, that's worth just north of $165 million."

Sam said nothing. He just sat there. Andy and Keiley kept a close watch, if only to be sure he was still breathing. Of that there could be no doubt, because with his cold, Sam's breathing was not quiet. Betty, who wasn't privy to the dynamics inside the office, couldn't help herself. She pushed the door open just a little and peeked in, then quickly withdrew. It wasn't the hoot and holler she had expected, but she saw enough to know that Sam was trying to process the news he'd just received.

"Uncle Frank," he managed to stammer, "was worth more than a hundred million dollars?"

"Yep, and that doesn't even count the lamps and the ring," Andy said with a smile. "Congratulations!"

"That's a lot to take in. He was so frugal."

"Well, you have to remember, Sam, that he didn't know. I mean, yes, he had the lamps, but there's no telling if he understood their value. As for the stock, he couldn't have known about that.

"But we're not quite done yet. There was one more thing in that cylinder."

At this, Keiley's head jerked upward. Had Andy been holding out on her? That would be a discussion for later in the day, after Sam had left. But, depending on what next emerged from Andy's overladen desk drawer, discuss it they would.

"Since we are now talking about IBM, I read that back when companies started using computers for billing customers' accounts, they would send out the bills on IBM punch cards to be returned with a check. You know, so the payments could be automatically credited to the correct account by reading all the data from the punched holes. It was much more primitive than all the optical readers and QR codes and the like we have today. And those cards wouldn't work if they came back all messed up, which meant the payments had to be processed the old-fashioned way—by hand. So the companies started printing instructions on the cards that said, 'Do Not Bend, Fold, Spindle, or Mutilate.' And it must have worked, because they did it that way for years. If you ever watch those old TV shows from back then, you'll know that it also became kind of a running joke for comedians back in the 1960s and 1970s.

"Well, Edison may have had some stock in the company, but he clearly wasn't a man to concern himself with such matters, even in the years long before that little meme took hold. Because as you'll see, this last item has pretty clearly been bent and folded, and after spending a hundred years in a round cylinder, it's fair to say it's been spindled. And from the look of it, mutilation isn't off the table."

And with that, Andy reached down one more time and pulled out an old photo, which, again, he laid upon the desk. It was a team photo of some baseball players, all clad in uniforms with the team name "Edisons." Clearly this was one of the inventor's industrial league, or semi-pro, teams. Most of the men in the photo appeared to be in their twenties or thirties. All save one. For in the very middle of the photo was an older man, dressed not in a baseball uniform but in a business suit. The man in the middle was Thomas Edison.

Andy pointed to the lower right-hand corner of the picture. "You can see down here that the photo was taken by someone named Lueder. I looked into that, and it turns out that Lewis Lueder worked for the Edison Company, and for a long time he was Thomas Edison's official photographer. So this is almost surely a photo of one of the company's industrial league baseball teams, of which they had quite a number. We haven't been able to tie down the year. But it seems to square with that baseball you've got there."

After Sam (and Keiley) had had an opportunity to study the photo, Andy reached over and, as he had with the stock certificate, flipped it to reveal the back side. Written on the back of the photo in a hand that had

become familiar to Andy and Keiley in the course of their research, but not to Sam, was an unsigned note that read:

Francis,
I thought you might enjoy having this old photograph of your father's baseball team.

Sam read the inscription, then asked if he might flip back to the picture itself. Andy nodded his assent, not that it was needed, and Sam turned the bent, folded, spindled, and mutilated paper over, looked again—long and hard—at the photograph itself, then smiled with recognition.

"There," he said, "in the front row. Second from the left. That looks just like some of the old photos of Grampa John."

"Everything in life depends on will. I never had an idea in my life. I've got no imagination. I never dream. My so-called inventions already existed in the environment—I took them out. I've created nothing. Nobody does. There's no such thing as an idea being brain-born; everything comes from the outside. The industrious one coaxes it from the environment; the drone lets it lie there while he goes off to the baseball game."

—Thomas Edison

"After [Thomas's son Theodore's] death in 1992 the name of Edison lingered only among descendants of the Sloane family. Of old Sam Edison's lusty blood, no patrilineal trace remains."

—Edmund Morris, *Edison*

The Box Score

Acknowledgments

This book, like any other work of fiction, bubbles up out of a stew of facts, ideas, guesses, and suppositions, all cooked up by the author from ingredients supplied by many others. When a project on this scale nears its completion, it is at once pleasing and humbling to acknowledge their assistance.

I want to thank Rita DiMatteo, the resident historian of Llewellyn Park in West Orange, New Jersey, for her insights into that community. Ms. DiMatteo also served as editor of the Westheimer book cited below.

In assigning a contemporary value to the one-percent fictional interest in the initial ownership of the company we now know as IBM, hypothetically gifted to Thomas Edison by founder Charles R. Flint, I am indebted for the assistance of Neal Chalkley and the mathematical whizzes of Edward D. Jones & Company, LP. It was they who calculated the number of contemporary shares in IBM that such a holding in the CTRC Company would have yielded through subsequent splits and reinvested dividends.

This tale would have been far less richly textured without the resources of the Thomas A. Edison Papers Project at Rutgers University, a collection that is at once amazing in its scope and depth and exceptional in its accessibility. For that we, and I, owe a debt of gratitude to Paul Israel, the real Director and General Editor of the Project, who bears substantial responsibility for the quality of the archive. I particularly appreciated his prompt and on-point responses to my queries while I was writing this book.

Every so often an author is lucky enough to happen upon a person who will go out of his or her way to help locate or interpret information that is critical to the project. In this instance, it was my great good fortune to find Leonard DeGraaf, Archivist at the Thomas Edison National Historical Park, who helped me understand the procedures of the National Park Service and the nuances of the relationship between that particular park and the Llewellyn Park community in which one of its prize components is embedded, introduced me to some of the holdings of the Park's archives, and, importantly, helped track down information about a particular photograph that proved essential to the plot. Lenny, thank you.

Special thanks as well to Alexandria Edwards, Marketing and Public Relations Coordinator of the Edison and Ford Winter Estates, and to David Dyte, co-creator of the remarkable website BrooklynBallParks.com, for their assistance in tracking down some hard-to-find photographs.

As with the earlier volumes in this series, I have had the good fortune to work with the editorial and production superstars at Sunbury Press. I could not pass on this opportunity to acknowledge and express my appreciation to publisher Lawrence Knorr, editor Sarah Peachey, and designer Crystal Devine.

This project has offered a wonderful opportunity for the author to demonstrate his ignorance of several technical fields. For example, I make no claim to being a chemist, though I did marry one. I am by no measure an expert in radar, though I have watched every episode of *M*A*S*H* more times than I care to admit. And I am most certainly not an engineer, though I once considered model railroading as a hobby. And that brings us to the law.

In Andy Dennum's previous appearance in this series, *The Federal Case*, I pointed out that he was a young and inexperienced attorney, and that I was no kind of attorney whatsoever. Together we begged the forbearance of anyone who had a better grasp of the law than the one reflected in the story. Andy has returned here, still young but slightly more experienced, yet nevertheless fictional. I cannot vouch for his having learned any more about the law, given that he is, after all, not real, and I can say with assurance that I remain as ignorant as before. In planning the current volume, though, I had the good sense to consult with my son-in-law, Michael Harwin, who is, in fact, an attorney, and he had the good sense not to render any legal opinions. But he did educate me as to the many layers of law and regulation that poor Andy would need to surmount if he were to be successful in ensuring that his client was well served. For that, and for his subsequent valuable comments on the manuscript, Andy and I, as well as Sam Patrick, are grateful. Michael also cautioned that, unlike Andy, no real attorney would pile up billable hours researching a case unless it was clear that some client would be paying the tab. Perhaps this is one of those times when fiction holds the high ground?

Finally, as always, thanks to my patient and supportive wife, Amy, who has survived yet another book. How she does it I will never know. But she is always my first reader, and in this instance, my chemistry consultant as well, and her comments invariably shape the final product more than I care to acknowledge. Oh, wait. . . .

Notes

viii   The definition is excerpted from Paul Dickson, *The Dickson Baseball Dictionary*, Third Edition (New York: W.W. Norton & Company, 2009), pp. 479-480.

x   "Thomas Alva Edison was widely viewed" — Michael Schein, "Thomas Edison Was A Cranky Dude (And Other Reasons You Should Follow His Lead)," *Forbes*, October 2, 2018, found online October 25, 2022, at https://www.forbes.com/sites/michaelschein/2018/10/02/thomas-edison-was-a-cranky-dude-and-other-reasons-you-should-follow-his-lead/?sh=15bcd1a01305.

x   "Years later" — "Thomas Edison," Wikipedia, found online October 25, 2022, at https://en.wikipedia.org/w/index.php?title=Thomas_Edison&oldid=1117454513.

x   "Edison's commitment to practicality over theory" — Frank Crane, "An Edison Story," *New York Globe*, June 14, 1919, found online July 4, 2023 at https://edisondigital.rutgers.edu/document/SC19034A#?c=&m=&s=&cv=&xywh=-765%2C-83%2C2729%2C1671. Provided by the Thomas A. Edison Papers at Rutgers University.

xi   "one-time prospective customer" — See Jenks's December 12, 1892, letter to Edison requesting guidance on the selection of equipment, together with Edison's hand-written response, found online October 25, 2022, at https://edisondigital.rutgers.edu/iiif/2/251812/full/776,/0/default.jpg. Provided by the Thomas A. Edison Papers at Rutgers University.

xi   "I beg to state" — This letter, dated April 9, 1901, provided by The Thomas Alva Edison Papers at Rutgers University, found online October 25, 2022, at https://edisondigital.rutgers.edu/iiif/2/416123/full/1472,/0/default.jpg.

xii   The hand-written original of this letter that appears here, provided by The Thomas Alva Edison Papers at Rutgers University, was found online October 25, 2022, at https://edisondigital.rutgers.edu/iiif/2/409626/full/1392,/0/default.jpg. Provided by the Thomas A. Edison Papers at Rutgers University.

A typescript of the letter, dated December 31, 1907, was auctioned by Swann Auction Galleries to an unidentified buyer on July 30, 2020. An image of that version of the letter was found online October 25, 2022, at https://catalogue.swanngalleries.com/Lots/auction-lot/EDISON-THOMAS-A-Typed-Letter-Signed-to-IBM-founder-Charles-R?saleno=2543&lotNo=14&refNo=772310.

Notes

xiii   "By the time in question" — The author acknowledges that there is at least one rival hypothesis worthy of note. One of Edison's projects in his West Orange laboratory was the development of an improved—which is to say, functional—rechargeable battery for use in automobiles. And around 1911, at the same time he was creating the future IBM, Flint had organized a company to manufacture submarines of a French design. In January 1911, Edison did write to Flint to apprise him of the work being done to develop batteries that might have applications in submarines. See the letter found online October 25, 2022, at https://edisondigital.rutgers.edu/iiif/2/419360/0,268,1664,1261/1664,1261/0/default.jpg. Provided by the Thomas A. Edison Papers at Rutgers University. However, the text of that letter makes clear Edison's assumption that Flint was unaware of the project, which would seem to eliminate this as the subject of the earlier 1907 correspondence.

xiv   Excerpted from Thomas A. Edison, "Baseball Greatest Game, Says Edison: Inventor Lauds Cobb as Fine Manhood Type, Urges Youths to Follow," *The Palm Beach Post*, February 23, 1927, p. 2. Found online August 12, 2023, at https://www.newspapers.com/image/130093929/?match=1.

3   "he produced his first lampshade" — For an extraordinarily detailed chronicling of the personal and professional life of Louis Comfort Tiffany, see "The Louis Comfort Tiffany Chronology," found online June 28, 2023, at https://morsemuseum.org/louis-comfort-tiffany/chronology/about/.

3   "The last fruit in Thomas Edison's orchard" — To be clear, the premise here is fictitious. Edison is known to have fathered six children, three by each of his two wives. The author is aware of no evidence that he fathered others out of wedlock.

10   "Edison could hear his wife's words clearly" — See "All Edison's Interests Now Cling to His Wife," an *Associated Press* article published on the eve of his death in the Chattanooga *Daily Times*, October 10, 1931, p. 1, found online August 14, 2023, at https://www.newspapers.com/image/604395765/?terms=%22Theodore%20Edison%22%20baseball&match=1. The article states: "In the past, because of the peculiar timbre of her voice, her words have been clear to Mr. Edison, despite his deafness."

12   "And you are telling me this" — Though it might strike the reader as unlikely that a man of Edison's age at the time would have retained both his interest in sexual activity and his virility, we know from the direct testimony of his wife, Mina, that he remained active at least well into his seventies. "It puts a bright hue on everything when he is happy and makes love to me as he is doing now," she wrote in a letter to her son Theodore in April 1921. Quoted in Morris, p. 29.

13   "I remember one game" — For a history of Sprague Field and of early baseball in the Bloomfield and East Orange area, see Society for American Baseball Research, "Sprague Field (Bloomfield, NJ)", March 12, 2019, found online May 2, 2023, at https://sabr.org/bioproj/park/sprague-field-bloomfield-nj/.

15   "subsidize my worthless children" — The narrative in Morris is replete with examples of the demands made by his children, particularly Thomas, Jr., and

William from his first marriage, and Edison's resentment of their seemingly constant importuning.

18   "How had he gotten into this mess?" — The beginnings of Edison's foray into redesigning his batteries for use in submarines is nicely chronicled in Morris, pp. 95-99, 108-110.

19   "Hutch wouldn't have known" — This story was related by Captain Cable to Charles Edison many years later, in 1940. Personal correspondence between the author and Leonard DeGraaf, archivist at the Thomas Edison National Historical Park, August 12, 2023.

20   "that got them looking at the bases" — The characteristics of genuine Tiffany lamps were detailed by Fontaine's Auction Gallery in "How to Spot Authentic Tiffany Studios Lamps," posted August 19, 2021, and found online June 18, 2023 at https://www.fontainesauction.com/how-to-spot-authentic-tiffany-studios-lamps/#:~:text=Look%20for%20a%20Patina%20on,brown%20or%20green%20in%20hue. A similar set of criteria for determining the genuine item is provided by Dakota Murphey of Heritage Auctions, "Tiffany Lamps: How to Tell Real from Fake," posted April 6, 2021, and found online June 18, 2023 at https://www.antiquetrader.com/antiques/tiffany-lamps-how-to-tell-real-from-fake.

21   "As for value" — These price estimates are supported by auction results found online, May 12, 2023, at https://www.invaluable.com/blog/inside-the-archives-tiffany-lamp-prices/.

22   "It's not, though there might have been some connection." — Though the Theosophy Society is separate and distinct from the Masons, it was nevertheless the case that, when the cornerstone for the movement's headquarters in Wheaton, Illinois, was laid, the group's president at the time, Annie Bessant, wore Masonic regalia and the stone itself was laid according to the rites of the Co-Masonic Order. See Theosophy World Resource Center, "Theosophy in America," Manila, Philippines: Theosophical Publishing House, N.D. Found online July 23, 2023, at https://theosophy.world/encyclopedia/america-theosophy.

22   "That design is the logo of the Theosophical Society" — For an illustration of the emblem and a thorough discussion of its elements and their respective significance, the reader is encouraged to consult "The Emblem of the Theosophical Society," an official posting by the Theosophical Society of Australia, found online July 23, 2023, at https://theosophicalsociety.org.au/statics/the-emblem.

23   "her full name was Georgine Shillard-Smith" — These biographical details were found online, May 12, 2023, at https://theosophy.wiki/en/Georgine_Shillard-Smith.

28   The letter from Edison Portland Cement regarding Otto Schott was found online August 4, 2023, at https://edisondigital.rutgers.edu/iiif/2/420807/full/1376,/0/default.jpg. Provided by the Thomas A. Edison Papers at Rutgers University.

28   "St. Joseph's Church" — For a chronology of Catholic churches in the Archdiocese of Newark, see https://www.rcan.org/offices-and-ministries/history-archives/chronology-parishes, found online, April 30, 2023.

Notes

30   "Otto Schott's name" — The discussion of Schott and of borosilicate glass is based on Ainissa Ramirez, "The Chemical History of Superior Glass," *American Scientist* 110:3 (May-June 2022), p. 178, found online April 25, 2023, at https://www.americanscientist.org/article/the-chemical-history-of-superior-glass. For a more general biographical portrait of the German inventor, see "Otto Schott," found online July 23, 2023, at https://en.wikipedia.org/wiki/Otto_Schott.

30   "For most of the day-to-day glassblowing" — See Paul Engle, "Thomas Edison's Lady Glassblowers," November 4, 2019, found online July 23, 2023, at https://www.conciatore.org/2019/11/thomas-edisons-lady-glassblowers.html.

31   "By some accounts" — This is one of several potential word-origin stories that are summarized in "The History of Shot Glasses," found online July 2, 2023, at https://www.glasswithatwist.com/articles/the-history-of-shot-glasses.html.

33   "found himself on the home page" — Found online May 23, 2023, at https://www.melfisher.com/default.html. The 2011 map in question just below was found online May 23, 2023, at https://www.melfisher.com/Library/InTheNews2011.asp.

34   "The ship was carrying" — For an overview of the *Atocha* see https://en.wikipedia.org/wiki/Nuestra_Señora_de_Atocha, found online May 23, 2023.

41   "his early nickel-iron batteries used thick glass housings" — For an illustrated and very accessible overview of the history and workings of storage batteries, see Edison Tech Center, "Batteries: Types and History," found online July 23, 2023, at https://edisontechcenter.org/batteries.html, and note especially section (2.d) on Edison's use of glass housings.

42   "I'm looking at a table" — The table in question was the Millipore Sigma ranking titled, "Relative Strength of Acids & Bases," found online June 23, 2023, at https://www.sigmaaldrich.com/US/en/technical-documents/technical-article/chemistry-and-synthesis/acid-base-chart.

42   "a project of the arts and sciences school" — For an early look at the potential of this archive, see McAuliffe, passim.

43   This photo of the 44 Road 3 Building that houses the Edison Papers Project at Rutgers University was found online June 5, 2023, at https://maps.rutgers.edu/#/?lat=40.523685&lng=-74.433124&selected=4053&sidebar=true&zoom=21.

45   Notebook page found online May 27, 2023, at https://edisondigital.rutgers.edu/iiif/2/363502/full/732,/0/default.jpg. Provided by the Thomas A. Edison Papers at Rutgers University.

46   "the very first motion picture" — Edison Studios produced "The Ball Park," a fifty-second-long clip showing a baseball game featuring a team from Newark, in 1898. The film, available through the Library of Congress, was found online May 27, 2023, at https://www.loc.gov/item/00563587/.

47   "a listing of all the guy's personality traits" — Morris, p. 756.

47   "a contemporaneous one by a guy named Kennelly" — Kennelly, passim.

48   This letter, which resembles in appearance a telegraph, was found online, May 27, 2023, at https://edisondigital.rutgers.edu/iiif/2/222823/full/749,/0/default.

jpg and https://edisondigital.rutgers.edu/iiif/2/222824/full/722,/0/default.jpg. Provided by the Thomas A. Edison Papers at Rutgers University.

49   "Inventor Abandons Science for Day of Games of Employees at Olympia Park," *New York American*, July 17, 1912, found online May 27, 2023, at https://edisondigital.rutgers.edu/iiif/2/492687/full/1000,1253/0/default.jpg.

50   "I discovered that there was an Edison Club baseball team" — This is documented in a letter dated January 29, 1914, from Clarence B. Hayes, president of the Edison Baseball Team, to Mina Edison, offering complementary tickets to an unspecified event, found at NPS Catalog # EDIS-73247 in the archives of the Thomas Edison National Historical Park. Hayes's position with Edison is documented at https://edisondigital.rutgers.edu/folder/E1664A-F#?cv=&c=&m=&s=, found online August 8, 2023, and confirmed in *Edison Laboratory Historic Furnishings Report, Volume 1, Historical Data and Furnishing Plan* (Harpers Ferry, WV: National Park Service, 1995), pp. v, 24, found online August 8, 2023, at http://npshistory.com/publications/edis/edis_lab_hfr.pdf.

50   "at least one of the other team officers" — See, for example, the letter from Meserlin to A.R. Rogers dated October 19, 1914, and found online August 8, 2023, at https://edisondigital.rutgers.edu/document/E1440AG#?c=&m=&s=&cv=&xywh=-442%2C-1%2C2083%2C1504. On Hutchison's position, see "Miller Reese Hutchison," found online August 8, 2023, at https://en.wikipedia.org/wiki/Miller_Reese_Hutchison.

50   The photo of the 1909 Brooklyn Edisons was found online May 27, 2023, at http://www.covehurst.net/ddyte/brooklyn/semipro_parks.html.

50   "a player named Joe Judge" — Daniel, M. Daniel, "Joe Judge, Native New Yorker: Washington First Baseman One Of The Few Big Leaguers Born In The Metropolis," *The Daily Record* (Long Branch, NJ), August 18, 1926.

51   "Brooklyn Edisons Nine Wins Intercity Contest," *Brooklyn Standard Union*, June 11, 1911, p. 7, found online August 14, 2023, at https://www.newspapers.com/image/543870318/.

52   The 1929 team photo is in the National Park Service archive and was found online June 4, 2023, at https://npgallery.nps.gov/EDIS/AssetDetail/0ee052190c9b49b3a3443d62bb558594. Courtesy National Park Service.

53   The photo of Edison throwing out the ceremonial first pitch, taken May 26, 1914, is in the National Park Service archive and was found online June 4, 2023, at https://npgallery.nps.gov/EDIS/GetAsset/744fccd853bb437c906ee7a4fc2a7d85/original.jpg?. Courtesy National Park Service.

53   The snapshot of Edison pitching to a live batter, taken July 16, 1912, is in the National Park Service archive and was found online June 4, 2023, at https://npgallery.nps.gov/EDIS/GetAsset/cd9889fd0db44ece8ce5127b8d7b9422/original.jpg?. Courtesy National Park Service.

54   "Stepping on the pitching slab" — "Edison Makes Merry at Picnic: 'Wizard' Takes Holiday and Romps and Plays with Employees," *Newark Star-Eagle*, July 17, 1912, p. 4, found online August 13, 2023, at https://www.newspapers.com/image/877035066/?terms=%22the%20edison%20club%22%20baseball&match=1.

54   "It certainly is wonderful to think of a man like Cobb" — Thomas A. Edison, "Baseball Greatest Game, Says Edison," op. cit.

55   The photo showing Edison with Ty Cobb and Connie Mack at the Fort Myers ballpark, taken March 7, 1927, is in the National Park Service archive and was found online June 4, 2023, at https://npgallery.nps.gov/EDIS/AssetDetail/2a2ba 1bfedc440889b09dd77e00576d4. Courtesy National Park Service.

55   "there's a fun story that goes with this picture" — The first version of the story was related by Dan Holmes in "When Ty Cobb and Thomas Edison met in spring training," January 15, 2018, found online May 28, 2023, at https://www. vintagedetroit.com/ty-cobb-thomas-edison-met-spring-training/#:~:text=Ty%20 Cobb%2C%20Thomas%20Edison%2C%20and,way%20to%20becoming%20 a%20millionaire. The second was told in the Edison and Ford Winter Estates Blog entry, "Baseball at Terry Park – From Edison to Today," and found online May 28, 2023, at https://www.edisonfordwinterestates.org/baseball-at-terry-park-from-edison-to-today/.

55   "There's even a third take" — This variation, with its rich detail, comes to us courtesy of Hughie Jennings, "Thomas Edison Lights Up Ty Cobb," found online May 28, 2023, at https://hughiejennings.com/the-ee-yah-blog/f/ thomas-edison-lights-up-ty-cobb.

56   The photo of Edison at bat, taken March 7, 1927, is in the National Park Service archive and was found online June 4, 2023, at https://npgallery.nps.gov/EDIS/ GetAsset/070a388c84b54a83bbc9613a7bbf9fdb/original.jpg?. The catcher in the photo is Connie Mack. Pitching that day, though not shown, was Ty Cobb. Courtesy National Park Service.

57   "Apparently, the Edisons invited the team" — This delightful tale was actually shared by Alexandra Edwards, Marketing and Public Relations Coordinator for the Edison and Ford Winter Estates. Personal correspondence with the author.

57   The photo of the team visit to the Edisons was found online May 28, 2023, at https://www.edisonfordwinterestates.org/baseball-at-terry-park-from-edison-to-today/. Mack is pictured to the right of center behind a shrub, with Cobb just off his right shoulder wearing a V-necked sweater. Reproduced with the permission of the Edison and Ford Winter Estates.

57   "the Brooklyn Robins were in Fort Myers during spring training" — "Dodgers Lazy; Fail to Call on Thomas Edison," *Los Angeles Evening Express*, March 20, 1931.

58   "And one more thing" — The article about Theodore's baseball card collection is, so far as I know, apocryphal, but the collection as described was quite real and can be found in the archives of the Thomas Edison National Historical Park. Edison's enjoyment of cigars and chewing tobacco is documented by Jeffery Sitts in *Pipe Line*, February 26, 2021, and found online August 8, 2023, at https:// www.smokingpipes.com/smokingpipesblog/single.cfm/post/thomas-edison-prolific-inventor-and-cigar-smoker; while his dislike for cigarettes is described in "Thomas Edison and Cigars," February 24, 2023, found online August 8,, 2023, at https://www.holts.com/clubhouse/cigar-culture/thomas-edison.

59 "The Edisons' home" — For a thorough discussion of the home and the Edisons' time there, see "Glenmont: Thomas Edison's Historical Home," found online April 27, 2023, at https://www.thomasedison.org/edison-s-home-glenmont.

59 "But more remarkable still" — See "Llewellyn Park Historic District," found online April 29, 2023, at https://www.livingplaces.com/NJ/Essex_County/West_Orange_Township/Llewellyn_Park_Historic_District.html. For much greater detail, see United States Department of the Interior, National Park Service, "National Register of Historic Places Inventory – Nomination Form," February 28, 1986, found online April 29, 2023, at http://npshistory.com/publications/edis/nr-llewellyn-park-hd.pdf.

60 "a cherished Halloween tradition" — This story, attributed to Marie von Lengerke Blaisdell, is related in Westheimer, p. 39.

61 "The Douglases" — Edison's neighbors are identified as of 1913 in the map of the Llewellyn Park Historic District included in the above-referenced National Park Service Nomination Form.

63 The first of these notebook examples is from page 49 of Edison's notebook number 128 that was found online May 27, 2023, at https://archive.org/details/taepnotebook-NP128/page/n47/mode/2up?view=theater.

64 The second notebook example is from page 9 of Edison's notebook number 124 that was found online May 27, 2023, at https://archive.org/details/taepnotebook-NP124/page/n8/mode/1up.

65 "a letter that Edison wrote to the shareholders of his battery company in 1908" — The text of this letter was found online May 9, 2023, at https://edisondigital.rutgers.edu/iiif/2/429077/full/1000,1198/0/default.jpg. Provided by the Thomas A. Edison Papers at Rutgers University.

65 "a park in Hoboken, Elysian Field" — A detailed history of this facility, both in general and as a baseball venue, was found online May 28, 2023, at https://en.wikipedia.org/wiki/Elysian_Fields_(Hoboken,_New_Jersey).

66 "The company was named for its founder" — For an overview of Frank Sprague and his company, see https://en.wikipedia.org/wiki/Frank_J._Sprague, found online May 28, 2023. For a fascinating story of the role of Sprague's technology in the development of modern subway systems, see Most, passim.

66 "As for the ball field" — See "Sprague Field (Bloomfield, NJ)," March 12, 2019, found online May 28, 2023, at https://sabr.org/bioproj/park/sprague-field-bloomfield-nj/.

67 In Edison's day, Olympic Park had been a massive complex — For an extensive history of the park, see Jeffrey Stanton, with Patrick McKinney, "Olympic Park -- Newark, New Jersey, 1887-1965," published by the National Amusement Park Historical Association and found online August 15, 2023, at http://lostamusementparks.napha.org/Articles/NewJersey/OlympicPark.html. The 1912 map Keiley located appeared in the same article and was found online at http://lostamusementparks.napha.org/Articles/NewJersey/OlympicPark-1912Map.html.

67 "she found a page that summarized the history" — That page was found online May 28, 2023, at http://www.brooklynballparks.com. Follow the bulleted link to "Many more amateur and semipro parks".

70 "There, it turned out, was Washington Park" — See Ross and Dyte.

71 The 1911 photo of Edison Field was found online May 29, 2023, at http://www.covehurst.net/ddyte/brooklyn/semipro_parks.html.

74 "a date that was shown beside his signature on a pledge card" — The pledge card, along with correspondence indicating that Edison had been invited to meet with Madame Helene Blavatsky, the founder of the Theosophy movement, was found online May 30, 2023, at https://www.theosophy.world/encyclopedia/edison-thomas-alva.

75 "Georgine Northrup Wetherill Smith" — This biographical information was found online May 30, 2023 at https://theosophy.wiki/en/Georgine_Shillard-Smith.

75 "Whistler is well remembered" — For a succinct summary of Whistler's lifestyle, artistic style, and influence, see Emily Snow, "James Abbott McNeill Whistler: A leader of the Aesthetic Movement," *The Collector*, March 30, 2021, found online July 26, 2023, at https://www.thecollector.com/james-abbott-mcneill-whistler-a-leader-of-the-aesthetic-movement-12-facts/.

78 "that fits with Edison" — Perhaps the most succinct summary of Edison's views on religion and immortality, some of them redolent of theosophical thinking but others not, is found in Morris, pp. 99-105.

78 "And sure enough, there they were" — There are several lists of prominent adherents, among them those found online November 30, 2020, at https://theosophy.wiki/en/Category:Famous_people; https://www.listal.com/list/famous-theosophists; and http://www. katinkahesselink.net/his/influence-theosophy.html.

78 "And guess which other painter had been a theosophist." — See Eleanor Heartney, "Spirituality Has Long Been Erased From Art History. Here's Why It's Having a Resurgence Today," *Artnet News*, January 6, 2020, found online July 26, 2023 at https://news.artnet.com/art-world/spirituality-and-art-resurgence-1737117.

78 "the Edison timeline" — See https://edison.rutgers.edu/life-of-edison/chronology/1911-1920, found online May 30, 2023.

83 This photo of the grounds at Glenmont, with the house in the distance, was taken October 21, 1960, is included in the National Park Service archive, and was found online June 4, 2023 at https://npgallery.nps.gov/AssetDetail/b2f5a7b7db-7141be822ee835e828a673. Courtesy National Park Service.

83 "Edison made another super short film" — See Edelman.

88 This photo of the nickel washing machinery in Edison's storage battery factory was found online, July 27, 2023, at https://www.nps.gov/media/photo/gallery-item.htm?id=8B2303FB-155D-451F-671CD3CAEEAD3149&gid=B802AEC1-155D-451F-67ED0AEDA440D760. Courtesy National Park Service.

96 The 1913 map of properties and owners in Llewellyn Park is reproduced in the National Park form, dated 1986, proposing Llewellyn Park for inclusion in the National Register of Historic Places, p. 54, and was found online June 30, 2023,

at http://npshistory.com/publications/edis/nr-llewellyn-park-hd.pdf. The same document provides the legal description of Glenmont on p. 259.

97 "this tool they call a 'Wetlands Mapper'" — The Mapper can be accessed online at https://www.fws.gov/program/national-wetlands-inventory/wetlands-mapper. The image shown just below was produced on June 26, 2023.

97 The landscape plan was found in National Park Service, *Cultural Landscapes Inventory*, p. 6.

98 The 1913 photo of the Glenmont grounds and house was found in *Cultural Landscapes*, p. 54.

100 "Park Way is paved now" — The details of the paving of Llewellyn Park's roads and the removal of the walking paths on the west lawn were found in *Cultural Landscapes*, pp. 74-76.

103 "Edison and Tiffany ever met" — See "How Thomas Edison Influenced Louis Comfort Tiffany," posted September 4, 2020, and found online June 17, 2023, at https://htdeco.fr/en/blog/lamps/how-thomas-edison-influenced-louis-comfort-tiffany#Thomas%20Edison. Additional detail found in "Enjoy Tiffany Lamps? Thank Thomas Edison," *Behind the Scenes*, New York Historical Society, June 20, 2014, found online June 18, 2023, at https://www.nyhistory.org/blogs/enjoy-tiffany-lamps-thank-thomas-edison.

108 Letter found online June 17, 2023, at https://edisondigital.rutgers.edu/iiif/2/201596/full/526,/0/default.jpg. Provided by the Thomas A. Edison Papers at Rutgers University.

109 "Some of his early prototype lamps" — See "Welcome to the World of Tiffany Lamps and Tiffany Style Lamps," posted March 25, 2023, and found online June 18, 2023, at https://tiffanylamplove.com/welcome-to-the-world-of-tiffany-lamps/.

109 The cover pictured here, along with the inside contents, were found online June 18, 2023, at https://edisondigital.rutgers.edu/iiif/2/376701/full/850,/0/default.jpg. Provided by the Thomas A. Edison Papers at Rutgers University.

110 The photo of Edison's Paris exhibit was found online June 18, 2023, at https://www.si.edu/es/object/what-did-1889-sound%3Aposts_f2d5bb6307669c-8936c431096e3f93c8. William J. Hammer Collection, Archives Center, National Museum of American History. Reproduced with permission.

111 "a fundamental amendment to the Deed" — This document was found online June 29, 2023, at https://llewellynpark.com/HOA/assn13266/images/Llewellyn_Park_Deed_of_Trust.pdf.

111 "the Rambles shall be preserved" — This obligation is spelled out in paragraph fourteen of the aforementioned document.

113 "chancery courts dealt with equity" — See "Chancery Court of New Jersey," Department of State, State of New Jersey, found online August 7, 2023, at https://www.nj.gov/state/archives/catsjchance.html.

113 "The next document Andy found" — See *Haskell v. Wright*, 23 N.J. Eq. 389 (1873). Found online July 28, 2023, at https://cite.case.law/nj-eq/23/389/.

114 "Next his search turned up another gem" — This document was found online June 29, 2023, at https://www.dropbox.com/s/nfdgs20n4xsyq22/Llewellyn%20 Park%20Master%20Plan.pdf?dl=0.

114 "This one came accompanied by" — Found online June 29, 2023, at https://www. dropbox.com/s/jwfoaqdcqdrrr0t/Llewellyn%20Park%20Master%20Plan%20 %28maps%29.pdf?dl=0.

114 "At least one of these" — This photo is found on p. 34 of the Master Plan. Additional period photos suggesting the same conclusion are found on pp. 38, 44, and 53.

114 "That possibility was brought home" — See the photograph of Glenmont in Westheimer, p. 39. The photograph is undated, but the caption and associated text suggest that it dated to the period of Edison's residence.

114 "For all of its detail" — This photograph is found on p. 38 of the Master Plan.

115 "The fourth document" — The full application was found online June 30, 2023, at http://npshistory.com/publications/edis/nr-llewellyn-park-hd.pdf.

115 "an online posting from a group called Strong Towns" — Andrew Price, "A Brief History of Setbacks," March 7, 2018, found online July 11, 2023, at https://www.strongtowns.org/journal/2018/3/6/a-brief-history-of-setbacks #:~:text=In%20the%20early%2020th%20century,enough%20to%20accom-modate%20a%20car.&text=As%20the%20car%20became%20more,all%20 sides%20of%20the%20house.

116 "he skimmed one of the books" — Ross, pp. 9-12.

116 See "Life in Llewellyn Park: Some of the Prominent People Who Have Homes Along Its Devious and Secluded Avenues – A Real Estate View of the Park," *The Kansas City Star* (September 13, 1887), p. 2, found online August 7, 2023, at https://www.newspapers.com/image/648369220/?terms=Llewellyn%20Park& match=1.

117 "Andy had recently read a book" — This was probably Garrett M. Graff's book, *Watergate: A New History* (New York: Avid Reader Press, 2022).

118 "Edison's copy of a 1916 letter" — Found online July 9, 2023, at https://edison-digital.rutgers.edu/document/E1644AB#?c=&m=&s=&cv=&xywh=-324%2C-84%2C1831%2C1662. Provided by the Thomas A. Edison Papers at Rutgers University.

118 "he also came across another letter" — Found online July 9, 2023, at https:// edisondigital.rutgers.edu/iiif/2/475285/full/1152,/0/default.jpg. Provided by the Thomas A. Edison Papers at Rutgers University.

120 "Llewellyn Park Trustees had gotten into a dispute" — *Trustees of Llewellyn Park v. Township of West Orange*, 224 N.J. Super. 342 (App. Div. 1988) 540 A.2d 868.

120 "sent around a notice of assessment" — Found online July 9, 2023, at https:// www.westorange.org/DocumentCenter/View/3290/LP-Assessment?bidId=.

120 "the group was required to file an IRS Form 990" – Found online July 9, 2023, at https://projects.propublica.org/nonprofits/organizations/221073790/ 202233189349304403/full.

122 "the name of the committee's chair" — Data for the actual committee was found online July 10, 2023, at https://www.causeiq.com/organizations/committee-managers-of-llewellyn-park,221073790/. Both the draft letter and the members and actions of the committee employed in this story are, as noted in the early pages of this book, entirely fictitious.

124 "He knew that Glenmont had been designated" — See the June 9, 2005, testimony of Joseph M. Lawler, Regional Director, National Capital Region of the National Park Service in support of H.R. 1096, the legislation that established the Thomas Edison National Historical Park as the successor entity, found online September 1, 2023, at https://www.doi.gov/ocl/hr-1096.

124 "the document did not contain any real surprises" — Memorandum of Agreement between the National Park Service, United States Department of the Interior . . . and the Trustees and Committee of Managers of Llewellyn Park, West Orange, New Jersey . . . , dated August 3, 1959, passim.

130 "When the radar signal goes into the ground" — For a discussion of how GPR technology works, see "GPR FAQ," found online July 11, 2023, at https://www.sensoft.ca/support/faq/. The author claims no expertise in this area, and hopes he has summarized the information found there with reasonable comprehension and accuracy.

133 "Then there was something called Preservation New Jersey" — For general information about this group see https://www.preservationnj.org, found online July 23, 2023. For information about the grant, see https://www.nj.gov/dca/njht/funded/sitedetails/LlewellynParkHistoricDistrict.shtml#:~:text=The%20Llewellyn%20Park%20Gatehouse%2C%20also,promoters%20of%20the%20Picturesque%20Movement, found online July 23, 2023.

139 "the property happens to be owned by the federal government" — The summary of interests and procedures described in the passage that follows is based in large part on several publications of the Advisory Commission on Historic Preservation, including "36 CFR PART 800 – Protection of Historic Properties," found online July 15, 2023, at https://www.achp.gov/sites/default/files/regulations/2017-02/regs-rev04.pdf; *Protecting Historic Properties: A Citizen's Guide to Section 106 Review*, found online July 15, 2023, at https://www.achp.gov/sites/default/files/documents/2021-01/CitizenGuide2021_011321.pdf.; "Section 106 Applicant Toolkit," found online July 15, 2023, at https://www.achp.gov/digital-library-section-106-landing/section-106-applicant-toolkit; and "Council Members," found online July 15, 2023, at https://www.achp.gov/about/council-members. Additional sources consulted include National Park Service, op. cit., passim; the New Jersey Register of Historic Places Act N.J.A.C. 7.4 (2015), found online July 15, 2023, at https://www.nj.gov/dep/hpo/1identify/nj_register_hist_plac_rules_07_02_2015.pdf; State of New Jersey, Department of Environmental Protection, "New Jersey Historic Preservation Office," found online July 15, 2023, at https://www.nj.gov/dep/hpo/; "Llewellyn Park Preservation Foundation," found online July 15, 2023, at https://llewellynpark.

com/Page/13266~103838/Llewellyn-Park-Preservation-Foundation; West Orange Historic Preservation Commission, "West Orange Historic Preservation Commission Archives 1977-2019," found online July 15, 2023, at https://www.westorange.org/DocumentCenter/View/7768/HPC-ArchivesFindingAid-#:~:text=Abstract%3A%20The%20West%20Orange%20Historic,files%20involving%20the%20maintenance%20of; and personal correspondence with Leonard DeGraaf, Archivist at the Thomas Edison National Historic Park.

In point of fact, the rules and procedures set out in this list are but a small subset of the laws, executive orders, regulations, and policy guidance documents that govern activity within the national parks, including this one. For a more comprehensive listing see National Park Service, *Foundation Document*, p. 15.

161 "open this meeting by reading the mission statement" — The TENHP mission statement was found online July 18, 2023, at https://home.nps.gov/edis/learn/management/index.htm.

162 "The Park Service has a memorandum of agreement with the Army Corps of Engineers" — "Memorandum of Agreement Between the U.S. Army Corps of Engineers and the National Park Service, P11PG00072," found online July 23, 2023, at https://www.usace.army.mil/Portals/2/docs/MILCON/IIS/P11PG0007_MOA_USACE_Executed_MOA.pdf. For an overview of the Corps and its potential role in this hypothetical project, see Samet, *passim*.

172 "U.S. Code, Title 40, Subtitle i, Chapter 5, Subchapter iii, Section 552" — The text of Title 40, which relates to public buildings, property, and works, was found online July 19, 2023, at https://www.govinfo.gov/content/pkg/USCODE-2011-title40/html/USCODE-2011-title40.htm. In the printed version of the law, the information on Section 552 is found on p. 52.

172 "36 CFR 2.22" — The portion of the Code of Federal Regulations applying to the National Parks was found online July 19, 2023, at https://www.nps.gov/cure/learn/management/upload/NPS-36-CFR-complete.pdf. Section 2.22 is found on pp. 24-25.

173 "the Uniform Unclaimed Property Act" — Found online July 19, 2023, at https://higherlogicdownload.s3-external-1.amazonaws.com/UNIFORMLAWS/a2ca86be-4d12-2c5e-46d4-48680af38c28_file.pdf?AWSAccessKeyId=AKIAVRDO7IEREB57R7MT&Expires=1689795353&Signature=X%2BHU1Hr%2FQh838VH1Cd6aGhbuVJM%3D. In reality, New Jersey still operates under an earlier version of this legislation that was enacted in 1989, and not under the 2016 revision. See the interactive map, ibid.

173 "Title 46 of the New Jersey Statutes" — For a gateway to the relevant New Jersey law, see https://casetext.com/statute/new-jersey-statutes/title-46-property/chapter-4630c-lost-or-abandoned-property, found online July 23, 2023.

176 "Andrew Mellon, who was the Treasury Secretary under Coolidge" — "Thomas Edison's Congressional Gold Medal," United States House of Representatives, Office of Art & Archives, found online July 20, 2023, at

https://history.house.gov/Historical-Highlights/1901-1950/Thomas-Edison-s-Congressional-Gold-Medal/.

179 "It was then that he had first heard about the sweet spot on a baseball." — For a discussion of the location and significance of the sweet spot on a baseball, see "How to Sign a Baseball – Pro tips and Proper etiquette for signing a baseball," *Pro Baseball Insider*, March 19, 2013, found online July 20, 2023, at https://probaseballinsider.com/the-proper-way-to-sign-a-baseball/.

180 The stock certificate shown here is fictitious and is based on a sample certificate issued by the Computing-Tabulating-Recording Company in 1915. The assignment of shares to Thomas Edison is a construct of the author.

184 "it wasn't Edison who formed that company" — For the history of CTRC and its component companies, see "Computing-Tabulating-Recording Company," found online July 20, 2023, at https://en.wikipedia.org/wiki/Computing-Tabulating-Recording_Company#:~:text=The%20Computing%2DTabulating%2DRecording%20Company,systems%20subsequently%20known%20as%20IBM.

187 "a report from 1936 from a hearing on the pooling of patents held by the House Committee on Patents" — "Pooling of Patents," *Hearings Before the Committee on Patents, House of Representatives, Seventy-fourth Congress, on H.R. 4523, a Bill Providing for the Recording of Patent Pooling Agreements and Contracts with the Commissioner of Patents, Parts 3-4*, pp. 3428-3430. Washington: U.S. Government Printing Office, 1936.

187 "Edison's shares amounted to one percent" — Here I have exercised a bit of artistic license so I could use the boilerplate stock certificate shown on page 180, the earliest I was able to locate. As noted above, that certificate, of a design adopted in 1915 in connection with an initial public offering some four years after the company's founding, was for one hundred shares. At the true point of origin in 1911, there was a total capitalization of ten thousand dollars, as noted in the text, but only one hundred shares were issued, each with a value of one hundred dollars. If Edison had received one such share, it would have been the same as his having received one hundred of the 1915 shares with a par value of one dollar. The IPO, incidentally, was made on September 24, 1915, and raised five million dollars in capital. For the details, see "What year did IBM Open their IPO or Initial Public Offering," found online July 20, 2023, at https://digifyr.com/what-year-did-ibm-open-their-ipo/.

190 "whatever the price is when you look online" — Edison's fictional share of CRTC was hypothetically issued in 1911. For practical reasons, however, the calculation of the present-day number of resultant shares could only be based on the change in the number of shares after the initial public offering in 1915. From that base, the holding was adjusted through time for all stock splits and with the assumption that all dividends would have been reinvested—a reasonable assumption for a share that lay undiscovered underground for more than a hundred years. Depending on the impact of the IPO on the original 1911 shares, the value of this

holding might vary significantly from the figure shown. The calculation of current-day value was determined with the assistance noted in the Acknowledgments above, and was broadly confirmed in Jing Cao, "Sure, IBM shares have gained 3,400,000% but are they a buy now?" a story from Bloomberg News published in *The Globe and Mail* (Toronto, Canada), November 11, 2015, and found online August 2, 2023, at https://www.theglobeandmail.com/globe-investor/investment-ideas/sure-ibm-shares-have-gained-3400000-but-are-they-a-buy-now/article27207458/.

198 This team photo, dated circa the 1920s, was found online July 9, 2023, at https://www.rswliving.com/events/199743/vintage-baseball-game-at-terry-park/. The photo was taken by Lewis Lueder, Edison's official photographer, when he was an employee of Thomas A. Edison, Inc., later McGraw-Edison. McGraw-Edison transferred copyright of all historical materials created by the company or its employees, including this photo, to the United States government, i.e., to the public domain. The author has been unable to locate the original of the photo. Accordingly, there is no reason to believe that the handwritten note on the back noted below was anything more than a figment of the author's imagination.

199 "Everything in life depends on will." — Quoted in Lucille Erskine, "Great Inventor Tells Former St. Louis Woman That Death Is Only Sleep and 'We Won't Know We're Dead,'" *St. Louis Post Dispatch*, March 10, 1912, p. 52, found online August 14, 2023, at https://www.newspapers.com/image/138926008/?terms=%22there%27s%20no%20such%20thing%22%20edison&match=1.

200 "After [Thomas's son Theodore's] death" – Morris, p. 633.

Sources Consulted

Edelman, Rob. "Baseball Film to 1920," Our Game Blog, May 22, 2012, found online May 27, 2023, at https://ourgame.mlblogs.com/baseball-film-to-1920-45a5491e669f.

Kennelly, Arthur E. "Biographical Memoir of Thomas Alva Edison 1847-1931," *National Academy of Sciences Biographical Memoirs*, XV: 10. Washington, DC: National Academy of Sciences, 1932. Found online July 23, 2023, at https://www.nasonline.org/publications/biographical-memoirs/memoir-pdfs/edison-thomas.pdf.

McAuliffe, Kathleen. "The Undiscovered World of Thomas Edison: Historians, sorting through a treasure trove of Edison's papers, are discovering revealing details that enrich our portrait of one of America's most accomplished inventors," *The Atlantic*, December 1, 1955, found online September 1, 2023, at https://www.theatlantic.com/magazine/archive/1995/12/the-undiscovered-world-of-thomas-edison/305880/.

Morris, Edmund. *Edison.* New York: Random House, 2019.

Most, Doug. *The Race Underground: Boston, New York, and the Incredible Rivalry That Built America's First Subway.* New York: St. Martin's Press, 2014.

National Park Service. *Cultural Landscapes Inventory: Glenmont Estate, Thomas Edison National Historical Park.* West Orange, NJ, 2011.

National Park Service. *Foundation Document: Thomas Edison National Historical Park.* West Orange, NJ, May 2018.

Ross, Andrew and David Dyte, "Brooklyn's Semipro Fields," found online, May 27, 2023, at http://www.covehurst.net/ddyte/brooklyn/semipro_parks.html.

Ross, Benjamin. *Dead End: Suburban Sprawl and the Rebirth of American Urbanism.* New York: Oxford University Press, 2014.

Samet, Melissa. *A Citizen's Guide to the Corps of Engineers.* Published by American Rivers and the National Wildlife Federation, 2009. Found online July 23, 2023, at https://biotech.law.lsu.edu/blog/A-Citizens-Guide-to-the-Corps-of-Engineers-Permitting-D.pdf.

Westheimer, Bill. *Greetings from Llewellyn Park.* West Orange, NJ: Petey Pie Press, 2012.

About the Author

JB Manheim is Professor Emeritus at The George Washington University, where he developed the world's first degree-granting program in political communication and was later founding director of the School of Media & Public Affairs. In 1995, he was named Professor of the Year for the District of Columbia. He learned his love of baseball watching Dizzy Dean on the Game of the Week and huddling with his grandfather for warmth on July nights at The Mistake By The Lake, AKA, Cleveland Municipal Stadium, and renewed it when the National Pastime finally returned to the Nation's Capital. Manheim brings to life his expertise in propaganda and strategic communication through his fictional stories of baseball behind the scenes. His writing will lead you to question whether what you think you know about the history of the game and about the powers who control it is real, or whether it's just a carefully nurtured product of lies, deceptions, misdirection, and propaganda. JB Manheim is a member of the Society for American Baseball Research, the Internet Baseball Writers Association of America, and International Thriller Writers.

www.ingramcontent.com/pod-product-compliance
Lightning Source LLC
Chambersburg PA
CBHW011347010726
47493CB00011B/2996